CAUGHT BY MENACE

Grabbed #2

Lolita Lopez

Night Works Books
College Station, Texas

Night Works Books
3515-B Longmire Drive #103
College Station, Texas 77845
www.roxierivera.com

Publisher's Note: This is a work of fiction. Names, characters, places, and incidents are a product of the author's imagination. Locales and public names are sometimes used for atmospheric purposes. Any resemblance to actual people, living or dead, or to businesses, companies, events, institutions, or locales is completely coincidental.

Cover Art © 2015 P Schmitt/Picky Me Artist

Grabbed By Vicious/ Lolita Lopez – 2nd ed.

Caught By Menace

Lolita Lopez

Grabbed, Book Two

Menace's plan to catch a docile woman is shot to hell when he's tackled by a darkhaired beauty who wants to save her friend from being Grabbed. Refusing to leave the planet's surface empty-handed, Menace claims the spitfire with his collar.

Naya clawed her way off the streets of Connor's Run and vowed to never let any man control her. She plans to make Menace so miserable he'll set her free, but the ruggedly sexy warrior disarms her with his unexpected patience and kindness.

Against her better judgment, Naya surrenders to Menace's masterful hands and mouth. Submitting to her new husband brings more pleasure and happiness than she'd ever imagined possible. For the first time in her life, she willingly trusts a man to protect her.

But when past misdeeds catch up with her, Naya puts the depth and strength of that love to the test. Determined to prove he's worthy of her trust, Menace will stop at nothing to save her.

CAUGHT BY MENACE

Lolita Lopez

Chapter One

NAYA KEPT TO the shadows and moved silently through the cool night. Not even the inky darkness could slow her feet. She had traveled this path enough times to memorize every inch of the back alleys and darkened streets of Connor's Run. Like most nights, the town's power grid had failed, plunging the place into blackness. Not wanting to garner attention, she used no flashlight and relied on the palest slivers of moonlight from the three moons orbiting Calyx to make her way to the rendezvous point.

She shook off the cold sensation of uncertainty slithering along the back of her neck. Once her mind was made up, she'd never been one to hesitate. Tonight was no different. As a wide-eyed twelve-year-old terrified by the talk of the government signing one of the Harcos bride treaties, she'd sworn a promise to her best friend Jennie. Eleven years later, Naya refused to break that promise, even if it meant leaving behind the only life she'd ever known.

And so she ran. She ran through the back streets of Connor's Run, skirting the squalid tenements and ignoring the stench of refuse from the poorly maintained water management systems. She kept close to the buildings, the brittle bricks and stones scraping against her thin jacket and leaving chalky marks on the worn, faded fabric. In a few hours, the lottery results would be official and it would be too late to save Jennie. She had to move fast if her plan had any chance of succeeding.

As she neared the meeting point, a ramshackle warehouse that had been long abandoned and scheduled for razing, Naya eased up on her pace. Her hand drifted to the weapon secured at her hip. Her father had always joked that this gun would be pried from his cold, dead hands—and she'd done just that. She'd been nine years old the night she'd inherited her first weapon. Looking back, it was a sad omen of the dangerous, often violent life she would be forced to lead, but to keep food in her belly and a roof over her head, there had been no other choice.

Creeping through the darkness, Naya listened carefully. She held her breath and hugged the nearest wall. She scanned the warehouse for any signs of life and spotted just one light. The eerie red glow of a light stick gave the warehouse a sinister appearance.

Recognizing Dankirk's signal, she pursed her lips and let loose a high-pitched, warbling whistle. The sound mimicking a night bird was quickly answered with a lower-pitched whistle in three short bursts. Assured the coast was clear, Naya hustled to the dilapidated building and darted between two busted-out boards. Once inside the warehouse, she pushed back the hood covering her face and kept her fingertips hovering just above her weapon. After being ambushed and betrayed more than once, she never let her guard down anymore.

"Naya." Dankirk's familiar voice cut through the darkness. "Over here."

She crossed the brick floor and came face-to-face with the Red Feather fixer. As a member of the underground group of political dissidents, Dankirk handled the logistics and "fixed" all the issues that arose during their risky missions. Like her, he had some serious skill in smuggling supplies and technologies that were forbidden in their society.

"You're late." He tucked away the eerie red chem-light and replaced it with one in bright-yellow that more clearly illuminated his face.

"The rumors of the Grab have already hit the streets. People are talking about rioting. I couldn't take my usual route."

Dankirk laughed, the sound so bitter and resigned. "Yeah, because the food riots in The City last month did so much good, right? Hell, people always talk about rioting over the Grabs but they do nothing. They'll serve up their daughters like lambs to the slaughter rather than risk the wrath of The City's secret police or the sky warriors."

Humming in agreement, Naya glanced around the warehouse. "Where's the alderman?"

"He's coming. Probably delayed the same way you were." Dankirk slipped the glowing stick into the holder attached to a lanyard dangling from his neck. His illuminated face showed his disbelief. "Are you sure about this, Naya?"

"Not really," Naya admitted, "but I can't let those sky monsters take Jennie."

He snorted with amusement. "Monsters? Shit, Naya,

look no further than Harper's Well if you want to see real monsters. Naw," he said, his low, country drawl dragging out the word, "those Harcos men aren't that bad. They keep us safe here on Calyx. Besides, they turn a blind eye to us sneaking folks off this hellhole of a planet to the colonies. They haven't stopped a single smuggling ship or medicine or technology shipment from landing here in over a year. They're doing a good thing for us."

She couldn't argue with him there. The Harcos were the dominant race in this solar system. Like her Earth ancestors, the Harcos were human but much larger and more terrifying. But she'd seen enough of them in the Free Market section of Connor's Run to know she didn't want one of them catching her in the Grab, the archaic chase organized every quarter to provide brides to these sky warriors.

Though they had women of their own on their home planet of Harcos Prime, they were tens of thousands of light years away. In exchange for policing the solar system, the sky warriors took payment in natural resources like minerals and food—and in women.

Unmarried women aged eighteen to thirty were eligible for the Grab. The officials from The City, the government center of Calyx, picked a town or village to host the Grab every quarter and calculated the quota required based on the number of sky warriors approved for the list by their superiors. This time it was nineteen young women who would be called. The mayor of Connor's Run had chosen them by lottery that afternoon. By sunrise, the list would be posted throughout the town.

But unlike the girls trying desperately to get their names off the list, Naya was willing to do everything in her power to get her name *on* that list.

"You know the odds of you pulling off this plan are like, zero, right?"

Naya glanced at Dankirk. "That's what we say every time we smuggle a family off Calyx to Jesco colony or Safe Harbor, Danny. We still try."

He slipped his hand into the front pocket of his jacket and produced the passports and travel permits she'd requested. "They're not as good as the old ones, but the Artist is long gone."

Naya tugged his chem-light closer so she could see better and quickly thumbed through the forged traveling papers. Here on Calyx everything was low-tech. All official correspondence was paper and ink. Only in the colonies did the Earth descendants embrace superior and more efficient technologies. When she and Jennie reached Safe Harbor in a few days, they'd meet with Dankirk's contacts and upgrade their papers to the implanted tags favored there.

"These are good. Good enough to get us through customs on the colonies," she added and stuffed them into the inner pocket of her jacket. "What happened to the Artist?"

Dankirk pointed up. "They Grabbed her."

Naya grimaced. "That's terrible."

"Not from what I've heard," he replied. "Besides, she came from Harper's Well. I don't know about you, but I'd rather take my chances on a sky ship than live in that backwards swamp. Maybe it's not so bad up there on their alien ships."

"How would you know? There's a communication blackout once you're taken. You never get to see or talk to your family or friends again."

"I don't think that's true. I've heard some girls have contact with their families. And the Artist has a sister that does some work for the Red Feather now. She was one of the last ones we successfully smuggled out of Harper's Well. I guess she figures she owes us a debt so she helps us place single or widowed mothers and their children in safe houses on Jesco colony and Safe Harbor."

"She does owe a debt. Every one of us that takes a favor from the Red Feather owes a favor in return."

"There you go with your honor code again." Dankirk shoved two pieces of chewing gum into his mouth and winced as he bit down. "Anyway, the sister in the colonies told me that the Artist is happy with her new husband on the *Valiant* and living the kind of life we can only dream about here."

Naya's gaze narrowed suspiciously. "Sounds like some kind of bullshit story to hide what's really going on up there in those sky ships."

"Believe what you want. I choose to believe the woman is happy. The moons only know that she deserves it, especially after being arrested and publicly humiliated for drawing that newsletter for us."

She remembered the horror of learning the woman, just a teenager back then, had been arrested for her crime of disseminating information. They had sentenced her to a public shearing, the same sentence given to prostitutes, and had shaved her head in the Harper's Well town square. It was such a cruel thing to do to someone so young.

Naya noticed the way Dankirk winced as he chewed. "That tooth bothering you again, Danny?"

He nodded. "Damn thing is killing me. The chewing helps. There's some kind of herbal oil in the gum that numbs the area nicely."

"You should see someone about that tooth before you get an infection and die. Go have Griff pull it."

He growled. "I am not letting some drunken bear of a bartender jerk a damn tooth out of my head, Naya!"

"Quit being such a crybaby! He did my wisdom teeth when I was like, sixteen."

"Yeah, well, you're a different breed, kid. My ancestors were wimps. I'm quite fond of the analgesics they offer in more civilized places like the colonies and The City."

She rolled her eyes. "Well, unless you plan to bribe one of the licensed dentists in The City just to get an appointment and then pay the exorbitant fees for pharmacy access and medical exemptions, you don't have a lot of choices. Just suck it up, get drunk and have it yanked."

Dankirk shuddered. "I'll suffer until I can see someone in Safe Harbor next week. There's a sick kid in Grogan's Mill that needs some kind of major surgery. The hospital on the Harbor can help him so I'm smuggling them out."

"Are you taking the whole family?"

He shook his head. "Just the mother."

"Is it too expensive for the whole family to travel?"

"Hardly," he said in frustration. "It's just mom, dad and the kid, but the dad is one of those no-intervention nutters. It's crazy. This kid will have a totally happy, healthy and productive life if he has the surgery but his dad is ready to start digging a grave and lighting memorial candles. I just don't understand it."

"Different cultures, Danny. That's why our people settled here in Connor's Run. They sure as hell knew they weren't going to find the kind of freedom they wanted in places like Harper's Well or the Mill."

"You ain't lying." Danny's head snapped to the far wall of the warehouse. "I think we have company." He pushed her toward a dark corner. "Hide behind those boxes until I give you the signal."

Naya didn't argue. Silently she crept to safety and crouched down. Controlling her breathing and listening intently, she experienced such a surge of sadness. It wasn't supposed to be this way.

All those centuries earlier, when her ancestors had left Earth for the promised land in the stars, they'd believed they were going to a place of peace and prosperity. After their generational ship limped into this end of the galaxy, the Harcos took pity on them. They'd been given a beautiful planet by a race of sky warriors to start their new civilization—but it had all gone pear-shaped. Religious disagreements, corruption, a famine and an epidemic had gutted their new world.

Their civilization had fractured. Most of the wealthy citizens and nearly all of the scientists and physicians and engineers had fled Calyx for the smaller but habitable planets nearby to form the more progressive colonies like Safe Harbor and Jesco. All of the religious extremists had chosen to leave The City and form their insulated communities like Harper's Well and Grogan's Mill where women were property—under the guise of protection, of course—and penalties for breaking moral codes were swift and harsh. Places like Connor's Run, where people paid lip service to the laws of The City but not much more, had popped up in strategic locations to serve as marketplaces and trading posts between the backward villages and morally corrupt City.

This? Hiding in a warehouse to bribe an official while planning to make a daring escape off the planet to save her friend from a forced marriage to some juiced-up sky warrior? No, this wasn't the way it was supposed to be.

A low whistle pulled her from the hiding place. She rose slowly, quietly, and waited until she could see Dankirk and the gray-haired alderman clearly. Certain it was safe, she let her hand fall from her weapon and went to meet them.

Dankirk made the necessary introductions. "Naya, this is Alderman Crane. Alderman, this is Naya."

"We've never met but I know you." Alderman Crane extended his hand. "You did a favor for my niece a few years ago."

Naya frowned and shook his hand. "I did?"

"She came to your pawnshop asking for a weapon because she was afraid her husband was going to kill her. You told her a gun wasn't the answer and gave her something even better—a way out."

Naya's eyes widened as the memory resurfaced. "Lilac, right? Blonde? Late twenties?" She nodded. "I remember her." *And the bruises on her face…*

"She's doing well now. You helped save her life. I'll do whatever I can to return the favor."

"I want my name on the Grab list."

The alderman blinked. "You want me to put your name *on* the list?"

She nodded. "I know how crazy it sounds, but I have my reasons. I need my name on that list. It's of the utmost importance." She took a step closer to the man. "I happen to know your daughter's name is on the list."

His expression grew solemn. "She is."

"Give me her number. It's an easy fix. It's been done plenty of times. You give me her number and put me on the list. She takes my number and stays off the list. That gives her at least another year of freedom before the Grab comes back to Connor's Run."

The alderman looked shocked. "Why?"

"Because I made a promise to a friend," Naya replied. "I never break a promise."

"She's big on that whole honor thing," Dankirk murmured.

"It's an admirable quality," Alderman Crane remarked. "I'll do it, Naya. I'll switch the numbers." He hesitated. "How much do you expect me to pay for this transaction?"

"Nothing. I want a favor," she said simply. She gestured toward Dankirk. "You'll owe us a favor."

"Us? The Red Feather?"

"Yes," she clarified. "Someday, someone will come to you and ask for help. You'll do whatever you can to make it happen. You'll remember how I helped your niece and your daughter and you'll pay it forward."

"Of course," Alderman Crane promised. "I'll do whatever it takes."

Naya shook his hand and slipped the piece of paper with her identification number against his palm. "Thank you."

He squeezed her hand before pocketing the paper. "Good luck with whatever it is you have planned. May you find happiness in wherever this takes you."

Dankirk walked the alderman outside. When he returned, he sighed loudly. "Well that's that. You're going to be on the list. You're going to have to run."

"That's the plan." Naya tried to ignore the wobbling anxiety burning in the pit of her stomach.

"It won't be easy to get from the surface of Calyx to the colonies," Dankirk warned.

"We've got our papers." She touched her pocket. "Jennie's boyfriend will land his surface-to-sky cruiser in the woods just beyond the safe zone. Jennie and I know the woods like the backs of our hands. We'll evade the Harcos men, get to the safe zone and make a mad dash right to the waiting ship."

"Why not run now? Run tonight. Run tomorrow. Don't wait, Naya."

"We can't. You know the government has this place clamped down tightly. Those damn riots in The City have made it impossible to even travel between towns. Even if we could evade the local police force and get Josef's ship into orbit, those guys?" She pointed toward the sky and shook her head. "They keep a close watch on the planet leading up to their Grabs. They'll never allow two women chosen by the lottery to make a run to the colonies. They'd probably arrest Josef for trying to steal something they consider theirs. It's too big of a risk."

Dankirk rubbed the back of his neck. "What about Jennie's boyfriend? Does this guy have the necessary permits to get to the surface?"

Naya nodded. "He's a research scientist from the colonies. He's got a permit to fly his surface-to-sky cruiser in and out of Calyx airspace four times a week. His end of things is squared away."

"And yours? What the hell are you going to do with your shop?"

"What I should have done years ago when Nattie left me here," Naya replied, the memory of her older brother's betrayal still so painful. "I'm selling out—lock, stock and barrel."

He chuckled. "I see what you did there."

She rolled her eyes. "I haven't run weapons in a long time, Danny. Once the Splinter terrorists came here and their civil war with the Harcos," she pointed skyward again, "started to spill into our world, I gave up that rather lucrative side business running cargo for the Sixers. Once those two groups got into bed together, it wasn't worth the risk or the hassle. I need to get tangled up with their insurgency problems like I need a hole in the head."

"Agreed." Dankirk shuffled his feet. "So—you headed home?"

Naya's chest tightened. "I'm sorry, Danny. I just… We can't."

"Not even once? For old times' sake?"

"We did once," she reminded him. There was such hope in his voice. She didn't have the heart to add that it had gotten weird and awkward so fast. Afraid this might be their last meeting ever, she stepped close and wound her arms around his waist. Rising on tiptoes, she pressed their lips together in a gentle, lingering kiss. "Good night, Danny."

"Night, Naya." He caressed her face and dropped a kiss on her forehead. "Be safe."

"I'll try." She couldn't promise anything else.

"I'll catch up with you in the colonies." He rubbed her earlobe between his forefinger and thumb. "I can't decide if you're incredibly brave or just really stupid."

Laughing softly, she pecked his cheek and started to walk away. "Probably a bit of both."

Out in the cool night, Naya kept to the shadows again. Her mind raced as she cut across Connor's Run. She tried not to focus on how badly things could go wrong. The alderman might be unsuccessful in his quest to switch numbers. Or, even worse, he might sell her out to the authorities as a political dissident to curry favor with someone higher up the food chain.

Even if she made it into the Grab, either she or Jennie could be snatched up by one of the Harcos warriors. If Jennie were caught, Naya would have to let herself be taken so they could stay together and escape at some point. Getting off one of those warships wouldn't be easy but Naya had gotten out of trickier scrapes.

The very thought of being caught made her shiver with

fear. There were few things that truly scared Naya. Being dragged to one of those Harcos sky ships was one of them. She'd heard the stories of how they treated their wives. She figured there were some embellishments tacked on to those stories—anything she heard via gossip typically had something salacious added to it—but they all began with a seed of truth. It was the possibility of truth that scared her.

What went on in Harper's Well and Willow's Tears was bad enough, but up there? Oh, hell no. They put collars and leashes on their women and forced them to do all sorts of perverted things. They were abusive and cruel to their wives.

And huge. She'd never seen such big men. The massive giants of the Harcos race stood seven feet tall on average and weighed hundreds of pounds. They were solidly built men, all lean muscle and brutal strength. Most had pale hair and eyes, but she'd seen the occasional dark-haired man among them.

The face of one of the men, the only one she'd ever spoken to, flashed in her mind. His pale-green eyes and white-blond hair left her shivering—but not with fear. With need. With desire.

She still didn't understand it. Their chance meeting nearly three months earlier had shaken her. Apparently he'd been on a mission to find flowers. For a friend? For a woman he loved? She didn't know. Somehow he'd ended up at Jennie's flower stall in the open market. By chance, Naya had stopped by and the giant Harcos warrior hadn't seen her approaching. He'd turned so quickly he'd knocked her off balance and into the street, where she'd almost been crushed by a rolling cart.

To say they'd exchanged some furious words was an understatement. The look on his face when she'd told him to fuck off had been priceless. No doubt he'd never had any woman speak to him in such a way. For the briefest of moments, she'd been sure he was going to snatch her right up, toss her across his lap and spank her backside. Instead he'd tossed a handful of coins at Jennie, grabbed his bouquet and stormed off in a huff. Naya had laughed so hard at the sight of the massive warrior flouncing off and clutching his bouquet of fragile flowers to his chest.

He'd started plaguing her dreams that night. Of all the men who crossed her path day after day, why did it have to be him? He was everything she loathed and nothing she wanted. Yet so many nights she'd bolted upright in bed, ripped from the wildest dreams and hovering on the verge of climax. It stunned her that a few moments with an intimidating stranger could have such an astounding effect on her. In real life, she rarely came close to having an orgasm.

But she couldn't think about that now. She had to focus. She couldn't risk overlooking even the simplest step in the plan.

Finally reaching her shop, Naya took the alley stairs up to the second-floor apartment she shared with Jennie. She let herself inside the small place and found Jennie sitting on their lumpy couch. Hugging her knees, she glanced up, her eyes red from crying. "Well?"

Naya locked the door and smiled. "It's done, Jennie. We're getting out of here."

Chapter Two

MENACE STEPPED OFF the elevator into the med bay of the *Valiant*. He checked his watch again to make sure he still had time. The last week he'd been swamped with weapons shipments and inventory. Twice he had rescheduled his medical clearance for today's Grab. Even now, he was cutting it close. Only his rank and his reputation as a man who shouldn't be crossed were going to save him from being struck off the list.

He caught sight of Vicious, his close friend and the *Valiant*'s highest-ranking land corps officer, leaving a private exam room with his wife Hallie at his side. Vicious held her hand and tenderly swept his fingertips down her cheek. Not wanting to intrude on a private moment, Menace dropped his gaze. He had a feeling their visit to the med bay had to do with her inability to conceive but Menace didn't dare ask. He and Vicious had been friends since childhood but there were some things that even friends didn't discuss. This was one of them.

"Menace," Vicious called to him as he walked Hallie to the elevator. He smiled knowingly. "Sneaking in at the last moment for your med check?"

"Of course." Menace nodded in Hallie's direction. "Ma'am."

She grinned up at him, her smile warm and friendly. "I hear you're running today. Good luck, Menace."

Vicious chuckled. "If the women running today are anything like Hallie, you're going to need it."

She smacked her husband's chest. "Be nice."

He feigned injury and rubbed the spot his wife had whacked. "Yes, Kitten."

Menace still couldn't believe how gentle and sweet Vicious was with her. Vicious was one of the most feared of their kind, a true warrior who had proven himself in some of the worst battles of the war and their constant skirmishes with alien life forms. Somehow Hallie had wrapped him around her little finger. As far as Menace could tell, Vicious had never been happier.

Hallie stepped into the waiting elevator. "I'll see you at dinner."

Vicious nodded. "I'll call if I'm running late."

Menace wondered at the domestic scene before him. As little as six months ago, he would have been repulsed by such a sight. Now he yearned for these little moments of sweetness Vicious shared with his wife. All the long, hard years of unending war had taken their toll. He was tired of the loneliness and the bachelor quarters. He wanted a real home. He wanted someone to protect and love. He wanted a woman to support and love him back.

Alone now, Vicious turned his full attention to him. "You're going to Connor's Run?"

Menace nodded. "It's a midsized Grab today. Less than twenty girls, apparently."

"Good odds," Vicious commented. "You want my advice?"

Menace laughed. "Not really, but you're going to give it anyway."

"That's what superior officers do, Menace. But seriously, pick a woman and stick with her. Don't change your tactic halfway through the Grab. Listen to your gut. You won't be led astray."

"Did your gut tell you to Grab Hallie?"

Vicious chuckled. "I had this crazy idea that I wanted some tall, blonde, buxom beauty. My head told me that this imaginary woman was the perfect match for me. You know, someone with similar genes to complement my own." He shook his head. "But the moment I spied Hallie with that dark hair and those dark eyes?" Vicious touched his chest. "I felt it here. I knew she was the one."

Menace couldn't help himself. He let the image of that young woman from the flower stall in Connor's Run invade his thoughts. With her soft brown skin and black hair, she was so unlike the typical Harcos woman. One look at her and his heart had stuttered in his chest.

But that mouth of hers! He'd been wrong to knock her over but she'd bitten his head off before he could apologize for his accidental collision. The string of expletives that had left those pouty lips had blitzed his instant attraction, but her friend, the sweet brunette with dark eyes who had sold him the flowers? Now that was a woman he wouldn't mind catching. Modest, quiet, friendly, sweet. Maybe he'd look for someone just like that.

"Are you taking the full honeymoon period?"

Pulled from his thoughts by his commander's question,

Menace shook his head. "Raze and the SRU boys have some weapons recertification needs. I'll be doing those during my days off just to get them out of the way. Terror and his crew will probably need rearming at some point. You know how they are about running through weapons and ammo."

Vicious grunted at the mention of his best friend's name. Terror excelled in his work with the Shadow Force the silent, secret arm of the military that carried out all the covert operations required to keep their people safe, but he was such a difficult man. The war hadn't been kind to him and he seemed to grow colder and more withdrawn with each passing year.

"Try not to work too hard during your bonding period," Vicious instructed. "Hallie and I weren't able to have any kind of honeymoon and it made things difficult in the beginning. You should take the time to get to know your new wife. You only get one chance to do things right."

"Understood."

Vicious clapped him on the back. "Let me know how it goes."

"Will do." Menace headed toward the reception desk and checked in for his physical. He was in and out in twenty minutes and on his way to the departures deck for the trip to the surface. He eyed the small crowd of waiting men and judged his competition. Only three were fellow officers and all of them lower ranking. As the highest-ranking officer taking part, the younger, lower-ranking soldiers would defer to him. He would have the pick of the litter, so to speak.

An hour later, a quiver of excitement pierced his belly. Menace leaned against the railing of the hastily erected stage and gazed down into the group of women who had been picked by the lottery to participate in the Grab. He scanned the offerings and tried to find a woman who piqued his interest.

A few of the women were much too young to tempt him. He wanted someone equal to the task of being his partner and someone with enough life experience to relate to him. He instantly skipped over their faces in search of just the right woman. He only had once chance to find his life mate. He had to choose just right or risk years of un-happiness.

A familiar face caught his eye. His gut clenched. It couldn't be—but it was.

Menace frowned at the sight of the young woman who had cussed him out in the market that day. From the stunned look on her face, she remembered him too. Her dark eyes narrowed to a piercing glare that silently warned him to back off and leave her be. She shouldn't have wasted the energy. He planned to avoid her at all costs. One taste of that waspish tongue was quite enough for him.

His searching gaze skipped to her right. He spotted her friend, the one from the flower stall who had enthralled him with her sweet smile and kind voice. She was exactly the kind of woman he had in mind. There was no doubt now. He was chasing that one.

Menace's brow furrowed as the bratty one leaned over and whispered in her friend's ear. They glanced furtively his way. From the way they talked behind their hands, it was clear they were strategizing. Vicious had told him all about Hallie's battle plan for the day she'd run. She'd almost beaten him. What if the mouthy one helped the woman he wanted evade him today?

Bold as brass, the young woman with the dark, impish eyes flashed him a big smirk and gestured rudely in his direction. The crude one-fingered salute was a silent version of the nasty remark she'd tossed his way that day in the market.

He couldn't believe her audacity. She laughed and glanced away from him. Her behavior grated on his nerves. He planned to tell the man who Grabbed her to spank her—and often. Clearly she needed a little discipline in her life.

The mayor of Connor's Run climbed onto the stage. One of the Harcos liaisons, who monitored the Grabs and ensured complete cooperation by the people of Calyx, joined the mayor. While the mayor read from a piece of paper, the Harcos bureaucrat held his touchscreen tablet at the ready. The liaison would make sure all the rules of the Grab were followed to the letter. No violence against the women. No underhanded or devious means to catch them. No bribing or trading money or gifts to entice them.

Menace noticed the two women inching their way toward the starting line. They obviously planned to be the first out of the pen. The moment the mayor whacked the bell, the pair sprinted from the crowd and quickly left the other women in their dust.

Impressed, Menace stretched his neck and glanced at his watch. The women had three full minutes of running before the men could enter the race. His hand drifted to his shirt pocket. He felt the raised outline of the white bride's collar tucked safely there. It was the generic collar given to every man boarding a shuttle bound for one of the Grabs.

"Hey, Gunner!"

Without tearing his gaze away from his intended target, Menace answered to the nickname usually given to his rank and specialty. "Yes?"

"You have your woman picked out, sir?"

Menace nodded and pointed toward the two women he'd been watching. Little Miss Mouthy and her gorgeous sidekick were sprinting into the tree line now. "The one in the red shirt is mine."

"And the sexy one in gray?"

"You can have her." *And good riddance.*

"WE AREN'T GOING to make it."

Naya glanced at Jennie. There was no time for a reassuring smile as they sprinted through the woods. "We stick to the plan, Jennie."

"It's a long way, Naya." Jennie wasn't breathing hard yet. Naya took that as a good sign.

"We have adrenaline working for us today." She cast another glance over her shoulder. The coast was still clear but soon they would have to evade the grabby hands of those giant, tattooed men in their frightening black uniforms and boots.

A shiver coursed down her spine. She couldn't believe *he* was here. He had recognized her the same moment she'd spotted him. The way he had looked at Jennie unsettled her. He wanted Jennie. That much was clear. No doubt he would be running their way soon.

She tried to ignore the frisson of unwanted jealousy that stabbed her belly. The fact that he had skipped over her so easily hurt her pride, but she would never admit that aloud. It wasn't easy to swallow that the man who had starred in her dirtiest fantasies found her utterly unattractive.

But this was so *not* the time to even think about that.

"Just keep running, Jennie. Josef is waiting for you. That's all that matters." She shot Jennie a quick grin. "We're going to make it."

A loud war cry of a whoop shattered the stillness of the woods. Naya's heart leapt into her throat. The men were loose and they were gaining ground.

"Is this where we split up?" Jennie asked, her voice unnaturally high and anxious.

"Yes. Remember the plan, Jennie. We've run this route a dozen times. We're going to make it."

Jennie nodded and took off one way while Naya ran the other. Even though she'd just given Jennie that pep talk, her stomach pitched violently. This was nothing like the dry runs. There were men hell-bent on capturing them hot on their tails. One mistake and their plan was toast. *They* were toast.

The crackle of ground covering snapping under heavy boots echoed in the forest. Naya gulped and pushed herself to run even faster. She took a chance glancing back and spotted one of the Harcos men a hundred yards or so behind. He wasn't as big as the man from the market but he ran fast. Too fast, she realized and turned her attention forward.

Her gaze jumped around the forest. She hooked a quick right and ran straight for a tricky spot in the terrain that only the locals knew well. A dry creek bed, some fallen logs and shifting, loose rocks were a disaster for the uninitiated. The idea of causing an injury to the monstrous man wasn't one she relished but she wasn't about to be Grabbed by him. Hopefully he'd be smart enough to sense the danger and stay back.

Sure-footed as a rabbit, Naya hopped from log to rock and crossed the dangerous creek bed with the speed and efficiency of practice. The monstrous hulk in his black uniform didn't let the new obstacle slow him down. Stupidly he leapt onto a log that quickly began to roll. He fell forward and cracked his knee on a rock. His roar of pain filled the air. Naya winced at the discomfort he must have been feeling but didn't stop to render aid. She had to keep moving.

Cutting through the woods, Naya checked the forest for signs to help her navigate. This tree, that rock formation, the winding empty creek beds—all of them helped her stay on course. She estimated she was less than ten minutes from the safe zone and the spot they'd chosen to rendezvous with Josef.

"Naya!" Jennie's bloodcurdling shriek ripped through the forest. Spurred into action, Naya sprinted even faster in the direction of the scream. Her stomach clenched so tightly she was sure she would heave her guts. Legs burning and sides aching, she burst through some thick underbrush into a clearing. The slap of the thorny branches left her bare calves nastily scratched, but she couldn't think about that now.

Naya's stomach dropped at the sight of Jennie trying to evade the clutches of the sky warrior with the pale-white hair and green eyes. Refusing to let him Grab her best friend when they were this close to the safe zone, Naya reacted without thinking. She raced across the tall grass separating them and slammed into the man's side, wrapping both arms around his upper thighs and taking him to the ground.

His shocked grunt ricocheted off the trees. Stunned she'd been able to throw him off balance, Naya scrambled to her feet before he could recover and grabbed Jennie's hand. She roughly tugged on her friend. "Move. *Now!*"

They ran as if the flames of hell licked at their heels. Naya ignored the pain accompanying every breath. She was certain she hadn't broken anything, but she'd definitely bruised her shoulder and right side tackling that behemoth.

"Come back here!" he growled menacingly and chased after them. "You won't make it. Not both of you!"

Naya refused to even consider that possibility. They were so close to making their escape. She couldn't give up hope now.

"Jennie!" Josef appeared at the tree line. He sucked in ragged breaths, his sweatsoaked shirt clinging to his lean frame. "Jennie! Hurry!"

Relieved by the sight of Josef, Naya shoved her friend forward. "Move, Jennie. Move! We have to—*aargh!*"

"Got you!"

Naya lurched forward and then snapped back as a massive hand gripped the back of her shirt. She heard fabric tearing as her momentum was cruelly arrested. As if in slow motion, she fell backward, her shoes sliding on the dewy grass and her hands snatching at empty air. "No!"

Jennie grabbed her hand and jerked but she wasn't strong enough. "Naya! Naya!"

"Leave her," Josef shouted as he rushed toward them. He frantically forced Jennie's fingers open and hauled her up into his arms. Eyes glistening and chest heaving, he sobbed, "I'm sorry, Naya. I'm so sorry."

Panicked and overcome with dread, Naya screamed for help. "Jennie! *Jennie!*"

But Josef didn't stop. He ran. He ran with the woman he loved tucked safely in his arms. Yet again Naya had been left behind.

Naya shuddered in revulsion as the warrior tried to flip her over. She balled up her fist and whacked him on the jaw as he finally succeeded in forcing her onto her back. He hissed in pain but didn't strike back. Instead he captured her smaller hand in his and restrained her arm overhead. Shockingly he didn't try to hurt her.

"Enough," he whispered harshly. "It's done. You're caught."

"Please," she sobbed, her emotions overwhelming her. "Please let me go. My friends—"

"They left you. They're long gone." The briefest flash of sadness crossed his face. "You're mine now."

Naya dragged a slow, shaky breath into her lungs. She

hated herself for crying in front of him. Showing a man—especially one as dangerous as this—weakness was a terrible mistake. "You're going to regret Grabbing me."

"Probably," he agreed with a sharp laugh. "The same way you'll regret coming to the aid of your friend. You could have been halfway to space by now if you'd just kept running."

"I will never regret saving Jennie from you. She loves Josef. She belongs with Josef."

"And now you belong to me," he reminded her.

"Not for long," she warned.

He laughed again, the sound so cruel. "You aren't the first bride to threaten that and you won't be the last." His fingertips trailed her cheek. "It won't work. It never does."

She choked back the sob that threatened to escape her lips. As if curious, he lowered his face until their noses nearly touched. Eyes closed, he inhaled deeply, drawing her scent into his lungs. When his eyes opened again, he tilted his head. "I'm Menace. What's your name?"

"Naya," she whispered. Menace? What the hell kind of name was that? She studied his face but it was pointless. Try as she might, she couldn't read this man. The unsettling feeling of being completely at his mercy made her stomach lurch.

"Naya," he repeated slowly. His fingertips moved down her jaw and along the side of her neck. "I like that. It's different."

Her breath caught in her throat as his fingers glided across her collarbone and down the center of her chest. Her ripped shirt displayed too much flesh. Menace took advantage and swept his fingertips across her bare belly. His touch, so intimate and possessive, caused goose bumps to blossom on her hot skin.

Pinned beneath his powerful frame, Naya could barely move. Trapped and terrified, she tried to slow her panicked breaths. She fought the claustrophobia gripping her chest.

Menace must have read the fear in her face. Caressing her arm, he urged, "Easy, Naya. Deep breaths. You're safe with me."

Despite his surprisingly kind voice, she chortled sarcastically. "Safe? With you?"

His jaw tightened. "Your people may think we're all monsters, but it isn't true. I've never harmed a woman in my life. I won't allow you to be harmed either. Do you understand? You are mine now. *Mine.*"

The possessive word rang in her ears. Her new reality washed over her like cold water, chilling her right to the bone. Unlike many women in her world, she'd been able to live a fairly independent existence. Even as a homeless, orphaned teenager, she'd found a way to escape the clutches of men who wanted to make her their own. To now be owned by someone—by this stranger—left her feeling ill.

"I don't want to be yours."

His lips settled into a grim line. "It's too late for that. I've Grabbed you. It's done."

Putting an end to the discussion, he reached into the front pocket of his black uniform shirt and withdrew a thin white collar. Squeezing her eyes shut, Naya cursed the tears that dripped from her lashes onto her cheeks. The collar was slipped around her throat and fastened, not too tightly, but snug enough to remind her that she was this man's property now.

"Don't," he rasped and wiped the wetness from her face. "I gave you my word, Naya. I'll take care of you."

"Take care of me?" She laughed caustically. "If stealing me away from my planet and forcing me to be your sex slave is your idea of taking care of me, I'll pass."

"Luckily for me, I'm not giving you the option." He rose to his full height, reached down and swept her up off the ground. His pale eyes fixed her with a warning stare. "Don't even think about trying to kick or hit me or run away, Naya."

She arched her brow and informed him of the obvious. "You'll have to put me down sometime."

Menace snorted and patted her backside. "Don't worry about that. I've got cuffs and a gag waiting on the ship."

Her jaw dropped with shock. Indignant, she whacked his arm. "You're a pig, you know that?"

"Is that the worst you've got for me?" Laughing, he shifted her in his arms and threw her over his shoulder.

Forced into the awkward position, she stiffened in fear of being dropped right on her head. "What kind of a dirt-bag carries around cuffs and gags?"

"The kind who plans to protect his investment," he replied matter-of-factly. "I survived some of the nastiest, most brutal battles of the war to gain enough points to Grab a wife. I'm not about to let you run off or get taken by another male. You might not have been the one I wanted, but you're pretty enough for a consolation prize."

His words wounded her more than his fists ever could

have. Not the one he wanted? His consolation prize?

Suddenly she was taken back to the night her mother had packed her bags and left with the sky trader. Only six years old, Naya had tearfully begged her mother to take her along, to please not leave her behind, but the answer then hadn't been any different than Menace's cutting remark just now. Her mother had revealed she'd never wanted her and had viewed her as little more than an obstacle in her path to happiness.

And then there had been her older brother, Nattie. What had he told her the night he'd chosen to take Sindee, his girlfriend, to the colonies instead of her? *I love her. She's everything to me.*

Because, in the end, Naya had meant nothing to him. After she'd risked her life to make the money they needed to run, she'd been disposable. Nattie had easily discarded her in his quest for freedom and a new life with his girlfriend in the colonies.

Forced to relive some of the lowest memories of her life by Menace's cruel remark, Naya fought the urge to punch him in the kidneys. Just the knowledge that his three hundred pounds of dead weight would crush her on the forest floor stopped Naya from taking some revenge for his hurtful words.

All the fight left her then. She sagged against his powerful shoulder and let his thick, corded arms bear her full weight. This would go down as one of the worst days of her life. She'd been abandoned by the last person she'd loved and trusted and captured by a man who didn't even want her. Now he was taking her back to his ship where he would force her to do all kinds of degrading and perverted things.

But that didn't mean she had to go quietly. She'd make him so miserable he'd trip over himself to put her on a transport ship bound for the colonies just for some peace and quiet. Oh, she'd let him think he'd won this battle, but their personal war? It was far from over.

Chapter Three

M ENACE RUBBED THE back of his neck and paced back
and forth in his bedroom. He had the door to the
playroom cracked open so he could hear Naya and come to
her aid if she needed him. Not that she'd let him help her.
The woman was so stubborn and rude she'd probably
refuse his help even if he were the last man in the universe
and she faced certain death.

He blew out a frustrated breath and tried to figure out
what the hell to do next. He had been warned that some
brides could be testy after a Grab, but nothing had prepared him for this. Carrying her out of the forest, he'd felt
the fight leave her. He hadn't been stupid enough to believe
she'd willingly submit herself to him as a wife, but he had
hoped she would be amenable to giving their new situation
a try.

All that hope had been shattered the second he'd taken
her onboard the transport ship. Such a string of filth and
cursing he had never heard! And that was saying something coming from a man who had served on the front
lines with the infantry for nearly two decades. The colorful
combinations that she abused him with had left more than
one fellow soldier snickering.

Not even gagging her with one of the soft training gags

had been enough to shut her down. She had simply grunted and kicked and jerked at the cuffs he had used to keep her in her seat. Worried she would injure herself, he had been on the verge of requesting a sedative from one the medics. Apparently the idea of being drugged scared her because she had quieted down almost instantly.

After the nightmare trip from the surface to the docking station on the *Valiant*, Menace had dreaded taking her through the intake procedure and medical exam. To his utter shock, she'd behaved herself. It wasn't until she'd nearly completed intake that he realized why she was being so cooperative. That sharp, intelligent gaze of hers was scanning the ship. He'd almost been able to hear the gears turning in her head.

Concerned she would try to run—or worse—Menace had blindfolded her for the trip to his private quarters. As smart as she was proving to be, Menace doubted it would even slow her down if she escaped his quarters. He was certain she'd memorized every step, every turn and every ding of the elevator as it moved between the floors of the med bay and the housing section. Just in case, he had put travel restrictions on her ID chip to prevent her from leaving his quarters without him or one of the escorts on his emergency contact list.

It wasn't supposed to be this way. After seeing the way Hallie made Vicious smile and laugh, he'd let himself dream of this moment. With envy, he had watched their gentle interactions, the soft words and lingering touches, and yearned for it. He'd yearned for a woman to ease his burdens, to bring him happiness and show him love.

Instead of finding his helpmate, he'd Grabbed a woman who seemed intent on making his life miserable.

But it didn't have to be this way. She wanted control, right? Well, he'd give her a choice and then she'd be free to choose to be happy with him.

He strode to his closet, pushed aside the sliding silver door and rifled through his sock drawer for the one pair of white socks he owned. A white flag of surrender wasn't standard issue for the duty uniform. A sock was the best he could do.

Nearing the door to his playroom, Menace realized Naya was being awfully quiet. The fine hairs on the back of his neck stood on edge. He tapped the doorframe, activating the mechanism that pulled it wide open, and stepped into the room. The sight that greeted him left his mouth gaping wide open. "How the hell did you get loose?"

"Oh, nice of you to come check on me now!" She shot an angry glare his way. With one ankle still cuffed to the chair where he'd placed her after her shower, Naya frantically worked to pick the lock. "What if I'd passed out chained to this chair?"

"There are sensors in the cuffs. They measure your pulse and respiratory rate. If you'd been in any distress, I would have been alerted." Menace shook himself from the stupor of finding her nearly free. "How the hell—"

"For a soldier, you're really bad at frisking." She stuck out her tongue at him. "Always check the cheek, Menace. You'd be surprised how easy it to hide something like, oh, a hairpin in there."

He remembered the small black pins she'd been wearing in her hair during the Grab. He'd been sure he'd taken them all when he'd pushed her into the bathroom for her shower. Apparently he'd been wrong.

In a flash, she worked the final cuff free and jumped to her feet. She raised her hands as if prepared to fight him. "Get back, Menace!"

"Or what?" He laughed and shut the door. He pressed his thumb to the keypad there, activating the biometric lock. "You'll stab me with a hairpin?"

She glared at him, her dark eyes flashing with such intense hatred. "Don't tempt me." She snatched up the chair and wielded it like a bat. "Maybe I'll knock you upside the head with a chair. How does that sound?"

"Like first-degree assault," he muttered.

"Exactly! Now get my clothes and get the hell out of my way."

Menace let his interested gaze rake her naked form. His cock instantly responded to the sight of so much silky, brown flesh. The memory of her struggling beneath him in the forest sent heat rolling through his stomach. So small and hot, her body had instantly called to him. The sight of her naked skin made his heart race.

Her perky breasts heaved with every shallow breath. Her nipples had drawn tight to dusky peaks. Not from arousal, of course. Fear. Cold. All those things could elicit the same response.

His needy gaze moved lower. His fingers just itched to ride the gentle slope of her curving waist to her full hips and thighs. Though petite, she carried more weight than most of the women he'd seen from her planet. She had the sweetest curves he'd ever seen. What he wouldn't do for the chance to worship between her thighs.

"Are you deaf? Where the fuck are my clothes?"

Her waspish tongue ripped him from his lusty thoughts. Frowning, he said, "They're in the laundry. I'll give you clean clothes in the morning. If you cooperate," he added, figuring this might be one of the few bargaining chips in his arsenal.

"Cooperate?" She scoffed loudly and let the chair drop with a noisy clatter. She gestured to the wall of implements he'd so carefully organized. Some of the floggers and crops and canes he'd had for years. Others, like the gags and clamps and toys, he'd chosen in preparation for bringing home a new wife. "Look, I don't know what you think is going to happen tonight, but I'll tell you this, Menace. The only person getting their ass beat tonight is *you*."

And there it was. Under all that bravado, she was afraid. She was scared. *Of me.*

The knowledge hit him hard. Realizing he'd gone about this all wrong, Menace quickly reassured her. "Naya, I told you earlier today that I will never hurt you. I meant that. Never will my hand or any of those things," he pointed to the wall, "touch you without your consent."

"Well, don't hold your breath! My consent to be battered and abused will never come."

"Battered? Abused?" He reeled in shock at her strong language. "Naya, domestic discipline and a little rough love between a husband and his wife is not abuse. So long as there is consent," he added. "It's sexy. It's exciting. It's intimate and loving."

"Sexy? Intimate? *Loving?*" Eyes wide, she vehemently shook her head. "I'm sorry but this torture chamber isn't inspiring any feelings of sexiness or intimacy."

"That's because I've screwed this up," Menace admitted. He took a cautious step forward. "I should never have followed the usual protocol for claiming a wife. I should have done this differently." He exhaled roughly and ran his fingers through his hair. "Can we just—can we call a time-out here?"

Her expression softened. The fists that had been raised and ready to pummel him slowly dropped. "All right."

"Thank you."

She gestured to his hand. "Why the hell are you carrying around a sock?"

He glanced at the white sock and sheepishly smiled. "I came in here hoping to offer you a truce. I didn't have anything else white in my quarters."

Surprise filtered across her beautiful face. "A truce? Why?"

"Because this isn't the way it's supposed to be, Naya. I don't want a war with you.

That's the very last thing I want from you."

She swallowed hard. "What do you want from me, Menace?"

"I want…" He faltered and search for the right words. "I want a wife and a family. I want you to be here when I come home in the evenings, Naya. I've spent the last twenty-four years of my life training, fighting, training some more and trying not to get killed. I've earned the right to some comfort, to some happiness. I want—I want that with you. Let me make you happy."

She moved closer, the caginess gone from her once-mistrusting gaze. Now she looked at him with sadness in her dark eyes. "That's not the way happiness works, Menace. The people in a relationship have to be happy by themselves before they can be happy together." She hesitated. "Are *you* happy, Menace?"

"I am," he replied honestly.

"But?"

"But I'm lonely," he admitted, baring his secret to her. "Were you happy in Connor's Run?"

"Most of the time," she confirmed.

"But?"

"But it's a hard life down there on Calyx," she said.

Menace seized his opening. "I can give you a better, easier life here, Naya. You'll never be hungry. You'll never be cold. You'll have access to medicine and technology. You'll never be alone again. I will take care of you."

"Why?"

"Because owning a wife, mastering a woman, it's a precious thing. It's the one thing I've strived for all these years. Owning you is my reward."

Her voice grew tight and annoyed. "I don't want to be owned."

He understood her frustration with her new classification. "The laws are the laws, Naya. I own you now, but that doesn't mean you're property. It simply means that I'm responsible for you. I will never treat you any differently."

"Yeah, sure you won't."

"I won't," he insisted.

"You *own* me, Menace. We're different."

"On paper," he said. "In real life, it's nothing like that. Don't think of yourself as being owned. Think of yourself as my partner."

"Your partner?" she repeated in disbelief. "You just said that mastering me is something precious. How can we be partners if you're my master?"

"I want to be your master when we're in here or in my—*our*—bedroom. The rest of our relationship would be equal."

She rubbed her cheek and shook her head. "I don't understand, Menace. It doesn't make sense to me."

"It's because we're from two vastly different cultures." His gaze skipped around the playroom as he tried to think of a way to explain this to her. Noticing the way she rubbed her upper arms, he unbuttoned his uniform shirt and slipped it off his shoulders. "Here. Take this. You're cold."

She eyed the offered shirt for a distrusting moment before finally taking it. "Don't think this is winning you any favors."

He chuckled softly. "Believe me, Naya. I'm starting to understand just how hard I'm going to have to work to earn your trust."

"Good luck," she said grumpily and slipped into his shirt. "That extra appendage between your legs has automatically put you on my shit list."

He grimaced. "Could we maybe tone down the language a bit?"

She blinked at him. "You have a problem with cursing?"

"I do."

"But you're a soldier. You're, like, a soulless killing machine. You hunted me down like a rabbit and dragged me back to your ship like a prize. I'm supposed to believe someone cold enough to do that to me doesn't like to hear a good *fuck you* once in a while?"

He gritted his teeth at her description of him. "I am *not* a soulless killing machine. Every single life I've taken in battle has stayed with me." He tapped his chest. "I carry the horror of war with me every day. It's not a game to me, Naya."

Her cheeks flushed with embarrassment as she finished buttoning the shirt. "I'm sorry. I shouldn't have said that."

He sighed and slashed his hand through the air. "It's fine. It's forgotten. I'm sure you've spent most of your life hearing awful things about my people."

She nodded. "So far most of them have proven true."

He followed her gaze to the wall of impact-play implements. Remembering her earlier statement, he clarified, "This isn't a torture chamber. This is a playroom."

"Playroom?" She laughed. "I think words may not have the same meaning in your culture as they do in mine. A playroom is where kids keep their toys."

"Well, this is a playroom for adults. These are our toys."

"Your toys, maybe," she replied hotly. Pointing at the wall, she said, "I am brutally aware of what *those* felt like on my bare ass. I assure you there was nothing playful about it, Menace."

His gaze moved to the thin, snappy cane. "You've been

caned?"

"Yep."

"By a lover?"

She snorted. "By a principal and a teacher." She pointed out a long leather strap. "My mother was rather fond of one of those."

He was taken aback by the idea she'd been struck by her mother and in school.

"Your teachers hit you?"

She stared at him as if he were the dumbest man in the universe. "Well, yeah. It's called corporal punishment, Menace. You know, that thing you want to do to me."

"No," he said quickly. "I don't want to beat you as punishment. What adults do in the privacy of their playrooms is in no way comparable to a grown adult beating on an innocent child."

"To be fair, I wasn't always innocent."

Menace grunted in irritation. "It doesn't matter. We don't strike children in my culture."

"But you go to military school at like, five, right? You honestly expect me to believe no one at the academy ever knocked you around?"

He shook his head. "Never. Not once."

"You were obviously luckier than me."

He was beginning to see that. Her obstinate behavior made more sense. "Why did your teachers strike you?"

She shrugged. "Sometimes it was for fighting. Most of the time it was for code infractions. My mom…" Her voice trailed off to nothing. "I didn't always have a clean uniform for school. That was a big no-no. I finally figured out how to do my own laundry. Then, after my dad died, I missed a lot of school or I was late. Eventually I just decided it was easier to leave school than have a permanently black-and-blue ass."

Menace let that tiny glimpse into her childhood sink in and take hold. The similarities to Hallie's miserable childhood were so obvious. He finally understood why Vicious had taken such a drastically different route with Hallie—and why he was so overly protective of her.

Wordlessly Menace strode to the wall and started yanking down the canes and crops and striking implements. He stuffed them in one of the drawers in the corner cabinet. Glancing back at the wall, he spotted the floggers. Those would have to go too.

"What are you doing?"

He started to take down the floggers. "I'm putting away the things that scare you. There's no reason to keep them out if I'm not going to use them."

She stepped forward and hesitantly touched one of the soft tendrils of a flogger crafted for teasing and warming up a sub. "Why do you do it?"

The siren call of her body heat filled him with need. This was the closest they'd been without cursing or fighting. Calm and curious, she tempted him even more. He couldn't help but compare her to the friend who had escaped him. He'd considered that one the epitome of his desires. Standing this close to Naya, gazing down into her dark eyes and breathing in her scent, he realized his first instinct had been dead wrong. It wasn't the docile, sweet thing he needed. It was this young woman, this spitfire who drove him crazy.

"It's our way," he said finally.

She frowned at him. "What does that mean?"

"It means that our women are different than yours." He placed his armful of floggers on the nearby restraint table. He selected the one she'd touched, the easy warm-up flogger, and handed it to her. "This is a flogger. It's used for hitting fleshy parts."

"Fleshy parts?"

"Buttocks, thighs, breasts…"

"I see."

"There's some new research that shows that the bio-chemical makeup of our Harcos women is vastly different than yours. Your bodies react much differently to endorphins, adrenaline and oxytocin."

She glanced away from him. "I don't really understand what that means. I never—I didn't finish school, remember?"

His gut clenched at the shame filling her voice. Daring to touch her, he tipped her chin and forced her to meet his gaze. "It's all right. You may not have book smarts, but you clearly have street smarts."

She didn't pull away from his touch. "You learn quickly how to survive. I can do math and I can read, obviously. I just don't have much of a science background."

"Would you like one?"

She looked surprised. "What do you mean?"

"Some of the wives have lobbied for a school program. It starts in a few weeks, I think. I'm sure Hallie can fill you in on the details."

"Hallie?"

"My friend's wife," he explained. "She was Grabbed six months ago. She's from Harper's Well. That's close to you, right?"

She made a face. "It's nearby—and a hellhole. I mean, even when my life was at its shi—crappiest," she hastily corrected, "I gave thanks that I wasn't born in Harper's Well."

His lips twitched with amusement at the way she'd skipped over the profanity. There was hope for her yet.

"So tell me about these endorphins," she instructed.

He let his fingers drop from her chin. "Women from our planet require pain to find pleasure. It's just the way their body chemistry works. It might be something as simple as a nipple pinch to send them over the edge into climax. It might even require something as hard as a thorough caning and predicament bondage. But your women?" He eyed her carefully. "Your bodies respond much more quickly and easily to pleasure."

"I guess." The prettiest shade of pink colored the very tips of her ears. She kept her gaze averted and gestured with the flogger. "So people—my people—really enjoy this?"

"So far," he confirmed. "The locker room talk is that most of your women enjoy multiple orgasms under the hands of their mates."

Her shocked gaze snapped to his face. "Multiple? Is that even—I mean—no way, right? That has to be bullshit tall tales between friends."

Menace decided it was now or never. He fingered one of the long, wide strands of the flogger and held her disbelieving gaze. "Let me show you good I can make you feel, Naya. Hop up on that table and give me an hour. We'll test out the locker room stories."

Chapter Four

MOUTH DRY, NAYA licked her lips and stared right back at Menace. Was he serious? He looked deadly serious. Emphasis on the deadly. She marveled at his thickly corded arms and ridiculously broad chest. With his gray undershirt stretched across his muscled form, he looked a little less intimidating. She noticed the heavy tattoos running from the edge of his neck to his wrist but only on the right side. The long stretch of tanned skin on his left remained unmarked.

"Naya?" he prompted gently and took the flogger from her hand. "What do you say?"

She considered his dare. Multiple orgasms? Surely that couldn't be true. She had a hard enough time finding one climax on her own and had never been able to find one with a partner. Of course, she'd never had a partner as dangerously sexy as this man. Menace scared her with his hulking size and fierce features, but he exuded such raw sexuality. If any man in the universe could coax two orgasms out of her, it was probably this one.

To be at his mercy terrified her. Could she really trust a man she'd known less than a day to make love to her? She examined his honest face. He'd promised he would never hurt her and she believed him. The way he'd taken down those canes was proof enough of his desire to be good to her. The cynic in her screamed that it was all for show, but she didn't believe that. He'd come in here with a white flag of surrender. That had to count for something.

Her gaze jumped to the cold metal table where his hand rested. She shook her head. "Not there."

His eyes widened slightly. He seemed just as surprised by her acceptance of his offer as she was in giving it. Was she really going to do this? Was she really going to let this stranger touch her?

"All right." Menace gestured around the room. "Pick a spot that seems comfortable."

Gulping nervously, Naya gripped the tough fabric of the uniform shirt covering her nakedness and scanned the room. She spotted a black couch-like contraption against the other wall. It had a curved shape, the sleek fabric gently sloping and rolling like an S. It looked comfortable enough and as close to a bed as she was going to get. "What about that?"

Menace followed her pointing finger. "I think that's a perfect choice. Come with me."

She gazed at his outstretched hand. Asking her to come with him seemed a huge improvement over being Grabbed and tossed over his shoulder. She gathered her courage and placed her hand in his. She gripped his fingers. "Don't make me regret trusting you."

His lips twitched in a smile. "Never."

Naya let him tug her along beside him. When they reached the big curving couch, he dropped her hand and moved to one of the cabinets lining the wall. He tossed the flogger with the wide, soft strands onto the countertop. He opened a bottom door and retrieved a wedge-shaped cushion that he placed in the lowest curve of the couch.

"To support your back," he explained. "You Calyx women are a lot smaller than our women. So many of our supplies are made with them in mind but the manufacturers are starting to add supplements like these to make them work for your kind."

Naya anxiously nibbled on her thumb. She'd just noticed the numerous loops adorning the edges of the odd furniture piece. There was only one reason for them and it wasn't decorative. "Are you going to cuff me again?"

"Why do you sound so worried? You still have that hairpin, right?" Menace glanced at her and smiled as he secured the extra cushion in place. "Do you want me to cuff you?"

She shook her head and pinched the pin between her fingertips. "No."

"Why not?"

She blinked. "Because it's weird."

He frowned at her and gestured for her to hand over the hairpin. She hesitated before giving it to him. He slipped it into his pocket. "Weird? That's not very helpful. Do you mean uncomfortable? Do you mean frightening?"

"All three," she replied. "It's weird that a grown man wants to cuff a woman and restrain her for sex. Where I come from, men restrain women so they can hurt them. It's as simple as that."

"But what if I ask for your permission to restrain you and I promise not to hurt you?"

She couldn't help but laugh. "Are you trying to negotiate with me? You realize that I ran one of the most successful shops in Connor's Run, right? You can't beat me when it comes to negotiation."

Menace looked surprised. "I didn't know that you were a businesswoman."

"You didn't ask."

He had the decency to look chagrined. "You're right. What did you sell?"

"Everything and anything I could make a profit on, but my main business was pawning."

"That's loaning money, right?"

She nodded. "A customer brings in something of value and asks for a loan. I keep the item until they repay the loan plus a small amount of interest. If they don't come back for the item, I sell it in my shop. Simple. Easy. Uncomplicated."

"Were you very wealthy?"

Naya laughed. "Hardly."

"But you said your business was successful."

"It was, but the only way to get wealthy on Calyx is to deal dirty and do people wrong. That's not my style. No, I ran a clean shop and treated my customers right. I earned a comfortable living."

"What happened to your shop?"

"I sold it the morning they announced the lottery results and had the money transferred to a bank in the city. A friend of mine will transfer it to the colonies in a week's time."

His eyebrows arched. "You must really trust this friend

to give him complete control of your funds."

"I do."

"More than me?"

She eyed him carefully. "You're not my friend."

"I could be," Menace countered. "I could be more than your friend."

More than her friend? Her lover? Her confidant? Her support system? She doubted any man would ever be able to be all of those things to her. "You're my captor. Let's not get ahead of ourselves."

Menace grunted in annoyance. "I thought we were past that."

"How about we go back to your planet and I'll hunt you down and take you back to Calyx where you'll be my property. Let's see how quickly you get beyond that."

"Fair enough," he finally conceded. "But we are together now. You're mine. That collar around your neck makes us mates."

Naya fingered the offensive circle of white leather. Rather glumly, she said, "Not exactly a silver wedding band, is it?"

Menace instantly perked up. "Would you like one? If it would make things easier between us, I'll get two in the morning and find someone to perform a ceremony."

His enthusiastic response shocked her. She hurriedly shot him down. "No, I don't want to get married."

His face fell. "I see."

Seeing the hurt etched on his face made her ache. "No, I don't think you do.

Marriage is forever. It's a real commitment."

"I made a real commitment to you the moment I put that collar around your neck."

"We must have different ideas of what commitment means. Where I come from, it means love and affection and dating and laughter and all that wonderful stuff." Judging by the look on his face, she was only making things worse by pointing out everything they didn't share. "Look, I'm sure you're a nice guy, but I don't plan to stick around here."

"Are we back to that? To threats of escape?" He shook his head. "It's a foolish dream, Naya. No one ever escapes. Ever." He reached out and grasped her hand. His fingers brushed the raised bump along her wrist where they'd implanted one of their damn ID chips. "You're being tracked around the clock. You're on restrictions until I give word to security. You can't even get out of this room."

His words circled round and round in her head. The ominous threat left her sick and cold. She snatched her hand away and turned her back on him. "You're a real miserable bastard, you know that?"

A long, painful moment of silence stretched between them. When Menace's hands touched her shoulders, she flinched. Dwarfed by his big, hard frame, she couldn't run. Maybe she didn't want to run. It was maddening really. One moment she wanted to bop him right in the nose for being so infuriating. The next she wanted to fall back against him and enjoy the strength of his arms holding her tight.

Menace gently kneaded her tight shoulders, his powerful hands easily manipulating her sore muscles. His body heat penetrated the fabric of the uniform shirt she wore and soothed her raw nerves. "I'm sorry. I shouldn't have said that."

"It's the truth."

"It is, but now you think I'm a controlling jerk."

"To be fair, I thought that before you told me about the chip implanted in my wrist."

He snorted with amusement. "Thanks."

A white-hot frisson pierced her core as his thumb stroked the side of her neck. Trying to ignore the wonderful sensation he caused, she asked, "Why are you so intent on keeping me? Why not let me go and try again at the next Grab?"

"I want *you*. I'm *keeping* you."

Recalling his ugly remark in the forest, she wondered aloud, "Even though I'm just the consolation prize?"

His hands stilled on her shoulders. With one swift step, he moved in front of her. Hands cupping her face, Menace gazed down at her, his expression one of concern. "Naya, do you think I meant that?"

"You said it," she snapped back. "I learned a long time ago to believe what people tell you, even if it's said jokingly."

"Naya, I *was* joking. I was smiling when I said it."

"Yeah, well, I couldn't exactly see your face, could I?" she grumbled unhappily. "You'd thrown me over your shoulder, remember?"

"Yes." He exhaled roughly and wiped a hand down his face. "I can't seem to get anything right with you."

Naya noticed the vulnerability in his expression. The

depth of his remorse left her questioning everything she'd believed about this man and his culture. Sure, he'd Grabbed her, gagged and restrained her in flight and cuffed her to a chair in this torture chamber, but he hadn't shown her any violence, not even when she'd struck him first. She'd been rude and nasty and had verbally abused him so badly his fellow soldiers had been laughing openly—and still he hadn't raised his voice with her.

It occurred to her that maybe she was the one who had everything wrong. All along she had considered escaping to the colonies the ultimate goal in her life, that only in Jesco or Safe Harbor could she find happiness. What if she'd been wrong? What if Danny's tale of the Artist who was Grabbed living a life of luxury and happiness was true? What if *this* was her chance?

Fingers trembling, she placed a hand on Menace's chest. His pale eyes flashed with uncertainty. Considering how badly she had behaved, he probably thought she was going to strike him or try to shove him backward to flee. She held his gaze and rose on tiptoes to kiss him. He was still much too tall for her to reach his mouth but he got the message and dipped his head.

Their lips finally touched. The bright burst of bliss filled her chest with such warmth. For the first time since meeting Menace, she relaxed completely. His lips were softer than she'd expected and moved gently across hers. She put her other hand on his chest and gripped the thin fabric of his undershirt. His scent, completely natural and unadorned, filled her nose. He smelled of man and soap and nothing else.

As if he feared spooking her, Menace cautiously placed his hands on her neck and face. He caressed her skin with his calloused fingers. The rough sensation of his fingertips gliding over her neck and cheek ignited her desire. She couldn't remember ever being this aroused by a man. Maybe it was the danger of the unknown or the primal maleness of Menace, but she practically vibrated with lust.

His tongue stabbed between her lips. She welcomed the invasion with a swipe of her own. His heavy breaths fanned her face. Their tongues dueled, but Naya quickly realized this was a battle she wasn't going to win. She didn't want to win it. For the first time in her life, she *wanted* to give up control.

"Menace…" She breathed his name as need gripped her.

"Tell me I can have you," he instructed, his voice husky. "Give me permission to have you, Naya."

She didn't think twice. "Yes."

With a low hum of excitement, Menace swept her up in his arms and carried her to the oddly shaped couch. He placed her on it and knelt near her feet. Even on the floor, he loomed over her. Those long arms could reach every part of her body.

Overcome with nerves, she licked her lips. He grasped the bottom of his shirt and pulled it up and over his head. It was tossed over his shoulder and disappeared from sight. He removed one boot and sock and then the other. His tactical pants quickly followed.

When he stood up to push his boxer briefs down his strong thighs, she couldn't take her eyes off him. She'd seen a few naked men in her time but none compared to Menace. Tattoos emblazoned the tanned skin of his right side. Myriad scars, some puckered and pink and others a glossy white and extremely thin, dotted his body. This man had known such immense pain and violence. Maybe they had something in common after all.

Her gaze slid to his cock. She tried to hide her shock, but his smug smile told her she wasn't successful. She couldn't blame him for being smug. It was a huge cock. Thick and long and erect, it commanded her attention. Her pussy pulsed as she imagined what it would feel like to have that massive tool inside her. Very, very good, she guessed.

Menace knelt down at the edge of the couch again. He picked up her foot and caressed her calf. His fingertip traced some of the scratches she'd received from running through the woods. "Do these hurt?"

She shook her head. "They're just ugly."

"I've got something in my med kit that will help them heal." He lowered his head and kissed each and every one of the scratches. She held her breath as his lips danced up one leg and then the other. He placed her feet back on the cushion and let his hands glide up and down her thighs.

When he didn't go straight for the prize, so to speak, she was impressed. The few lovers she'd had in the past had always zeroed in on the secret spot between her thighs almost as quickly as her pants had been out of the way. But not Menace. He seemed to have other ideas about seduction—and she liked them.

With one knee on the couch, Menace nuzzled her neck. She closed her eyes and enjoyed the sensation of his hot breath tickling her earlobe and his big, warm hand stroking her outer thigh. A bit breathless, she remarked, "You're very good at this."

He chuckled against her throat and licked the spot where her pulse raced. "I want the first time to be good for you."

Her heart stammered but for all the wrong reasons. It wasn't his desire to make the experience wonderful for her that made her heart race. No, it was the realization that he thought she was a virgin. She'd heard stories about these Harcos men and their penchant for virgin brides—something she most definitely could never be.

Alarmed by his misconception, Naya put both hands on his chest and shoved him up off her. Frowning, he gazed down at her with concern in his green eyes. "Did I do something wrong? Am I moving too fast?"

"No." There was no easy way to break the truth to him. Best to just blurt it out, she figured. "Menace, I'm not a virgin."

His expression turned to one of amusement. "And?"

Confused, she replied, "You said you wanted the first time to be good for me."

"I do." He kissed her with such tenderness. "Our first time," he clarified. Holding her gaze, he asked, "Why would I care about the state of your hymen?"

His blunt question made her face burn. "I thought you sky warriors were big on the whole virgin bride thing."

"Some are," Menace confirmed, "but I'm not one of them." His fingertips followed the line of her jaw down to the curve of her throat. "You're fine just the way you are."

Naya couldn't believe this fearsome sky warrior who had stolen her away from her planet had just said the most romantic thing she'd ever heard. "Oh."

"Stop worrying," he urged. "Don't think. Don't question. Just feel, Naya." *Don't think? Don't question? How about asking me not to breathe?*

Menace claimed her mouth in a sensual kiss. He left her dizzy and trembling when his mouth finally broke away from hers. If he kept kissing her like that, it would be almost impossible for her to think or question. She might not even be able to draw air into her lungs.

He flicked through the buttons on the shirt and pushed the fabric off her shoulders. She sat up just enough to allow him to whisk it away. Naked again and at his mercy, she balled up her hands and placed them on her thighs.

Menace spotted them instantly and clasped her wrists. "No. *Relax.*"

"I can't help it."

"Do I need to cuff you?"

Her stomach lurched as the memories of being cuffed and arrested flashed before her eyes. She didn't want those ugly thoughts to intrude on this moment. "Please don't."

Menace tilted his head. Had he seen the fear in her eyes? Probably. To his credit, he didn't mention her weakness. Instead he lifted her hands overhead and carefully pried her fists open. He pushed her fingers against the big wide loops of braided material above the couch. "Hold on to these."

Relieved not to be cuffed, she gripped the fabric loops. "I won't let go."

He chuckled and placed a noisy kiss right above her breast. "I'm sure you won't."

"Ah!" she moaned as Menace traced her nipple with his tongue. The sensitive flesh puckered as he laved her dark skin. He sucked her nipple between his lips and licked across the tight bud. Inhaling sharply, she tried to press her knees together as her clit throbbed to life. Menace's position between her legs made it impossible.

"You have extremely sensitive breasts," he remarked. A light graze of his teeth against her supple flesh made her shiver. "So beautiful," he whispered, his voice filled with awe.

She groaned when he pinched her nipple between his fingertips and concentrated all his oral efforts on the other one. Back arching, Naya surrendered to Menace's tormenting fingers and mouth. She'd never experienced anything like this. Every nerve ending in her body burned. Down below, her clit pulsed almost painfully. She felt sure that if she reached down and touched the pink pearl, she'd come instantly.

When Menace suddenly moved, she protested with a whimper. "Where are you going?"

"Easy, sweetheart," he murmured and rubbed her lower belly. "I'm just grabbing something from this drawer."

She followed his hand to the cabinets and drawers lining the wall. He tugged open the second drawer from the top of one cabinet and retrieved something shiny and metal. Swallowing hard, she stared at the object he displayed on his flattened palm. They were two bright-blue, tiny clips with black, padded tips hooked together on a chain. She'd never seen anything like it. "What is that?"

"They're nipple clamps."

Her gaze jumped to his face. "Excuse me?"

He laughed at her shocked expression. "They're nipple clamps. They squeeze your nipples."

"But—why?"

"It feels good."

"For whom?'

"For you."

She narrowed her gaze. "Says the man who isn't having his breasts tortured by them."

"There you go again with the torture claims." Menace shook his head. "If I was torturing you, would I ask your permission?"

"Well…no."

"Would you like to try them?"

"No." The answer jumped from her lips. "Absolutely not."

"Are you sure?" He didn't seem the least bit daunted by her refusal. "You might really enjoy them." He shrugged. "You might hate them. You won't know until you try."

She pursed her lips. "You're not going to let this go, are you?"

He grinned mischievously. "No."

Rolling her eyes, she sighed dramatically. "Fine. I'll try them—but if they hurt, I'm taking them off immediately."

"Fair enough." Clamps in hand, Menace crawled over her on the couch and skimmed her neck with his lips. He didn't go straight for her breasts but took his time licking and kissing and nibbling until she was burning hot again.

As he played with her left nipple, he asked, "What's your favorite color?'

The odd question threw her for a loop. "What?"

"Your favorite color," he repeated. "What is it?"

"Blue. Why?"

"I'm going to give you a safeword. It's the word you'll say when you're feeling overwhelmed or frightened or uncomfortable when we're together. We can safely explore your boundaries that way."

"Blue," she repeated skeptically. "Why can't I just say stop?"

"Because sometimes we say stop when we really mean *go*."

"That's the most ridiculous thing I've ever—*oh*!" She gasped when Menace applied the first clamp to her nipple. The sharp pinch of pain took her breath away. "Ow!"

He adjusted the pinching power of the clamp to a more tolerable level. "How's that? Are we blue?"

Were they? She didn't know. She just knew that the clamp squeezing her nipple felt so strange. Not bad, exactly, but really weird. "No."

"All right. Let's try the other one." He adjusted the tension before placing it around her right nipple. "How's that?"

She made a face. "Okay."

"Okay good? Okay bad?"

"Okay good? Maybe?"

He laughed. "Well you're not trying to whack me upside the head and you're not screaming *blue*, so I think we're all right."

Naya hissed when Menace grabbed the chain between the two clamps and pulled it taut. The tug on her nipples sent a bright flash of discomfort arcing through her chest. He squeezed the large ring dangling from the front of her white collar. There was some kind of opening mechanism in the hoop, because he was able to loop the nipple clamp chain onto the loop and close it. The new tension on the chain accentuated the tugging pull of the clamps around her nipples.

Menace kissed the tip of her nose and then her mouth. He massaged her breasts in his huge hands. Her nipples throbbed but it wasn't painful. She felt more aware of her breasts than ever. Goose bumps prickled her skin. Menace playfully flicked the clamps and made her gasp.

After a deep, lingering kiss, Menace made his way slowly down her body again, kissing here and teasingly biting there until he was on his knees at the edge of the couch. He grasped her thighs and pushed them wide apart. She gulped at the realization her pussy was on full display now.

"Put your feet here." He pressed them into place, bending her knees and opening her thighs even wider. "That's it, Naya. Just like that."

Her belly wobbled as Menace swept his palm over her sex. She kept the area neatly groomed with just a small, perfectly trimmed triangle crowning her mound and the rest of her pussy bare. Menace ran his fingertips down her smooth slit. "I like this. I think I'll let you keep it."

She rolled her eyes. "Oh, that's so kind of you."

He chuckled and carefully parted the lips of her sex.

She could feel the cool air in the room against her hot, slick flesh. He framed her swollen clit between two fingers. "You have the prettiest clit I've ever seen."

Well, that was a compliment she'd never imagined receiving! Uncertain what to say to such a remark, she simply watched him as he explored her most intimate region. There was no mistaking the hunger darkening his eyes.

"Wouldn't a piercing look so beautiful right about here?" He brushed his fingertips across the hood protecting her clit.

She slammed her knees together and trapped his hand there. "I don't think so!"

His mouth curved in a smile. "It's just an idea."

"It's a bad idea."

He laughed and forced her thighs apart again. "We'll table it for now."

Naya glared at him. "Table it? If you think—*ah!*"

Menace swiped her clit with his tongue. Her head fell back and the issue of piercing her genitals faded into the background. When the shock of being licked *there* faded, she experienced a wave of embarrassment. He shouldn't be doing that—but it felt oh so good *and* he seemed to be enjoying himself.

Until now, all of her sexual experiences had been rather perfunctory and short. None of her lovers had ever put his mouth between her thighs. Maybe that was why she'd never been able to climax with any of them. All the thrusting in the world couldn't compare to the wickedly delicious sensation of Menace's tongue circling her clitoris.

Gripping the loops of fabric, she gave way to instinct

and lifted her hips. Menace groaned against her pussy and shoved her thighs even wider apart. His tongue traced one side of her sex and then the other before returning to her clit. He lapped at the bundle of nerves and sucked it between his lips. When he rolled his tongue over the inflamed bud, Naya saw stars. "Oh! Men—Menace!"

A flutter of panic shook her core. The realization she was so close to an orgasm stunned her. Even in bed at home, it could take her fifteen or twenty minutes of fantasizing and rubbing to get even close to a climax. Half the time that was as good as it got for her. Somehow Menace and his magic tongue had obliterated whatever mental roadblocks normally prevented her from coming.

Menace found the perfect rhythm with his tongue. Naya's breathing deepened. Her breasts ached and the clamps pinching her nipples suddenly changed from a minor annoyance to a surprising accentuation of the pleasure rippling through her belly. Eyes closed, Naya concentrated on Menace's soft, pliable tongue flicking her clit and his big hands pushing her thighs wide open. It was the image of being fully at his mercy that sent her over the edge.

"Menace!" She shouted his name as the first wave engulfed her. Fighting to surface from the wild pulses of ecstasy, Naya held tight to the fabric loops above her head and undulated atop the low couch. "Oh! Oh! *Oh!*"

Just as the first ripples of pleasure started to slow and spread out, Menace changed his tactic. He sucked her clit, using hard, long tugs on the swollen pearl to bring her right back to the edge again. He released the bud and used his now firm tongue to swipe side to side across it.

Naya lost it. "Ah! Ah! *Unnnnhhhh!*"

The guttural groan that left her throat echoed off the playroom's walls. She snapped her hips and pushed her pussy even tighter to his mouth. Menace hummed excitedly and lashed her clit until she thought she just might die. The waves of pleasure overwhelmed and drowned her.

Menace finally backed off. His licks slowed and decreased in pressure. He kissed her clit twice and wiped his mouth on her lower belly. She still shuddered with aftershocks when he pushed back onto his knees and grabbed the flogger from the nearby countertop.

Even through the haze of lust, she realized what was going to happen now. She should have been scared. She should have tried to roll of the couch and flee but she didn't. Mellowed out by those powerful orgasms, she felt more inclined to trust him. He'd shown her nothing but pleasure so far, hadn't he?

Menace caressed her leg. "Keep your hands over your head and your thighs wide open. I want those feet planted right there. Don't move when I strike you. That's the first rule you have to learn when we're playing impact games. Understood?"

"Yes sir."

His eyebrow arched in surprise. "Sir?"

She gave a little shrug. "It seemed appropriate. You remind me of the headmaster at my old school with all the rules you're spouting and that scary thing in your hand."

He snorted with amusement. "Remind me to hit up the shop tomorrow. I think some costumes might be in order."

She frowned. "Costumes?"

"I'll explain later." He leaned forward and kissed her. "This won't hurt. You're going to love it."

She wasn't so sure about that, but she'd been skeptical about the multiple-orgasm thing and he'd proven her wrong. He'd been right about the clamps too.

Sitting back on his heels, Menace gathered the long, wide tendrils of the flogger in one hand and gripped the handle with the experience of a master. Her personal experience with being beaten by others told her that he wasn't far enough away or high enough up to really harm her. There wasn't enough room for him to get a good swing going.

The tendrils thwacked her left inner thigh first and then the right. The soft tongues licked at her lower belly and then her thighs again. With each flick of his wrist, Menace increased the pressure and the speed. The slow, thudding beat soon became something a bit snappier. Her skin erupted in a blush of heat. It was the strangest sensation and one that she quickly began to enjoy.

It stunned her that something she'd once loathed with the fury of a thousand suns now made her pussy ache with need. What the hell was happening to her? Maybe Menace had it wrong. It wasn't the Harcos women who were aroused by and needed these kinds of games to climax. It was *she*.

Menace had scooted back enough to put some power into the hits. She moaned as the fast-flicking tongues of the flogger smacked the sensitive skin of her belly and thighs. When they brushed across her breasts, she gasped. Her already throbbing nipples cried out for more stimulation but she didn't dare let go of the fabric loops she gripped.

And then Menace shocked her by directing the last three whacks right onto her pussy. She cried out at the unexpected thwacks. On instinct, she started to close her legs to protect her vulnerable flesh but remembered at the last second that she wasn't supposed to move.

Menace caught the quick correction. "Good girl."

His compliment and pleased smile left her feeling so incredibly proud. He tossed aside the flogger and fell between her legs again. His skin felt cool against the red-hot patches on her thighs. He attacked her pussy with his tongue. It took less than a minute before she shrieked his name and came hard. "Menace! Menace! *Yes!*"

He lifted his lips from her sex and crawled over her. Mouth hovering just above hers, Menace removed one nipple clamp and then the other. The rush of blood into her pinched nipples made her growl. He smothered her with passionate kisses but didn't stop tormenting her breasts. He pulled and lightly twisted her nipples as she panted against his throat. Her clit clamored for attention.

"Menace! *Please.*"

"Beg me, sweetheart."

Any other man asking her to beg would have gotten punched right in the gut, but Menace's raspy instruction made her so wet. She wanted to beg him. She wanted him to master her. "Make me come, Menace."

With a groan, he captured her mouth again. His punishing kiss stole her breath. The hand tormenting her nipple left her breast and dipped between her thighs. Two wide, long fingers penetrated her slick passage. He thrust slowly at first, allowing her to acclimate to his invasion, but then he found that spot along her inner wall that made her cry out and tense. He laughed triumphantly and began to forcefully fuck her pussy with his digits. His fingertips rubbed that spot again and again.

Legs trembling, she dug her toes into the couch. "Please. *Please!*"

Menace kissed her cheek. His lips moved to her ear. "Let go, Naya. Come for me. Come for your master."

Her master? Oh, if anyone could ever possibly earn that title with her, it was Menace, the man who had mastered her body with such ease.

Menace brushed his thumb across her clit. Once, twice—and then she climaxed. Head thrown back, she screamed with delight. Menace buried his face in her neck and nipped at her flesh. The combination of the sharp sting of his bite and the thrusting, strumming fingers between her thighs pushed her into a stratosphere of ecstasy she'd never known existed. She rocked and bucked and shrieked his name. "Menace. Menace. *Menace!*"

On and on the climax went. When she could take no more, when she was limp with pleasure, she pushed her face against his shoulder and pleaded, "No more, Menace. No more."

His hand went still between her thighs. Very carefully, he pulled free from her body. His fingers glistened with her nectar and left wet trails along her belly as they moved up her torso. He turned her face toward his and claimed her mouth in a gentle kiss.

Overcome with warring emotions, she gazed up at him.

The tenderness reflected in his pale-green eyes left her feeling so confused. Her hatred and frustration with Menace for ruining her plans and taking her away from her friend and her future in the colonies had all but vanished. How was that possible? How had Menace managed to change her mind so quickly?

Amazing as it had been, it wasn't just the sex. Oh, he'd rocked her world all right—but there was more to it than that. Other than her father and Dankirk, Menace was the only man of her acquaintance to show her such kindness and patience. She wasn't naive. She understood that Menace was showing her the very best of him in the hopes she would acquiesce to his desire for her to stay and be his mate.

The idea of choosing him and this new life on the *Valiant* didn't terrify her anymore. She wasn't silly enough to think they were soul mates or anything ridiculous like that but she was wise enough to see that Menace offered her something she'd always wanted. Stability. Happiness. Security.

He caressed her cheek. "Are you all right, Naya? Was it too much?"

She shook her head and teased her mouth across his. "It was perfect. You blew me away."

His eyes widened in mock shock. "Was that a compliment?"

Naya narrowed her eyes. "I can be nice sometimes."

"Only sometimes?" Menace palmed her breast. Her nipples were still sore from the clamps but he was gentle with her. "We'll have to work on that."

If this was his idea of behavior modification, she couldn't wait to sign up. "When?" Menace shifted on the couch and pinned her beneath him. His hard cock nudged her lower belly. "How about right now?"

His playful grin made her laugh. "Was all that just foreplay?"

Dipping his head, Menace whispered, "Sweetheart, we're just getting started."

Chapter Five

ENACE RELISHED THE look of utter satisfaction on
Naya's beautiful face. A faint flush colored her
luscious body. To show her that she was capable of such
sensual passion filled him with great joy. When they'd
started, he'd sensed that she was uncomfortable with her
body and unfulfilled by her past sexual experiences. He
hoped that what he'd shown her tonight would convince
her that they could be happy together and to give him a
chance.

His ears still rang with the sounds of her passion. She'd
howled like such a wild thing when she climaxed. Her taste
and scent still called to him. He could spend an eternity
with his face buried between her thighs and never tire of it.
The way she responded to him left him slightly shaken.
He'd had good times with women before, especially the
pleasure girls who worked in the sky brothels that catered
to the land and sky corps, but it hadn't ever been like this.
Vicious was right. There was something innately different
about making love to one's mate.

"Menace?" Naya sounded breathless and excited.

"Yes?"

"You're squashing me."

"What?" He blinked twice and realized that he was, in

fact, squashing her right into the couch. "Shit! Sorry."

She giggled as he quickly rolled off her and onto his side. "It's all right. You're just really big." Her gaze dropped to his waist. "All over."

His rock-hard cock throbbed incessantly. It took all his willpower not to part her thighs and sink into her hot, willing flesh. Naya made him harder and hungrier than any other woman. Though seducing her had proven more difficult than he'd expected, he'd enjoyed the challenge of persuading her to submit to his hands and mouth. What they'd shared eclipsed the rather businesslike transactions of negotiating with a professional girl from a brothel ship.

Menace noticed her interested gaze lingering on his cock. Her fingers moved just the tiniest fraction of an inch toward him before retreating. He snatched her hand and dragged it toward his erection. "It's normal to be curious. Touch me."

Her gaze skipped to his face. "How?"

"However you want," he said, hoping to encourage her sensual discovery.

She hesitated before trailing her fingertips up and down the length of his shaft. A shiver of anticipation coursed through him. Her light touch ignited his need. She grasped his cock and slowly stroked him. His leg muscles flexed as the whisper-soft caress of her fingers sent heat rolling through his stomach. Her hand moved lower and he held his breath. She cupped his sac and brushed her fingertips over his ultrasensitive skin. He swallowed the groan of pleasure threatening to choke him in the fear that any noise might scare her away.

Her hands moved from between his legs to his lower belly and chest. She swept her palms over his torso and traced some of the more gnarly scars dotting his skin. "You've been in a lot of battles?"

He nodded. "It's been a long war."

"But you're an officer now, right? You don't see much combat, I assume."

"I haven't been on the front lines in two years, but I spent twenty-two of them right there in the thick of it. But how did you know I'm an officer?"

"Your uniform." She touched her chest and indicated the spot where his insignia would have been. "I know enough about you sky warriors to know what all those patches and embroidered symbols mean. Was I wrong?"

"I am an officer," he confirmed. Certain she wouldn't understand all the rankings, he added, "I'm the top land corps weapons specialist aboard the *Valiant*."

Her fingers went still. "Weapons?"

Knowing her people tended toward the pacifist end of the spectrum, he steeled himself for an argument. "Yes. You dislike weapons?"

"Me? No."

Her clipped reply unsettled him. Her gaze skipped from his face to his chest. What was she hiding? Perhaps she was afraid to tell him just how much she disapproved of weapons. "I keep weapons in my—our—quarters but they're safely secured. You'll never have to see or touch them."

Her expression turned to one of amusement. She touched his jaw. "Menace, I'm not your typical Calyx human, okay? Connor's Run is a tricky place to live, so I owned weapons of my own for protection."

His chest tightened. "That's illegal."

"It's a gray area," she said carefully. "It's illegal to possess any kind of firearm in The City and the smaller villages like Harper's Well and Willow's Tears. Connor's Run has its own set of city ordinances that make possession of weapons legal if they're registered."

"And were yours registered?"

This time she held his gaze. "Most of them."

The startling realization that he knew almost nothing of Naya's history hit him right on the chin. "When we're done here, we're going to have a talk."

"Are we?" She didn't seem very thrilled by that idea. Instead she pushed up on her knees and straddled his leg. Her hand moved to his cock again. She grasped him a bit tighter and stroked him slowly. "I don't think we're close to being done here yet. Do you?"

Clearly she had something in her past that she wanted to hide. He wanted to know what kind of trouble she'd encountered that necessitated owning multiple weapons for protection but he was willing to overlook it for the moment. Her stalling tactic felt too damn good. "No, not even close."

She smiled. He was taken aback by how stunningly beautiful she was when her lips curved and her eyes lit up with amusement. Making her smile just like that would become his new mission—and he never failed a mission.

Placing his hands on her waist, he tried to sit up so he could capture her sweet mouth in a kiss but she pushed on his chest and kept him flat on his back. He frowned up at her. "What?"

"Have you ever been cuffed?"

His eyes widened. "During sex? Absolutely not!"

"Why?"

"Because I'm not submissive."

"Neither am I."

He wasn't so sure about that. The way she'd responded to being under his control couldn't be faked. She'd been highly aroused by his orders. There was also a touch of the masochist about her. The careful application of discomfort and slight pain had enabled her to orgasm so easily. Discovering the depths of her submissive nature would surely provide the two of them with years of pleasure.

But that kind of sensual journey required trust. It was clear Naya's trust was hard to earn. Unless...

"Do you see that second column of drawers? Open the top one and grab the green cuffs. They're the only ones with enough adjustable length to fit me."

She reeled back in surprise. "Are you serious? You're going to let me cuff you?"

Menace caressed her side. "I trust you."

Her eyes narrowed suspiciously. "Why?"

He laughed at her cynical response. "Is everything a conspiracy to you?" Shaking his head, he explained, "I'm not stupid or naive, Naya. I'm quite aware that you're still unhappy about our circumstances, but I trust you not to hurt me. You're not a malicious person."

Her expression softened. "I would never hurt you."

"I know." He cupped the back of her head and pulled

her down for a deep, lingering kiss. "Now get the cuffs before I change my mind."

She grinned again and nuzzled their noses together. "Be right back."

He enjoyed the view of her bare bottom as she climbed off him and took the couple of steps to the cabinets. With her short stature and small arms, she didn't have nearly the range he did. She retrieved the green cuffs and returned to the couch with a bounce in her step. His appreciative gaze moved to her perky breasts. He couldn't wait to get his hands and mouth on them again.

She knelt between his legs on the couch and waved the cuffs. "Now what?"

He took the cuffs from her and showed her how they worked. The hook-and-loop closure strips made a tearing sound as they ripped apart. "You just press these two pieces together." He tapped the shorter straps on the undersides of the cuffs. "Connect these to the loops on the top of the couch."

She nodded. "Got it."

Menace handed her the cuffs and stuck out his hands. She had a wickedly impish smile on her face as she wrapped the first cuff around his arm. There was only just enough length in the cuff to encircle his thick wrist. She fixed the other cuff and then lifted his hands overhead. To get his hands into position, she leaned against him and accidentally pushed her breasts close to his face.

Unable to help himself, Menace flicked his tongue across her nipple. She gasped and pulled back. Annoyed, she glared down at him. He faked a contrite look. "Sorry."

"Why don't I believe you?"

"Because you're brilliant?" He latched on to her breast and sucked gently. She inhaled deeply, as if trying to master her arousal, and continued fastening his hands in place. He teasingly bit down on her nipple and made her groan. He chuckled softly.

Naya's fingertips grazed his jaw. She gazed down at him with a mischievous glint in her eye. "Keep on teasing me, Menace, but just remember you're completely at my mercy now."

He decided not to tell her that he could easily bust out of the cuffs if he wanted. Besides, his curiosity raged. What would she do to him now that she thought she had complete control of the situation?

"Do you get a safeword?"

Her question surprised him. "Do I need one?"

She shrugged. "You gave me one."

"You're new to all this. I want you to feel safe and secure when we're trying new things."

"Is that your way of telling me you already feel safe and secure?"

"Yes."

She shook her head. "For a battle-hardened soldier, you are way too trusting."

"I trust my intuition. My intuition tells me I'm perfectly safe in your hands."

She didn't disagree with him but he sensed she thought he was a little crazy or maybe even slightly stupid. His assessment of her stood. She wouldn't hurt him or put him at risk.

Naya's mouth dropped to his chest. She took her time exploring his chest and arms with her fingertips and lips. The ticklish kisses along his collarbone and just below his ear made his heart stutter. She traced his nipples with her tongue and made sure to nip him a few times. He hissed at the brief, sharp bites but had to admit it felt rather good in a strange sort of way.

As Naya kissed her way down his body, Menace tried to control his breathing. Even though he knew he could break out of his restraints at any moment, the vulnerability from having his hands bound heightened the sensations he experienced. White-hot currents streaked through his lower belly and into his chest. His groin tightened with anticipation as she slipped down between his thighs and wrapped her fingers around his dick.

A growling moan escaped his throat. Her wet, soft tongue swiped the head of his cock. Nostrils flaring and arms captured overhead, he stared down at her. The comfortable tilt of the restraint couch made it possible for him to watch her performing oral sex on him. The sight of her pink tongue gliding up and down his pulsing flesh made his heart race.

"Naya," he whispered "That feels so good."

She smiled up at him before sucking him between her lips. She took only the very tip of his erection into her mouth but it was enough to leave him dizzy. Her lips were stretched around his girth, the sight one that would remain forever imprinted in his mind. She eased off his cock and painted his shaft with her tongue.

When she pulled him into her mouth this time, he

curled his fingers toward his palms. He needed something to grip but there was nothing. Hands fisted above his head, he drew measured breaths into his lungs and tried to regain some control over his response to her hot mouth moving up and down on his shaft.

His cock popped free from her mouth. She stroked his length with one hand and used the other to push his thighs wider apart. When her tongue touched his balls, he gasped. She licked all around his sensitive sac and sucked on the plump flesh. Every tug of her mouth sent his need skyrocketing.

"Naya!" He wished he could sift his fingers through her dark, silky hair. Instead he lifted his hips in silent urging. She laughed and continued to tease him with her tongue and fingers.

The moment she pulled his cock back into her mouth, he exhaled roughly. Lifting his hips again, he carefully thrust into her willing mouth. He was much too big for her to take completely but she gave it her best try. The crown of his cock nudged the back of her throat. The quick flash of tightening as he pinged her gag reflex left his balls aching and his cock throbbing. Primitive as it was, he couldn't deny his response to her slight gag.

She didn't abandon his cock. Using her fingers to control the depth of his oral penetration, Naya kept her mouth on him. He fought to breathe normally and wondered how much longer he could flirt with danger. Every stroke of her tongue pushed him closer and closer to the edge. As much as he wanted to spill in her mouth, he wanted to come deep inside her, marking her as his much, much more.

"No more," he said finally and let his hips fall back to the couch. Naya continued to lick him lightly and suck the head of his cock gently. "Naya," he said with a moan. "I want to come inside you."

Her gaze jumped to his. "You could get me pregnant."

Cold crept into his chest. "Yes."

"Is that how this works? You seduce me, get me pregnant and then I can't leave?"

The frustration lacing her voice began to deflate his lust. "Are we going to argue about this now?"

She sat back on her heels. "I don't see how we can avoid the conversation."

"Naya, the Grabs exist so soldiers who have earned enough points through skill and bravery can build families."

"But so quickly? We hardly know one another!"

He couldn't argue against that fact. She hugged herself and a slight shiver of panic stabbed his belly. She was pulling away from him emotionally. All the trust he'd built with her was threatening to shatter. "What can I do to make this easier for you?"

"Give me time, Menace." She caressed his naked thigh. After a moment, she finally spoke. "I'm willing to give this thing between us a try, but I can't risk making a child with a man I hardly know. That's not right, Menace. I know what it's like to be unwanted."

His eyes widened. "No child of mine would ever be unwanted."

The look in her eyes told him she wanted to believe him. "You say that now, but I've seen what resentment does to a kid. Being told that you're the reason someone was trapped isn't a good feeling. I lived it for years. I won't—I can't—do that to my child."

It was obvious someone had hurt her deeply. Her mother? Her father? Both? "You would never resent your child." He believed that with every fiber of his being. "Neither will I."

"Menace…"

"I won't come inside you. I'll pull out." He bargained with the only chip he had. "If I could go down to the infirmary and get birth control for you, I would, Naya."

"Why can't you? I thought your society was all about technological and medical advances."

"We have population issues. The war has lowered our birthrate dramatically. A couple can only gain access to birth control after the birth of one child or the presentation of medical issues in the female. Very rarely they'll grant waivers for other reasons. I'm willing to put in the paperwork, but it could be months."

"Months?"

He nodded and tensed his jaw. It killed him to offer, but he refused to force her into a situation she didn't want. "If you would prefer, we can abstain from intercourse until I get an answer on a petition."

She tilted her head. "You're serious?"

"I am."

With a little sigh, she said, "There are other ways."

He frowned. "Other ways?"

She nodded. "I was taught to chart my cycle by a midwife in Connor's Run."

"Chart your cycle?" He had no idea what that meant.

"You keep track of certain signs and your temperature so you can anticipate your fertile window and avoid sex during that risky period."

"And it works?" It seemed too simple to be true.

"Beautifully," she said with a slight smile. "There's a reason Connor's Run and some of the wealthier sections of The City have such low birthrates. When you use charting with a sponge soaked in certain solutions, you have an almost foolproof recipe for family planning."

He jumped on this new bit of information. "I have a thermometer in my med kit."

She laughed and rubbed his stomach. "You only check your temperature in the morning."

"Oh."

"But we're safe tonight."

"You're sure?" He didn't want her to feel pressured tonight. The mistrust and resentment that would breed could kill their fledgling relationship.

She drew a lazy design on his leg. "My cycle is just a few days old. I typically have ten to twelve days in the first half of my cycle where I'm safe, five to six when it's risky and then fifteen to eighteen days before my period begins. But," her gaze skipped to his face, "nature isn't foolproof."

She couldn't have uttered a truer statement. "The choice is yours, Naya. I'll respect whatever decision you make."

She didn't say anything. Instead she slid back down between his thighs and stroked his cock. Their serious discussion had put quite a damper on his lust. With her supple lips and nimble fingers, Naya coaxed his erection back to life. He let his eyelids drift together as he enjoyed the wonderful feelings caused by *his* woman.

When she released his erection from her mouth, his eyes popped open. His breath arrested in his throat as she climbed up his body and straddled his thighs. Wordlessly she held his gaze and rose up on her knees. Naya reached down between their bodies and grasped his cock. She teased his ruddy, weeping crown through her slick folds. His pre-cum mixed with the shiny nectar seeping from her core. Without saying a word, she'd declared her decision to risk everything with him.

"Release my hands," he ordered, his voice husky with emotion. "I need to touch you. I have to feel you."

Her smoky gaze softened. With his hard shaft trapped between her thighs, she leaned forward and jerked free his bonds. Wrists free, he slid one arm around her waist and tangled the fingers of his other hand in her hair. Menace pulled her sweet mouth down for a kiss. He put every last ounce of emotion he could muster into that kiss. He needed her to know how precious he considered her gift of trust.

Breathing heavily, Naya sat back and moved into a better position. She lifted her ass and clasped the base of his cock. He didn't dare move a muscle as she aligned their bodies. Biting her plump lower lip, Naya pressed down on his shaft. He groaned when he finally breached her wet pussy.

"Oh!" Her eyes widened but she didn't pull away from him. "You're too big."

"I'm not," he assured her, his voice filled with desperation. Sweeping a hand down her back, he whispered, "You can take me."

"I can't." Even as she spoke her denial, Naya braced herself with a hand on his chest and pushed down on his cock. Like him, she seemed aflame with the need to be joined so intimately.

"Easy, sweetheart," he murmured and kissed her mouth. "Take it slow."

Her slick honey coated his shaft. She'd inched down on his erection and then retreated until just the tip of him remained buried in her snug pussy. He'd never felt anything so perfectly tight and wet. In that moment he thought he might actually die from pleasure.

"Ride me, Naya." He gripped her waist, pulled her forward and then pushed her back.

"Menace!" She moaned loudly and placed both hands on his chest. Her lips parted on a long sigh as she followed his urging and rode him. Her lush breasts bounced with each swaying snap of her hips. Unable to help himself, Menace latched on to her nipple and tugged hard. She cried out and clawed at his chest, her short nails digging into his skin. He just laughed and sucked harder.

When her head fell back, he knew she was close. He could feel her slick passage gripping his cock. Wanting her to shatter with ecstasy, Menace licked his thumb and found her clit with the rough pad. She groaned and shuddered. "Please…"

He wanted to tell her that anything she wanted was hers, that all she ever needed to do was ask and he'd do everything in his power to make it happen. Instead of telling her, he showed her. With a few quick flicks of his thumb, he sent her over the edge. She shouted his name again and again while her pussy fluttered around his shaft.

The last spasms of her orgasm rhythmically gripped him. Menace held tight to her waist and planted the soles of his feet against the couch's firm surface. Knees bent against her backside, he pounded into her from below. The well-trained muscles of his abdomen and thighs flexed as he jackhammered her tight pussy.

"Menace! Oh! Oh! *Ooohhh!*" She came again, her shocked cry music to his ears. "Menace!"

There was no holding back now. He slammed balls-deep in her welcoming pussy and growled. "Naya!"

He shook with each burst of semen that left his body. His head ached from the sheer force of his climax. The muscles of his torso and legs burned from exertion but he didn't care. He'd claimed Naya now. He'd marked her as his own and made her his wife and mate.

Cradling her to his chest, Menace pressed a tender kiss to the crown of her head. Like him, she panted for breath. Her cheek rested against his chest and her warm, soft body felt so right curled up against him. Her silky, fragrant hair tickled his mouth.

Quite unexpectedly she laughed. The raucous, joyful noise infected him and left him grinning from ear to ear. "What in the world is so funny? Not my skills as a lover, I hope."

"Oh, no," she assured him. "That was the best sex I've ever had."

"Then what has you giggling like a fool?"

"I guess I'm not so bad for a consolation prize, huh?"

Even though the words he'd jokingly spoken had wounded her in the forest, he heard the teasing tone in her voice now. "No," he confirmed with a smile and stroked her back. "Not bad at all."

Chapter Six

N AYA STARED AT her reflection in the bathroom mirror and tried to get a hold of her wildly vacillating emotions. She had gone from infuriated and frustrated with Menace for snatching her away from her friend and her dreams of a new life in the colonies to…well…what?

Her feelings toward Menace were so tangled. She felt comfortable enough to admit that she liked him. Maybe more than liked him, but she didn't dare dwell on that issue. Menace had proven to be nothing like the imaginary sky warriors who had terrified her since childhood. No, he was sweet, kind and patient.

And trouble. Big, big trouble.

She'd known Menace for less than a day and already she was starting to wonder if the key to her future happiness was that shockingly huge, green-eyed, white-haired alien waiting for her in the other room. He'd offered her everything she'd always wanted—a home and security. All she had to do was try to make things work between them. That's all he'd asked.

She fingered the white collar encircling her neck. The thin strip of plain white leather looked so stark against her honey-brown skin. It had seemed such a savage and cruel thing when he had first put it around her neck. Now she had a better understanding of what this collar meant to Menace. He saw it as a symbol of the commitment he'd made to her in much the same way her people viewed matching wedding bands. She wasn't his slave or his sex toy. She was his wife.

Even though he'd been exceedingly good to her, Naya couldn't shake the idea that he was putting on an act. The contract she'd been forced to sign upon boarding the transport ship had so many clauses in such tiny print on the tablet screen. She hadn't been able to make any of them out but she was certain there had to be an escape clause of some kind. All contracts had them, right? The idea that Menace was simply going to keep her happy until some type of time limit passed wasn't one she could discount.

She'd gotten a good look at the spaceship during her processing. The sheer size of the *Valiant* stunned her. She couldn't even comprehend how so massive a ship could remain in orbit. The mechanics and engineering required were so far beyond anything she could understand. Even if she could escape Menace's quarters, she wouldn't get far. The chip in her wrist and the heavily armed guards all over the ship had dashed those hopes. If by some miraculous chance she managed to evade all of that she wouldn't have the first idea how to get from the ship to the colonies.

The realization that maybe she didn't want to flee—at least not yet—hit her hard. Menace's skillful seduction had done more than just show her that she was capable of enjoying sex in ways she'd never thought possible. No, he'd also shown her that the two of them shared an undeniable connection. Try as she might, Naya couldn't deny that she and Menace clicked on a level she'd never been able to reach with any other man.

Finally she admitted to herself that she wanted to stay and try. Maybe it wouldn't work. Maybe in a week or two the lust between them would fade and they'd both be looking for ways to get away from each other. More frightening for Naya was the prospect that things would be better between them. She wouldn't know the first thing about making a long-term relationship work. Every man she had ever known had fucked her over in one way or another. Even Dankirk, the man she had been friends with longest, had gotten her into scrapes that she had only just barely survived. Experience told her it was only a matter of time until Menace did the same.

"Naya?" Menace knocked twice on the bathroom door. "I left one of my undershirts on the bed for you. Come find me when you're dressed."

"Okay." She stared at the door. A quiver of embarrassment shook her belly. She had never actually done this part. Typically she would bounce from her partner's house or send him packing from hers as quickly as possible after sex. The second Menace had unlocked the door of the playroom and offered her the use of the bathroom, she had fled. She had milked this tidying-up business about as long as she could without rousing suspicion. Now what?

Gathering her courage, she opened the bathroom door and entered the spacious bedroom. Her entire apartment back in Connor's Run would have fit in Menace's master suite. He had dimmed the lights to a comfortable setting. She spotted the folded gray shirt sitting on the end of the bed. The fabric was a darker gray than the bedclothes. Apparently shades of gray and black were favored here.

Naya slipped into the too-big shirt. It skimmed her knees but she was glad for the extra length. It looked like an ill-fitting dress but gave her a sense of modesty. Running around without underpants wasn't something she did very often, but something told her Menace would probably prefer it.

Like the bathroom door, the bedroom door slid into the wall when she touched the frame. It was basically a high-tech version of the pocket doors used in her tiny apartment to save space. Unlike her apartment, these quarters were uncommonly roomy. Having been blindfolded earlier, she had missed the grand tour. She took a moment to scan her new, possibly temporary, home. The open living area was connected to a dining space and kitchen. On the far wall were more doors. She assumed they led to bedrooms.

The furniture was quite different from what she was used to back home. There were no woods or natural fibers. Everything was shiny and sleek and made of metal or the strange plastic she had spied in the bathroom and playroom. As she crossed the living area, she noticed the flooring beneath her feet felt soft and warm. It looked like slate but was actually a weird composite material. She swept her fingertips across the upholstery on the furniture. It had a slick, durable feel.

"That shirt looks better on you that it ever did on me." Menace stood next to the dining table and grinned at her. He held two plates in his big hands. "I hope you like scrambled eggs."

"I do." She couldn't quite believe Menace had made her something to eat. "No man has ever cooked for me."

"Well, I should warn you that I'm not much of a cook." He placed the plates on the table. "You might take one bite and wish I'd stayed in that category of men who never fed you."

"I doubt it." She moved closer to the table and eyed the food he had prepared. The bowl of fruit in the center of the table held her attention. It had been so long since she'd had an orange. They were some of the only native Earth fruits that had survived the long journey in the generation ships to be transplanted on Calyx. As such, they were precious and ridiculously expensive.

He must have noticed her lingering gaze. "Food supplies are stable here and my salary has a generous grocery allotment."

She decided not to point out that food supplies onboard the *Valiant* were so stable because they required such high quotas of food from Calyx as part of the treaty. Fruit and meat were so outrageously expensive in places like Connor's Run because the sky warriors here loved them so much.

Instead of arguing about political arrangements, she remarked, "You eat the same things we do."

He nodded and returned to the kitchen for a carton and two glasses. "You'd be surprised how similar foodstuffs are from planet to planet. At least in this end of the galaxy," he amended. "Your people prepare some foods differently than we do and we tend to prefer heavier use of spices, but overall our diets are similar."

"I'm glad to hear that."

He shot her a strange look. "Why? What did you think we eat?"

"Food in boxes, mostly."

"Boxes?" His expression turned to one of amusement. "You mean war rations?"

She shrugged and pulled out her chair. "I guess."

"When did you taste war rations?" He gestured for her to sit.

"There was a transport ship crash when I was a little girl. Your people came to our aid during the Merkorian invasion. One of your ships blew up over our heads. There were miles of debris. My father took me with him to scavenge."

"And you found rations," he guessed.

"They were terrible." She made a face as the memory of the salty, dry food resurfaced. "They kept me alive though. There had been a bad drought that summer and no harvest. The winter was especially harsh that year. When Daddy was killed, I hoarded them so I wouldn't starve."

"Your father died during the invasion?" He pushed a glass in front of her.

She sat down and reached for a fork. "He'd taken us— my brother Nattie and me," she clarified, "into the sewer systems under the town. For some reason those *things* couldn't hunt down there."

"It's their eyes," Menace said and gestured to his with a fork. "They need a certain amount of light to process shapes and colors and shades. It's why we developed weapons that target their faces. The skin is the secondary target on a Merkorian amphibicore. They require a certain amount of moisture to keep their scaly, slimy skins alive." He opened the carton and poured blue liquid into his glass. "How long were you down there?"

"Three weeks," she said and purposely pushed the gross memories into the farthest recesses of her mind. "We were in the storm drain sections mostly, so it wasn't too horrifying. I was only nine at the time. Daddy was able to make it into a big adventure at first so I wasn't too afraid, but then a week became two and I started to wonder if I would ever see sunlight again." She laughed as the good memories shone through for once. "Daddy came up with all these games and wild stories to keep me occupied."

"You loved your father."

"Very much," she said and poked at her mound of fluffy scrambled eggs. "He always did his very best to protect us, but it wasn't enough that day."

"What happened?"

"Nattie got into an argument with our father. He took off out of the sewers and Daddy went after him and, well, you know." She touched her neck. "I found him later that night, just after sunset."

Menace's eyes widened. "You went out alone? After dark?"

"Nattie and Daddy didn't come back. I had to do something. I couldn't just sit there alone and wait forever." Her eyelids drifted together as the tormenting memory of her father's gashed throat and bloodless body flashed before her.

"What happened after you found him?" Menace asked, his voice soft and gentle.

"I started digging."

"What? By yourself?"

She stared at him. "Well, who the hell else was going to bury him?"

"But your brother—"

"Is the fucking laziest, most irresponsible dickhead you'll ever meet."

Menace frowned. "Language, Naya."

She rolled her eyes. "He's a jerk, okay? Even back then he was a huge jerk."

"But you didn't see it?"

"No, I saw it all right. I was just dumb enough and naive enough to think that people change. They don't."

"No," he agreed.

Not wanting to talk about her brother or her father any longer, Naya changed the subject. "Your home is very nice."

"Thank you." Menace splashed the blue liquid into her glass. "I think you'll like this. It's juice from a fruit that grows on Harcos Prime. It's a little sweet and just the slightest bit tart."

She warily eyed the glass. "Is it mixed with water?"

"Yes."

"From your planet or mine?"

"Mine. Why?"

"Because I haven't been able to drink water in Connor's Run without boiling it since I was ten," she said and picked up the glass. After a curious sniff, she sipped the brightly colored juice. To her surprise, it was quite delicious. "Oh! This is nice."

"I'm glad you like it." He bit a piece of crispy bacon. "Why are water supplies compromised in your town?"

"The Merkorians destroyed most of the town's infra-structure. What they didn't screw up, you guys blew up during your aerial attacks on their ships. There hasn't been any money to fix it, so we boil water or we don't drink."

"You don't have to worry about that here. Water sup-plies are adequate and clean. The plumbing systems allocate a rationed amount per apartment per day but it's more than enough for the two of us to drink, bathe and do household chores."

She glanced around the space. "Your home is very clean. Do you clean it yourself?"

He nodded. "I'm eligible for a cleaning service, but I don't enjoy having other people in my space." He hesitated. "If you'd prefer, I can request those services."

Naya understood what he was asking. "I'm not going to lie. I'm not the world's worst housekeeper but I'm not the kind of girl who embroiders tablecloths and cooks five-course meals."

"Neither am I," he said with a smile. "Between the two of us, I'm sure we can make it work." He motioned to her plate. "Eat. It's getting cold."

"Yes, sir." She gave a mock salute and tucked into her meal. It was actually quite good. She looked around his home as she ate. "At least you don't have a lot to dust."

"I haven't been here long enough to clutter up the place."

"No?"

He shook his head. "I lived in a section set aside for bachelor officers until a month ago. When I put forth my name for this quarter's Grab, the housing department offered me a choice of married housing units. I picked this one because it's close to friends who have taken wives. I thought it would be good for you to have support nearby."

His consideration touched her. Even before he'd taken a wife, he'd put thought into how to make her transition to this new and scary life easier. "What made you decide to enter the Grab now? Earlier you said you'd been a soldier for twenty-four years. Why not do it earlier? Did you not have enough points?"

"I had the points." He drank some juice. "I've had enough points for years, but we were on the front lines for so long. Fighting in the field for months on end isn't conducive to building a new relationship. It's one of the reasons why they rotated our battle group out here. It's still dangerous but it's much quieter. It's our reward for fighting in the very worst battles of the war." He suddenly had a far-off look. "There were battles where less than twenty percent of our forces returned. It was more than the enemy, but just barely."

Naya tried to reconcile those figures. To go into battle knowing that only twenty out of one hundred men would survive must have been harrowing. Menace had been one of those lucky ones. Of course, she wasn't so sure if lucky was the right word for surviving an experience like that.

"I was happy living my single life. I didn't really see a reason to change anything until Hallie."

She remembered the woman's name from earlier. "Your friend's wife?"

"Vicious," he said. "He's a general and the highest-ranking member of the land corps in this sector."

"So he's your boss?"

Menace nodded. "He's a good one. There isn't a man I'd trust more with my life. Well," he hesitated, "maybe Terror. He's just as honorable and brave. The three of us were raised together at the academy and fought side by side in the worst of it." He took another drink. "I never thought Vicious would take a wife, but he found Hallie down there in Harper's Well and his whole life changed. In a good way," he added. "I grew envious of his happiness and thought, why not me? Why shouldn't I take my reward?"

Naya tried to process the idea that he considered her his greatest reward. "Menace," she said gently, "you shouldn't put so much stock in me. I don't want you to be disappointed."

His gaze snapped to her face. "How in the world could I ever be disappointed in you?"

She blew out a noisy breath. "I'm a nobody. I'm nothing, okay? I'm just some poor kid who never finished school. I'm not the kind of person most men would consider worthy of being deemed a reward."

"Don't say that." Menace looked irritated. "You're a survivor. You had a successful business. You showed loyalty and honor during the Grab. You're a good person."

"You don't know me." She dropped her gaze to the plate of half-eaten food. "I've done things that you would not understand."

"Look at me." She didn't dare refuse him. His gaze burned her skin. "We all have a past, Naya. I don't much care about yours. It's done. It can't be changed. Let's leave it where it belongs."

"You make it sound so easy. In my experience, the past has an ugly way of finding its way right back into the present."

"If it does, we'll deal with it." He spoke with such definitive finality.

She arched an eyebrow. "Just like that?"

He nodded. "Just like that."

She marveled at his certainty.

Menace reached for an orange. "What's that look?"

She shrugged and picked up the last bit of bacon on her plate. "I was thinking about how nice it would be to have an ounce of your arrogance."

Menace laughed and sat back in his chair. "It's a cultural thing, apparently. At least, that's what Hallie is always telling me." He jammed his thumb into the bright orange peel and nicked the skin. "I think you'll like her."

"We'll see." Naya didn't want to tell him that she'd never been particularly good at making friends, especially with other women close to her age. She had always been awkward and a bit strange. Other girls couldn't relate to her. "You said she was from Harper's Well, right?"

"Yes."

Naya shuddered to think what her life had been like. "She was lucky to escape that place."

"She'd been in trouble with their law once or twice. It didn't end well for her."

Her gut clenched. "Oh, Menace, you have no idea how barbaric their laws are. At least when I was arrested, I never had to worry about having my head shaved or being beaten in a public square."

The moment the words left her mouth, she regretted them. Naya bit her lip and dared to look at Menace. His hands had gone still. He leveled a calm stare at her. "You were arrested?"

There was no use denying it now. "Yes. Three times."

"I see." His jaw tightened. "I suppose that explains why you weren't thrilled with being cuffed."

"Basically," she agreed.

"You should have told me."

"When? Like right after you put a collar around my neck and carried me back to your warship? Or maybe when your doctors were asking me all those personal questions and jabbing me with needles? Or maybe later when you left me tied up in your dungeon?"

He frowned. "Playroom."

"You know what I mean."

"What were you picked up for, Naya?"

"Twice for theft," she reluctantly informed him.

"What kind of theft?"

"Food."

"Food?"

"I was hungry," she answered honestly. "I was eleven the first time and thirteen the second time."

His expression softened. "You were a minor. Those wouldn't count against you in our society. I hope you learned your lesson."

"To steal with more stealth? Yeah. Sure did."

He didn't appreciate the humor. His lips settled into a grim line. "You will not steal aboard this ship, Naya. Is that understood?"

"As long as you provide me with food and clothing or a way to earn an honest living, I won't have to, Menace."

"I'm not being funny, Naya. I'm deadly serious."

"Yes, I got that." She placed her fork back on her plate. "I haven't stolen a damn thing since I was fourteen."

"Then what was your third arrest for?"

"It wasn't officially an arrest."

"What was it?"

"I was picked up and held for three weeks without charges. They released me and that was that."

His face slackened. "You were held for three weeks without charges?"

She didn't understand why he was so surprised. "Sure. I mean, the secret police don't exactly have to abide by the laws. That's why they're the secret police."

"Why?"

"Well, they do the bidding of the central government and they don't officially exist so—"

He shook his head and interrupted her. "No, I meant *why* were you held?"

"Oh." She figured a watered-down version of the truth was in her best interest. She didn't know Menace well enough to really and truly trust him with all the sordid details of her life. He said the past was in the past, right? "I was suspected of smuggling."

"Smuggling?" He laughed. "You?"

Naya bristled at his insinuation that she was some stupid, helpless little thing. "You don't know me, Menace. You don't what I'm capable of or what I did to survive."

His eyes narrowed. "So it was true?"

"Of course it was true. I was helping smuggle people off the planet and moving medicine and other contraband around Connor's Run and the nearby towns from the age of ten."

His jaw dropped. "Ten?"

"I had to eat. My parents were gone. My brother was totally useless. It was the only way I could make money to keep us alive. I was quick. I was smart. It was good work for me."

"Good work?" He spluttered and sat forward, slamming the orange down on the table. "You were engaging in criminal activities, Naya."

"Yeah, Menace, I know. I was there, remember?"

"You're lucky you were a child when you were doing these things."

"Why? Because you'd turn me in for being a criminal?"

He looked aghast at the very thought. "I would never—"

She put up her hand. "Spare me. I've heard that line before and both times it ended with me getting royally fucked over by someone."

That time he didn't correct her blue language. Voice laced with irritation, he declared, "You should never have been put in that situation. Someone should have been looking out for you."

She scoffed. "And who would that be? My dead father? My loser brother?"

"What about your mother?"

She stiffened. "What about her?"

"Where was she during all of this?"

"Far away from me," Naya said and rose from her chair. She gathered together their dirty dishes. "I was six when she left with a sky trader from Jesco."

"She left you behind?"

Naya blinked rapidly to force away the tears threatening to spill. "I should have wised up then and realized she was just going to be the first."

"Your brother?"

She took his empty glass. "He hopped a transport ship to the colonies six years ago."

"But you would have been just a teenager then," he said in obvious confusion.

She felt his stare boring into her back as she carried the armload of dishes into the kitchen. "What can I say, Menace? I guess I'm just not the kind of girl people want to fight for."

"Put the dishes down right now and come here."

His angry tone shocked her. She complied instantly and slid the dirty dishes onto the closest countertop. When she spun to face Menace, he'd risen from his chair. The stony expression on his face struck fear in her chest. Swallowing hard, she made her way back to him.

Menace snatched her by the waist and dragged her close. He reached back and turned his chair around before sitting. He hauled her onto his lap and forced her to straddle his thighs. Those skilled fingers that had shown her so much pleasure cupped the back of her head and tangled in her hair. The pain in his pale eyes stunned her. "Naya," he said with force, "you are worth fighting for."

"Wh-what?" She could barely form the word.

"You are worth fighting for," he repeated just as firmly. "Those people? Your blood? They abandoned you, but I never will."

He seemed so honest and sincere. She had never wanted to believe a man so much in her entire life. She opened her mouth, but he shook his head and pressed his fingers to her lips.

"I know what you're going to say, but I'm not those men." He seemed to be struggling for the right words. "Do you have any idea what you mean to me? What I went through to get you?"

Menace gripped the bottom of his shirt and pulled it up and over to display the right side of his body. Those tattoos she'd studied earlier were in clear view now. "Every mark I carry on my body is a reminder of the hell I've survived. These tell the story of my history as a soldier." He touched his left side, the bare side. "But here? This is where I'll tell the story of us. Someday soon, your mark will be right here."

Menace touched the space just above his heart. The implication hit her hard. He would wear her mark on his heart because she meant more to him than anything in this world.

"When we have children, their marks will join yours. I will carry you on me forever because you are mine. *That* is what you mean to me." Menace caressed her cheek. "Do you understand now?"

"Yes." The depth of his devotion both terrified and warmed her. No one had ever spoken to her in this way. If any man in creation had the audacity to be everything he promised, it was probably Menace.

He stroked her jaw and smiled sadly. "I know you don't believe me. Not completely, at least." He kissed her tenderly. "That's all right, sweetheart. I know what I'm up against and I'm willing to take on the challenge of convincing you."

Naya didn't know what to say to that. Menace reached for the orange he'd peeled and popped off one segment of juicy fruit. He teased it across her lips. "Eat your dessert so I can have mine."

His sexy, playful meaning didn't escape her. She happily allowed him to slip the citrusy flesh between her teeth. She munched on the delicious orange and felt the first tendrils of anticipation unfold in her core. Only one thought circled round and round in her head. *I could get used to this.*

Chapter Seven

MENACE ENJOYED WATCHING Naya sleep. Her relaxed face showed the slightest hint of a smile. Considering the way he'd ravished her after she'd finished that orange, he wasn't surprised. Hell, he'd had a smile on his face when he'd finally drifted off with her secure in his arms.

He studied her full lips and dark hair. The first soft rays of faux sunlight spilled out of the recessed lights above the bed. His people had long since mastered the art of long-term space living by fooling the body with specially filtered UV lights set on timers that mimicked a daily solar cycle. By eating a specialized diet high in vitamins and exercising regularly, the Harcos lived in space for years without suffering negative side effects.

Menace wondered how well Naya would take to her new lifestyle. Hallie had struggled with living in full-time orbit. Vicious sent her to see her sister in the colonies whenever possible so she could have a few days with her feet on solid ground. If Naya needed that, he'd find a way to make it work. There were years of vacation days banked in his account waiting to be used.

He trailed his fingertip along her collarbone to the very tip of her throat and then lower to the valley between her breasts. Their discussion from last night still troubled him. That she had a criminal past as a juvenile delinquent was the least of his worries. The women of Calyx were faced with ugly choices. To survive, Naya had made the choices she felt necessary. He would never hold those against her.

No, what troubled him most was the way the people who should have protected her had treated her so abominably. A mother who ran out on her and a brother who left her behind to struggle for survival? It was an absolute disgrace.

He now understood what he faced in earning her trust. It wasn't going to be easy, but then none of the things in life worth having ever were. Naya was worth it. He had to make her see that she was truly a person who deserved happiness and love and security. If it took his last breath, he'd show her that.

Remembering a promise he'd made about giving her time before they took a step toward parenthood, Menace carefully slipped out of bed. To his amusement, she reached for him in her sleep. He patted her seeking hand until she settled back down. Smiling, he headed into the bathroom and went through his usual morning routine. Before returning to bed, he opened up the med kit in one of the cabinets and found the thermometer.

He slid back in bed and activated the thermometer. Before she'd gone to sleep, Naya had explained that her temperature had to be taken at roughly the same time every morning and after at least four hours of sleep. Considering the routine he kept, she would likely wake near this time every day.

Menace pressed the flat, circular tip of the thermometer to her temple. A split second later, Naya's eyes flew open in sheer terror. She grabbed his wrist hard enough to leave bruises. "Get that off of me!"

The thermometer beeped and he carefully tugged it away from her head. "Easy, Naya. It's just a thermometer."

Wild-eyed, she smacked at his hand and sat up. "The hell it is!" She rubbed the spot where he had taken her temp. "What did you do to me? Did you inject me with some kind of drug?"

Her misunderstanding would have been humorous if she wasn't so clearly gripped by paranoia. "Look," he said and thrust the thermometer into her hands. "It's just a temperature-taking device. You hold it to the forehead or temple and it takes a temperature in three seconds."

She took the device with trembling fingers and studied it. Her fingertip traced the flat probe and then the digital display. She swallowed hard as color crept into her cheeks. Obviously embarrassed, she refused to meet his gaze. "I'm sorry."

"Hey," he said softly and tipped her chin. "It's all right. I should have woken you first. I can't imagine how scared I would have been if some woman I'd only known for a day was jamming something strange against my head while I was in a dead sleep."

"I guess."

"Let's start this day over, okay?" Menace leaned forward and captured her lips. "Good morning, sweetheart."

Happiness filtered across her beautiful face. "Good morning, Menace."

"Smile for me," he murmured and brushed his knuckles across her cheek.

"What?" She laughed nervously but couldn't squash the bemused smile that tugged at the corners of her mouth. "Why?"

He kissed her forehead. "Because I like to see you smile."

Before she could ask him why he liked that so much, he claimed her mouth in a kiss that grew increasingly passionate. Mornings had always been the time that he was the most easily aroused. Having Naya's soft, warm body in his arms made it impossible for him to think of anything else but possessing her again.

He pressed her onto her back and threw a leg over her hips. Pinning her smaller body beneath his, Menace pushed up onto his knees and planted his hands on either side of her face. She gazed up at him with such apprehension on her face. He nuzzled her neck and nipped her sensitive skin. "Relax, Naya."

"It's hard sometimes," she admitted, slightly breathless. "I know you won't hurt me, but you're just so damn big. I've spent my whole life keeping away from big, scary men."

He couldn't blame her for experiencing an ingrained response. Not wanting her to be uncomfortable, he lifted off her and started to move to the side. To his surprise, she wound her legs around his waist and shook her head. "Stay on me."

"Are you sure?"

"Yes." She bit her lower lip and then admitted, "I like

the way it feels."

Now they were getting somewhere. "But it makes you feel conflicted?"

She nodded. "I feel like I shouldn't want to be powerless to you. I feel like I should be the one in complete control."

Menace caressed her naked breast and brushed his thumb over her nipple. The dusky-brown peak tightened under his touch. "You respond so wonderfully to being submissive to me, Naya."

"I know." She didn't sound happy about it.

He kissed the side of her neck and nibbled her earlobe. Coaxing pleasured sighs from her lips made his dick throb. Her hands roamed his sides, setting his skin alight. "I gave you a safeword, remember?"

Her hands went still on his ribs. "Blue?"

"Yes." He gazed down at her. "You have the power to make everything stop, Naya. Even if I have you cuffed to my bed and your feet suspended in midair, you're the one in control."

Interest flashed in her eyes. "Could we do that?"

He tilted his head. "You want me to cuff you to my bed?"

She gulped hard. "Yes."

"You're sure?" He was ready to pounce on her request but didn't want to regret it later if she wasn't absolutely certain.

"You said I'm in control, right? If it's too much, I can use the safeword you gave me."

He nodded. "It won't get to that point, Naya. The first

moment I detect any true fear from you, I'll cut you loose."

A sweet smile brightened her face. "I know you will."

She hadn't said the word *trust*, but they were getting there. She trusted him not to hurt her. She trusted him to behave honorably and abide by the rules. Knowing her history, it was a huge step forward in their relationship.

Menace kissed her deeply. "Wait here. I need to get some things."

"Um, may I use the restroom first?"

"Sorry," he apologized quickly. "I shouldn't have jumped on you the second you woke up, but you're just too tempting."

She laughed. "Well with an apology like that, a girl can forgive her big, sexy sky warrior for making her do the potty dance."

Menace frowned at her while she bounced off the bed and scurried to the bathroom. "The what?"

She touched the frame and opened the door. Glancing over her shoulder, she presented such a stunningly erotic picture. Her bare bottom and smiling face were the things of fantasies. "You haven't spent much time around toddlers."

He shook his head. "Children aren't very common aboard the *Valiant* yet. We've only just started an elementary school program for five- and six-year-olds. I understand it's a class of seven."

"Well, someday when you have a handful of rotten little Menaces running around this place driving you insane with their yelling and wild antics, you'll understand the term."

She disappeared into the bathroom and left him thinking about the very real possibility of such a thing happening in the not too distant future. An image of a young child with the same honey-brown skin and dark hair as Naya but his pale eyes appeared before him. The idea of someday walking into a noisy home to be greeted by the sounds of his wife and children filled him with the most desperate sense of longing.

For so long, he'd fought to preserve the Harcos way of life from those insurrectionists who wanted to ruin everything that was good and right and true about their society. He'd gone into battle ready to die to defend the lives of the men who stood on either side of him. Grabbing Naya had given him a chance to build something even greater to protect and defend—a family, *his* very own family.

Emboldened by his desire to cultivate a lasting, trusting relationship with the young woman he'd caught in the forest, Menace climbed off the bed and made his way to the playroom attached to their bedroom. He quickly chose the items he needed for the sensual torment he had in mind.

When he returned, he found Naya kneeling in the center of the bed. The ends of her hair looked damp. Had she showered that quickly? Anxiety and excitement radiated from her in waves. She chewed her lower lip and picked at the sheets. Telling her to relax wasn't going to help. The sooner he had her bound and completely at the mercy of his hands and mouth, the better.

"On your back," he ordered and dumped his armful of supplies onto the bed.

Her curious gaze scanned the items he'd dropped. She

pointed to a slim, short anal plug he'd chosen on a whim. "Do I even want to know what the hell that is?"

"Probably not," he said with a teasing smirk.

To her credit, she didn't instantly refuse to even consider the plug. She did as he'd asked and moved onto her back, her hands fisted at her sides. Gently he took her hands in his and pulled her arms up over her head. He hoped that in time she would grow to trust him enough not to tense up so badly. For now, he was willing to work around her fear. After the life she had lived in Connor's Run, he couldn't expect anything less from her.

When he pulled free the leather, padded cuffs hidden between the mattress and headboard, Naya's eyes widened. "Is that standard bed design around here?"

He laughed. "Yes. There are points along the bedframe that allow restraint connections."

She was quiet. "Is our bed the only place I need to worry about you whipping out the chains and cuffs? I mean, the dinner table is just a dinner table, right? It's not some weird piece of sex furniture?"

Menace snorted. "It's just a table."

He didn't tell her that even a simple table could be a perfect prop for some impromptu rough loving. He expertly applied the cuffs to her wrists and hooked the chain to a ring attached to the very top of the headboard. He pulled the chain taut, ridding it of any slack so she wouldn't be able to jerk her arms and potentially hurt her shoulders or wrists.

He checked the cuff tightness again. Vicious had been right about buying the extrasmall cuffs. The supply shop had started carrying them not long after Vicious Grabbed Hallie. They were much more expensive but provided such a good fit for Naya's slim wrists.

Menace swept his fingertips along the exposed undersides of her arms. She shivered and tried to squeeze her knees together but ended up squeezing his hips instead. He continued to tease and torment her with ticklish caresses and featherlight kisses as he moved down her body. The sight of her hard nipples and deepening breaths told him all he needed to know.

Skimming his way down her body, Menace became aware of the bright, fresh scent of the citrus soap he had bought especially for her. She had done more than just brush her teeth in preparation for their morning tryst. He found her actions a bit curious but wondered if this wasn't one of those slight cultural differences. He had heard that the women from Calyx were incredibly sensitive about cleanliness. Considering the attitudes many of the men down there held toward women's bodies, it wasn't surprising.

While he wouldn't blink twice at making love to his woman after a torrid night together, Naya clearly felt more comfortable after tidying up a bit. He made a mental note to start tomorrow morning by carrying her into a steamy shower. Just the thought of getting his soapy paws on her wet body made his balls ache.

But right now he had her bound to his bed, willing and ready. Menace grasped her ankles and latched the second set of padded cuffs around them. He hooked one end of a restraint to the ring dangling from the front of each cuff.

The other end of the restraint he attached to connection spots on the headboard.

"How do you feel?" He inspected the ankle cuffs and the restraint straps to ensure her legs weren't bearing any unnecessary weight.

"Vulnerable," she admitted.

"Good." He caressed her outer thigh. "Relax your muscles, sweetheart. Let the restraints do the work."

She inhaled slowly and closed her eyes. Menace sat back on his heels and let his needy gaze rake her sexy body. Trussed up in his restraints, she looked absolutely delectable. Her wide-open thighs invited him to delve between them and explore her slick, tight pussy. He couldn't wait to hear her moaning and panting and shrieking his name. If ever there was an ego stroke, it was the sound of his woman gripped in the throes of passion.

"Menace?" She spoke softly and uncertainly. "What happens now?"

"Now?" He let his fingertips trail along her inner thigh. "Now we play."

NAYA GULPED DOWN her anxiety. There was no mistaking the impish glint in Menace's eyes. With her wrists cuffed overhead and her legs in the air, no amount of wiggling or jerking would set her free. His searing gaze roamed her naked curves. He looked at her as if she were the most perfect and beautiful woman in the whole universe. No one had ever made her feel as craved and needed as Menace.

When he swept his rough, calloused palm along her skin, she shivered with desire. There was something about his big, warm hands on her body that made her lose control. His touch short-circuited the side of her brain that demanded she be tough and brave and dominant to the point of off-putting. There was a reason men back in Connor's Run weren't beating down her door. She came across as cold and aloof out of necessity. Showing weakness was the quickest way to becoming a victim in her neck of the woods.

But here with Menace, under his loving hands, she was slowly learning to accept her submission to him as a special kind of intimacy. She couldn't imagine any other man she would willingly allow to master her. Those honest green eyes showed no malice. Naya had always prided herself on being able to read people. Only once had she ever been truly fooled, but that instance was complicated by her sisterly affection and her childish belief that blood meant something.

Menace wasn't Nattie. Oh sure, she'd only known Menace for a day and yes, the mere sight of this feral beast of a man made her clitoris tingle with some kind of primitive need, but she believed with every fiber of her being that at his core Menace was honest and loyal and kind. Even though her heart raced and her gut clenched with nervousness, she recognized that Menace wasn't going to harm her. He considered her a precious gift that should be protected and cherished. Frankly the idea that someone wanted to protect and provide for her was more unsettling than being cuffed and bound to his bed.

"Menace," she whispered as he skimmed his lips over the swell of her breast.

"Naya," he replied just as softly, his amusement evident. A moment later he tugged her nipple between his lips.

She moaned at the sharp sensation his mouth caused. "The things you do to me…"

He chuckled against her breast. "You like them."

"I do." Admitting it aloud made her current predicament seem even more surreal. Had she really asked him to do this? To tie her up and use her? Just a taste of the sensual eroticism last night in the playroom had been enough to whet her appetite for Menace's brand of loving. She had no doubt that he would make good use of this opportunity to show her just how good he could make her feel.

Menace kissed his way down the sloping plane of her abdomen until he was between her thighs. Her lower belly pitched when his lips grazed her mound. She held her breath and silently willed him to put his tongue on her again. Already her clit throbbed incessantly. Menace had awakened a wanton sexual creature within her. She had gone from the girl who couldn't come to the girl who couldn't *stop* coming.

"Ah!" Head thrown back, she curled her fingers toward her palms. Menace had parted her silken flesh with his fingertips. His tongue invaded her secret place, dipping and swiping and driving her crazy. He flicked her inflamed bud a few times but didn't linger. His tongue moved even lower and entered her pussy. "Oh! *Oh!*"

He groaned with excitement and thrust his tongue in and out of her. The overwhelming sensation scared her a little, but she couldn't slam her thighs closed to force him to stop. Not that she really wanted him to stop. What was it he'd said last night? Sometimes we say stop but we really mean go? Oh hell. This was one of those moments.

Menace licked two fingers, moistening his skin, and penetrated her carefully. She bucked her hips and welcomed the thick digits filling her. His tongue fluttered across her clit as his fingers thrust deep and slow. Pulling at her bonds, Naya lifted her head and peered down at him. The sight of that big, strong man between her thighs sent her reeling over the edge.

Mine. The word echoed in her mind as she climaxed. Just as she belonged to him, he belonged to her. Moaning and crying out, she rode the waves of ecstasy. "Menace!"

He hummed against her clit and sucked the pink pearl harder. Her hips popped off the mattress and she shouted his name. His fingers curved inside her, the tips of them rubbing that spot inside her pussy that made her toes curl. He went wild on her clit, sucking the small bud and rolling his tongue across it until bliss burst inside her again. "Menace! Yes! *Yes!*"

His leisurely licks brought her down from the heights of ecstasy but she sensed he wasn't done with her yet. Limp with pleasure, she sagged against the bed. Menace's fingers slipped out of her. He drew a few circles around her clit and then allowed his fingers to glide down through her folds.

Her breath caught in her throat when his fingertips moved even lower. She clenched her butt cheeks. "What are you doing?"

"Stimulating your erogenous zones," he said matter-of-factly. "How does it feel?"

"Weird," she said. Her eyes widened when his wet fingertip circled the pucker hidden there. It still felt weird but it also felt...*good*? Naya licked her lips. The forbidden nature of his fingertip touching such a taboo place made her head pound.

"Your body is a treasure trove of erogenous zones. Not just the obvious ones like this," he said and licked her clit a few times. His fingertip tapped her anus. "This is another erogenous zone. This area is packed with nerve endings. You'll enjoy having it stimulated."

He spoke with such certainty. Voice trembling, she asked, "Stimulated how?"

"With my fingers, with toys," he informed her. "Someday maybe even with my cock."

She gasped and shook her head. "No, Menace. You're too big. Way too big."

"Easy, honey." Menace lifted his head so she could find his reassuring gaze. "You're nowhere close to being ready to penetrate that way. You may never be ready—and that's perfectly fine." Kissing her thigh, he said, "But let's not throw it off the table completely. There's no reason we can't explore it."

She was reminded of her fear of the nipple clamps. They'd been awfully pinchy at first but had started to feel really, *really* good once Menace touched her clit. He'd been right about the clamps bringing her pleasure. Maybe he was right about trying new things *down there*. He was the sex expert in their relationship, after all.

"You have your safeword, Naya. Use it."

"Now?" She glanced at him and frowned. "But I'm not ready to use it."

"I'm going to touch you here." His fingertip moved between her cheeks again. "I'm going to use a small plug on you. If you don't like it or if it hurts or if you just need to stop because it's overwhelming, you say *blue*."

The reminder that she was in control helped her face the unknown. Menace reached for the pile of things he had brought from the playroom. He picked up a tube and flipped open the lid. He squeezed a dollop of clear gel onto his fingertips. "Lubricant."

"Oh."

He picked up the strange black thing she had spotted earlier. "This is an anal plug. It's very slim and small. It also vibrates."

Naya couldn't wrap her mind around the idea of having that thing inside her. The detail about the vibrating confused her. "Vibrates? Why?"

Menace laughed. "You'll see soon enough."

Annoyed by his non-answer, Naya let her head drop back to the pillow. Menace slid down between her thighs again. He smeared the clear, cold lubricant on her rosebud. His tongue returned to her clit. All that talking had killed her arousal level but Menace's firm, flicking tongue soon ratcheted it right back up.

Sighing, Naya relished the feel of his tongue on her clit. When a well-lubed fingertip finally breached her virgin backside, Naya hissed. She tried not to tense. Menace sucked her clit a little harder and drew her attention away from the finger wiggling inside her ass. Heat filled her core.

The first twinge of a climax rippled through her.

Menace eased off her clit. His tongue brushed lightly across the swollen bud but he didn't use the rhythm and pressure that would normally set her off. Instead he started to thrust his finger in and out of her backside. She groaned in frustration but he didn't give her what she wanted…yet.

A second slick finger joined the first. She inhaled sharply at the full sensation. Menace's tongue fluttered over her clit, easing the discomfort of having two thick digits spearing her ass. He worked those fingers in and out of her, widening them just a bit. It didn't escape even her inexperienced mind that he was preparing her for something.

What he'd said about nerve endings was proving true. She throbbed and pulsed with need. It didn't seem possible, but the fingers thrusting in and out of her amplified every soft flick of Menace's tongue. Her swollen clit ached, but Menace wasn't about to give her the stimulation she needed to climax. Clearly the bastard enjoyed keeping her on the edge.

He pulled his finger free from her body. His mouth left her clit. She rocked her hips in a desperate move. "Menace, please. I want to come."

"Patience, sweetheart," he urged. "It'll be worth it in the end."

She couldn't see what he was doing but a few moments later the blunt, slippery tip of the plug he had shown her pressed against her anus. The muscles of her legs and arms tightened in an automatic response to being penetrated there.

"No," Menace ordered, his voice firm but gentle. "Relax. It's no bigger than the fingers that were just making you feel so good."

"I'm trying." She bit her lower lip and exhaled slowly. Menace didn't force her to accept the small toy. He applied just the slightest amount of pressure and waited patiently. It entered her at a snail's pace. He was right. It wasn't any wider or longer than his fingers. It felt cool inside her and incredibly odd.

Menace rubbed the back of her thigh. "Okay?"

"Yes."

"Feels weird?" He opened a small package and used the pre-moistened wipe inside to clean the slick lubricant from his fingers.

"Yes."

He leaned down to capture her mouth. "It's about to feel very, very good."

She arched an eyebrow. "Promise?"

"Have I let you down yet?"

"No." The answer came swiftly.

Menace kissed her long and hard. "Prepare to be awed, sweetheart."

From anyone else such a statement would have been silly or even joking but Menace actually meant it. Naya's stomach flip-flopped as Menace rose up on his knees.

His hand slipped down between her wide-open thighs. He touched the base of the toy embedded in her backside. A split second later, a wild buzzing sensation started to ripple through her. She gasped and lifted her hips in shock. "What the hell is that?"

"You asked why it vibrates." Menace's thumb moved

side to side over her clit. "This is why."

The delicious vibrations shuddered deep inside her. Menace strummed her clit with his thumb and palmed her breast. He squeezed her sensitive flesh and pinched her nipple. She hissed at the brief discomfort but didn't ask him to stop. The quicksilver flash of pain that accompanied his pinching, pulling fingers traveled right to her clit. The tiny bundle of nerves pulsed. When he finally let her come, she was probably going to pass out from sheer ecstasy.

Menace stroked the length of his massive cock. She panted at the sight of him working his big hand up and down his steely shaft. Gripped with the need to have him inside her, she jiggled her feet and curled her toes toward him. "Please, Menace. I need you."

Lust sparked in his pale eyes. Nostrils flaring, he moved even closer to her, pressing his rigid cock against her pussy. Skin-to-skin, she breathed hard and shifted her hips again. "I want you."

His eyes closed briefly. "Say it again, Naya."

"I want you. I need you, Menace." She wasn't parroting the phrases just for his benefit. She meant it. She wanted this man. She needed him. "Please…"

He planted his hands near her shoulders and hovered over her. "This may be too much for you. Tell me if it is."

"I will," she promised. "Just hurry. Put your cock in me."

He groaned as her filthy instruction registered. Grasping his erection, he dragged the ruddy crown through her dewy folds. She moaned with desire as he used the head of his cock to rub her clit. The vibrating toy in her ass tormented her.

Finally Menace pressed his cock into her. He moved at an achingly slow pace. His shaft filled her to the breaking point. She cried out as the sensation of being stretched and taken by his cock and the toy became almost too much. Menace froze his forward movement but bent his head. He nuzzled her cheek and coaxed a tender kiss from her lips.

Menace gripped the front of her bride's collar. The possessive, dominant action made her pussy clench. "Look at me."

Gazing into his light-green eyes, Naya lost herself. "Menace, I—"

He cut her off with a kiss. "You can take me."

Proving his point, Menace thrust forward just a fraction of an inch and then retreated almost completely. The gliding sensation of his huge cock made her moan. Nipples taut and tingling, Naya arched her back. His lips fell to her exposed neck. He nibbled and licked while rocking in and out of her wet pussy. Slipping his hand between their joined bodies, he found her clit. A few brushes of his thumb and she exploded.

"Menace!" Shrieking his name, she undulated wildly atop the bed. The climax punched the air right out of her lungs. Pure bliss spilled from her core, saturating her from head to toe. "Oh! Oh! *Ahhhh!*"

Still holding the front of her collar, Menace started to fuck her as if he were some feral beast. He snapped his hips and pounded her pussy. The small toy in her ass vibrated constantly and added to the wickedly erotic experience. Menace changed the angle of his shallow penetration. That was all it took to push her over the edge again.

When she finally surfaced from the deep waters of ecstasy, Naya practically sobbed for mercy. "Menace, I can't. *Oh!* Please. *Please!*"

With his lips against her ear, he slammed into her one final time. The force of his last thrust shoved her up the bed. Her name left his lips on a groaned sigh. "Naya."

She could feel his cock quivering inside her. The warmth of his seed eased the ache of his rough fucking. Boneless with pleasure, Naya shuddered with aftershocks. She buried her face against the crook of his neck and inhaled his pleasant scent. Eyes closed, she tried to memorize the feel of his body weight and heat pressing her into the bed. She never wanted this moment of intimacy to end.

Showing some reluctance to leave her, Menace carefully pulled out of her and removed the toy. He left her bound to the bed and made his way into the bathroom. She enjoyed the view of his chiseled backside and strong thighs. When he returned with a cloth and towel, she couldn't stop the goofy smile that curved her mouth. It didn't seem possible that he could be so ridiculously sweet yet so commanding and rough at the same time.

"What?" Menace asked as he cleaned her up and unlatched her cuffed limbs.

"I can't believe you're real."

He shot her a strange look. "What does that mean?"

She rolled her sore shoulders. "You're too good to be true."

"I assure you I'm not." Menace slid onto the bed beside her and leaned back against the headboard. He grabbed her by the waist and hauled her onto his lap. His strong fingers kneaded her shoulders and neck. "I'm just as flawed as any other man."

"I haven't seen a flaw yet."

He chuckled softly and skimmed his lips across the top of her head. "Give me time. I'm sure I'll disappoint or upset you soon enough."

She answered him with a *humph* and settled back against his broad chest. His massaging hands made her sleepy.

"How do you feel? Are your wrists or ankles sore? What about your bottom?"

Even though the man had just ravished her, she still blushed at his inquiry on the state of her backside. "I'm fine."

"Are you really? If you're not, I need to know."

Realizing he wasn't about to drop this line of questioning, she said, "I'm a little throbby down there but it's not painful or anything."

"Throbby?" He sounded amused.

"What? It's a word."

"I highly doubt that. It's not in any—"

A high-pitched squawk pierced the stillness of their bedroom. Startled, Naya jumped in his lap. Menace's reassuring arms embraced her. "It's just an alarm." She had never heard anything so loud or frightening. "An alarm? For what?"

"Abandoning ship," he answered calmly.

Her heart leapt into her throat. "What!"

"Sweetheart," he said gently, "it's a drill. We have them

once or twice a month."

The screeching alarm stopped but only briefly. A commanding voice shouted from the ceiling. "Now hear this. Now hear this. This is a drill. Proceed to your nearest evacuation area."

The message started to repeat. Menace shifted her in his arms and patted her thigh. "We've got to go."

Naya clambered to get off the bed. Shaking with adrenaline, she let Menace tug her into the closet. He pushed a pale-blue outfit consisting of pants and a shirt into her hands. The outfit was cut to fit a woman but one half a foot taller and much heavier than she.

He stated the obvious as he held them against her petite frame. "They're going to be a bit big, but they'll do until I can get you measured in one of the clothing shops."

Naya didn't care. She shook out the drawstring pants and shoved her feet into them. The shirt was just a smaller version of the undershirt Menace had let her wear last night while they ate dinner. She didn't miss the way he dressed so quickly. He pulled on the black uniform pants and a shirt with his insignia printed on both arms and on the left side of his chest. It looked like a more casual version of the uniform he had been wearing when he Grabbed her.

As if reading her mind, he explained, "This is my off-duty uniform."

Naya glanced at the closet. It seemed to be filled with various versions of the same uniform. Looking down at her somewhat ugly outfit, she couldn't help but wonder if she would have such limited choices for clothing too.

"Come on." Menace had shoved his feet into his boots.

He grabbed her hand and shot a quick look at her bare feet. "They were out of shoes in the size range that fits your women. I have them on backorder. Just keep close to me. I'll keep your toes safe."

Clinging to his hand and wincing with every squawk of that awful blaring alarm, Naya followed Menace out of their quarters. She had been planning to ask him to show her more of the ship, but not like this. He looked down at her and smiled reassuringly. Naya burrowed a little closer to his side and took a step across the threshold of his home into her strange new world.

Chapter Eight

MENACE WAS GLAD to be with Naya during her first evacuation drill. They had recently changed the schedule to coincide with the Grabs and the new brides coming onto the ship. Vicious had apparently heard an earful after Hallie had been forced to navigate her first abandon-ship drill alone.

Even though he wasn't absolutely certain Naya wouldn't try to escape, Menace showed her how to follow the red lines painted on the floors to the nearest evacuation-staging area. He pointed out the scanners mounted in the ceiling that would read her ID chip and confirm her movements during an evacuation. The records were instantly transmitted to the guard ships accompanying the *Valiant* to aid in recovery of the life ships.

"What happens if I can't make it to one of the staging points?" Naya hugged his side as he steered her down a corridor quickly filling with people.

Menace didn't want to lie to her. "The *Valiant* is designed to close off any damaged sections that pose a threat to the integrity of the ship. There are emergency life-support systems like that one," he pointed to a red box that contained an oxygen mask, "but those are a last resort. Once depressurization begins, death is inescapable."

Her fingers tightened around his. "And what happens if we get separated?"

Menace stopped so fast she slammed into him. He cupped her chin. "You keep moving to a life pod. Do you understand? You get to safety." Wanting to soothe her fears, he added, "If this ship was ever attacked, it's likely I would be on duty and you would be in our quarters. The odds of the two of us reaching separate life pods and safely leaving the ship are extremely high. I would find you as quickly as possible once we're rescued."

She looked reassured and squeezed his hand. He led her to their evacuation-staging center. Once there, he put her with the other wives and young children and moved to the front with the other officers. He outranked the pilot from the sky corps who lived on their floor by four months, so it fell to Menace to take control of the evacuation drill procedures. He assigned officers to each pod and quickly separated the groups of mock evacuees.

To make this as similar to real life as possible, he put Naya in a group headed by another sky corps officer. She frowned at him but got in line with the others and filed into the life pod. He took control of his group, ushered them inside and shut the door. Once everyone was in their seats, he contacted the bridge. They exchanged a series of transmissions and then checked his pod off the list.

Within half an hour, the all clear was sounded. Menace made sure his people were safely out of the pod, shut down the controls and exited the spacecraft. He searched the milling crowd for Naya's face and found her chatting with another woman. Both were wearing the white collar of a new bride. He hung back and let her have a moment to speak with someone from her past.

When they finished talking, Naya backed away and watched the other woman return to her husband. Naya stood on tiptoes and scanned the crowd. He raised his hand to catch her attention and strode toward her. The moment he was close enough, she reached for his hand and interlaced their fingers. Her smile and the way she clutched at his hand made his stomach flip-flop.

"Was that a friend from home?"

"Not exactly," Naya said and fell into step beside him. "An acquaintance is probably the right term. Her mother and I did business."

"Oh?" He liked hearing about her life back in Connor's Run.

"Zhaneh's mother ran a small bakery in town. Sometimes she'd come to me for short-term loans to buy supplies, especially when the prices on flour and butter and milk out of Harper's Well and Grogan's Mill skyrocketed."

"Why is there such a fluctuation in prices?"

She glanced at him. "Your quotas."

"My quotas?" He realized she meant his people. "Oh. I see."

She nodded. "There was a long drought that ended three years ago and some kind of fungus killed quite a few crops last year. I'm not involved in farming so I don't know the specifics, but I understand The City government takes the Harcos quota first. We have whatever is left over."

Naya's revelation made him feel uneasy. The intricacies of the various treaties his people made with other planets had never really interested him. Now he wondered what negative effects their terms had on other people. It didn't surprise him that some of the Harcos-controlled territories had risen up to fight with the Splinter forces threatening their way of life.

"Speaking of food," Naya said as they rounded a corner, "do you think I could maybe get some breakfast soon? I'm starving."

She said it with a playful grin but Menace still felt a twinge of guilt. "Yes. I'll feed you as soon as we reach our quarters."

She laughed and rubbed his arm. "That sounds like I'm your pet."

"Sorry." He caught sight of two familiar faces lingering near his front door. Vicious and Hallie waited in the hallway. Knowing Hallie, she'd probably pestered Vicious to bring her down to see Naya.

Menace knew the second Naya spotted them. Her step faltered. He glanced down at her and winked. Drawing close to the couple who had inspired him to take this step in life, Menace grinned. "Vee."

Vicious flashed the briefest smile. "Menace."

Menace made the introductions. "Naya, this is General Vicious and his wife, Hallie."

"Ma'am." Vicious nodded in Naya's direction. "Welcome to the land corps family."

Hallie rolled her eyes and stepped forward. She grasped Naya's hand. "It's nice to meet you, Naya. How did you like your first evacuation drill?"

Naya returned the handshake. "Not so much. The

alarm almost gave me a heart attack."

Hallie shot her a knowing smile. "I nearly fainted the first time I experienced one. Plus I was all alone in our quarters and I'd just gotten out of the infirmary. Someone," she glared at her husband, "forgot to tell me about the drills. Talk about a nightmare."

Vicious narrowed his eyes at Hallie but she just smiled. He turned his attention back to Menace. His expression became grim. "Menace, we need to talk. In headquarters," he added. "You'll need your uniform."

A chill raced down his back. "Am I being deployed?"

"No." Vicious' instant reply calmed him, but when his friend's gaze skipped to Naya, the worry returned. "It's about the Grab."

Menace slid an arm in front of Naya and pushed her behind him. He squared his shoulders. "You're not taking her from me."

Vicious clapped a hand on his shoulder. "Orion and his men will have to go through me before they take a bride away from one of my soldiers."

Menace frowned in confusion. "Admiral Orion? What does he have to do with the Grab?"

Vicious let his hand fall. "It seems your woman caused an injury on the field. A bad injury," he clarified. "Career-ending, possibly."

Menace turned to face Naya who looked shocked by that piece of news. He remembered the way she'd tackled him. She'd caught him unawares and taken him down, but she hadn't hurt him. It would take more than her small body weight to hurt a Harcos warrior. "Did you take a weapon into the forest?"

She reeled back, aghast. "No!"

There was no deception in her voice or on her face. "Did something happen to one of the men chasing you?"

"One of them fell," she said. "I ran across this tricky little spot in a dry creek bed. He followed me like a dumb-ass and slipped on a loose log. I saw him go down but I kept running because I didn't want to be caught." Her panicked gaze tore at him. "Menace, I didn't think he'd get badly injured. I only wanted to slow him down."

He brushed his fingertips down her face. "I believe you."

Voice lowered, she moved closer and raised fear-stricken eyes to his face. "Don't let them take me away from you."

Her pleading tone pained him. It must have taken a lot for Naya to ask that. "I won't. You're mine. That's not going to change."

"Naya," Hallie said gently, "would you like to come back to our quarters while the men sort this out? We could talk. It would be nice."

Menace was grateful for Hallie's kindness. He didn't want to leave Naya alone in their apartment while he was fighting for her. She was just nervous enough to rabbit on him. Hallie would keep her busy and secure.

Naya glanced at him and he communicated his approval with a nod. She smiled at Hallie. "Sure. Thanks."

Hallie pointed toward the end of the hallway and the elevator bank. "We're two floors up. I'll add your chip ID to our guestlist so you can come up to see me whenever you feel like it." Her gaze fell to Naya's bare feet. "Let me guess? Shoes on backorder?"

Naya managed a laugh. "Apparently."

"We'll raid my closet and find something that fits."

Menace watched Naya until she entered the elevator. When the doors closed, he steeled his jaw. "They aren't taking her from me, Vee. We've already spent a night together. Our laws are very clear on that account."

"I meant what I said, Menace. Even if you weren't one of my oldest friends, I would still fight for you. No whining little puke of a flyboy is going to order one of my men to give up his woman just because he tripped and fell." Vicious slashed his hand through the air. "It's not happening. Not on my watch."

Menace opened the door to his quarters. Vicious followed him inside. "I won't be long."

He made quick work of changing into his duty uniform and switching his boots. He found Vicious standing in the same place he'd left him. "I'm ready."

"She's very pretty," Vicious said as they left the apartment. "She suits you."

"Yes."

"She's not nearly as feral as I'd been led to believe." Vicious couldn't keep the smile from coloring his voice. "I hear she has quite a mouth on her."

Menace exhaled loudly and stepped into the elevator. "She's mellowed considerably since being Grabbed."

"Clearly."

Now it was Menace who smiled. "What can I say? Apparently I have the magic touch."

Vicious snorted. "Give it a week. I'm sure she'll be threatening to kick your ass again. Or was it shove that gag so far up your—"

"Yes," Menace interrupted. "I don't need a replay."

He remembered with extreme clarity the way she'd verbally abused him on the transport ride. She hadn't exactly shown the nicest side of herself. "I think she was just scared. Lashing out is her defense mechanism."

"And is she scared now?"

Menace shook his head. "I'm nurturing her trust in me."

"Smart move," Vicious said. "Take it slowly. There's no need to rush these things."

Menace figured there was no one else he could trust with the big issue in their relationship. "She wants to postpone conception of our first child." Vicious shot him a surprised look. "I see."

"Is that going to be a problem?"

"They'll bring you in for a mandatory reproductive health check if she hasn't conceived in six months."

Menace's eyes widened in shock. "They have that authority?"

Irritation crossed Vicious' face. "It's in the small print of our Grab contracts. I wouldn't have known either if Hallie…"

Menace heard the pain in his friend's voice. "I'm sorry, Vee. I didn't mean to bring up a sore subject."

"It's fine." Vicious inhaled slowly. "I don't care if it takes Hallie ten years to conceive our first child, but these fucking population laws are putting undue stress on her. It makes her feel like a failure. Knowing she's in pain and that I can't fix it makes me feel like a failure."

Menace was certain this was the first time in all the years he'd known Vicious that his friend had ever spoken with such emotion. "I don't know what to say," he admitted finally.

"There isn't much to say," Vicious replied matter-of-factly. "Biology is a bitch."

Another thought struck him. "Can they intervene in your bond?"

Vicious' jaw tightened. "The clause concerning that is vague. It's been threatened on other men."

"So if Orion succeeds in forcing me to give up Naya—"

"It would set a dangerous precedent," Vicious said.

"I won't let them take Naya," Menace vowed. It wasn't just his and Naya's bond at stake. It was Hallie and Vicious' too. "Can the doctors here do anything to help Hallie?"

Vicious nodded stiffly. "She's undergoing testing next week. We're hopeful."

"And if it doesn't work?"

"We have a sympathetic doctor. He and I have discussed an option that would give Hallie and me more time."

"I hope it works."

"It will. It has to." After a moment's pause, he asked, "Why doesn't your bride want children?"

"She wants them, I think, just not now. She's been on her own since she was a child. Her mother and brother abandoned her, and her father was killed by a Merkorian when she was only nine. She seems to have a hard time trusting and depending on another person. I understand her concerns with bringing a child into our union so quickly."

"Is this your way of asking me to sign your petition for contraception?"

Menace faced him. "Would you?"

"Of course." Vicious frowned. "Why would you think otherwise?"

"I know you're very traditional when it comes to things like this. Now that I know what you and Hallie are dealing with, I wasn't sure."

"Menace, my personal feelings on the issue have nothing to do with it. I have no business getting involved in the private discussions and decisions between couples. If you approve of her request, I'll expedite the petition through my office."

"Thank you."

Vicious waved his hand. "You're not just one of my soldiers, Menace. You're my friend. I want you to find the same happiness with Naya that I've found with Hallie. If getting her a contraceptive device does that, so be it. Just don't pin your hopes on an approval, Menace."

"I haven't. I made sure Naya understood how unlikely it was that permission would be granted."

"Even if I can manage to get the petition approved, they might only give you a few months reprieve. These damn population laws are so invasive."

The doors to the elevator opened. Menace fell into step behind Vicious, following the protocol of their ranks. Vicious crossed the lobby of the ship's headquarters but didn't go to his private space. Instead he took Menace to Orion's. A pair of medics sat in chairs just outside the ship commander's office. Both jumped to their feet and saluted Vicious who gave them a quick at-ease. The admiral's secretary rose from his desk and knocked twice on the door before opening it and announcing them.

Menace trailed Vicious into Orion's office. His gaze settled on the face of the sky corps pilot who wanted to challenge his rights to Naya. He'd seen the man around the *Valiant* but didn't know him well. The pilot sat in a motorized chair and had his immobilized leg in a harness. A small medication pump had been attached to his wrist. Menace wondered if he was even competent right now with all the painkillers running through his system. Broken leg or not, Menace was ready to kick the man's ass for distressing Naya.

Admiral Orion leaned back against his desk. Just as tall as Vicious, Orion had the brown hair and hazel eyes common in the first generation of children from Grabs in the Angolier sector of the solar system. With his arms crossed, he looked annoyed by the whole situation. "Vicious."

"Orion."

The admiral sighed. "Menace, you know why you're here?"

"I do, sir." Menace glanced at the pilot. "That man wants to take my wife."

"She fractured my damn knee so badly they can't fix it! What am I supposed to do now? Hobble my way through another Grab?"

"Flare," Orion sharply reprimanded his airman.

Flare gritted his teeth. "Sir."

Orion gestured to Flare. "He claims that the woman in question deliberately led him into a trap and caused him great injury. This injury prevented him from Grabbing a woman and may have even ended his career."

"That's the risk he took when he entered the Grab," Vicious countered. "We all signed the same forms. If he was reckless enough to follow Menace's woman across uncertain terrain, the consequence rests solely on his shoulders."

"Agreed," Orion replied, "but Menace can run again and find another bride. Flare has multiple surgeries and months of therapy ahead of him. They may have to send him back to Prime and you know the bride situation there isn't exactly thriving. If he's bounced out of the sky corps because of his injuries, his standing among prospective brides won't be nearly as positive."

"I sympathize with your man," Vicious said, "but you are talking about tearing apart a couple who have spent a day and a night together. If we were back on Prime, this kind of thing would ignite a blood feud." Vicious slashed his hand through the air.

"No. Menace Grabbed her. They're bonded. It's done."

Orion looked amused. "Is that a threat, Vee?"

"It's a fact, Orion. If you try to take Menace's wife away from him, you'll have every member of the land corps aboard this ship rising up in revolt. I shouldn't have to remind you that my force outnumbers yours three to one."

Orion's smile faded. "I'm quite aware of the balance aboard *my* ship."

Vicious exhaled roughly. "Let's not do this, Orion.

We've been friends and colleagues too long to allow something ugly like this to occur under our shared watch."

"Is that your way of telling me you have a proposal?"

"My wife remains in contact with friends on the surface. She's aware of a handful of women who desperately want to leave Calyx." Vicious addressed Flare. "Would you be willing to consider one of these women as a potential bride?"

Flare's angry expression softened. "There are women who want to be married to Harcos men?"

"The town Hallie comes from is a terrible place. Women there are given no opportunities. For many of them, being chosen in the lottery for the Grabs is like winning a one-way ticket out of hell."

"Flare, I'm going to urge you to consider the general's offer," Orion counseled the captain. "You've seen the general's wife?" Flare nodded. "She's very beautiful."

"And sweet and modest," Orion added. He shot Menace a disapproving look. "I hear the woman he was unlucky enough to grab is a shrew. You can take Menace's foul-mouthed harpy or you can choose a nice, gentle woman who actually *wants* to leave her home and start a new life with a brave Harcos man."

Menace bristled at the admiral's description of Naya but let it slide. He recognized that Orion was actually helping his case in trying to dissuade Flare from pursuing his claim to Naya.

"Is it legal?" Flare's question calmed Menace's frayed nerves. The man was considering Vicious' option.

"It is," Vicious assured him. "The arrangement would

be treated the same way as the matchmaking services from Harcos Prime."

Flare gestured to his ruined leg. "I can't go down to the surface to get her. How do I know one of the members of the team you send won't claim her for himself?"

It was a valid question. The tricky unclaimed-property laws made it very easy for another man to swipe a new bride. After the last Grab, there had been a massive brawl aboard the *Arctis* when a land corps sergeant had taken a pilot's new bride and barricaded her in his quarters. The Special Response Unit led by Raze had ended up blasting the door down to get them out but the bride was so enamored with the sergeant's brash "romantic" act that she'd refused to go back to the pilot. To say it had been a cluster-fuck of epic proportions was the understatement of the century.

"I'll go." Menace held Flare's disbelieving gaze. "I'm happily matched to Naya and have no reason to take your woman. I'll go down to the surface and safely escort your bride back to you."

Flare narrowed his eyes in suspicion. "Why should I trust you? Can you honestly say I'm not your enemy now?"

Menace scoffed. "Enemy? We're brothers-in-arms. Am I irritated that you scared my woman? Yes. Am I going to hold it against you? No. You've earned the right to a wife and a family. Naya didn't mean to cause such a traumatic injury, but she was partially responsible for your current predicament. My wife's debts of honor are mine. I intend to make this one right."

Flare nodded stiffly. "Thank you, Menace."

Orion pushed off his desk and straightened. "So it's settled? No more talks of blood feuds and mess-hall beat downs?"

Vicious smiled. "I think we've managed to head off disaster."

"Good." Orion shook Vicious' hand and clapped him on the back. He stepped forward and offered his hand to Menace. Voice soft, he said, "That bit about calling your wife a harpy? I didn't mean it."

Menace gripped the man's hand. "Understood, sir."

"I'll leave this to you, Vicious. Will Raze's team handle the extraction?"

"Yes," Vicious confirmed.

"I'll give you Zephyr for this mission. He's my best stealth pilot." Orion walked to his desk and tapped his communication unit. "Hunter? Send in the medics and call Zephyr into my office."

"Yes, sir."

A moment later, the medics entered the office. One of them used the controls on the back of Flare's chair. The other waited by the door. Menace watched the broken man leave the office. He couldn't shake the sympathy eating at him. It wasn't completely Naya's fault the man had hurt himself so badly. It was simply a freak accident, but for a military man in his prime to lose it all because of something as stupid as a rolling log? It was almost too painful to consider.

Menace received a nod of dismissal from Vicious and started out of the office. Just as he left, he heard Orion ask Vicious, "Are there truly many women who want to marry and leave Calyx?"

"There are. Why? Would you like one of them? I could make the arrangement for you."

"No, no," Orion quickly replied. He laughed nervously. "I was just asking for my men. There are some who have the points to enter a Grab, but not enough seniority to make it onto the lists every quarter. There are so many men aboard the *Valiant* with years of dedicated service, especially in the land corps, that the younger airmen among us don't have much of a chance…"

Menace didn't hear the rest of the conversation. The admiral's thought was an interesting one. Menace had bumped a younger pilot off the Connor's Run Grab list when he'd added his name. At the time, he hadn't much cared. He'd earned his spot, after all, but now he wondered if there wasn't a better way to do things down on Calyx. If Vicious was right and there were women who wanted to marry, why not give them access to matchmaking services like the ones on Prime?

"Well, that went better than I'd expected," Vicious muttered upon rejoining him. "Looks like Hallie has saved my ass yet again. The moons know she won't let me forget it."

Menace snorted. "I can't imagine your sweet Hallie crowing over such a thing."

Vicious shot him a warning glare. "Don't laugh too hard, Menace. The two of us made a huge tactical error earlier."

"And what's that?"

"We left our wives alone together."

Chapter Nine

"**D**ON'T WORRY, NAYA. Vicious will protect you and Menace."

Naya glanced at Hallie before stepping off the elevator into a private hallway. Her stomach was in knots. The idea of being taken away from Menace scared her. It wasn't as if she was in love with him or anything, but he'd been very good to her. He cared for her and would protect her. She couldn't say the same for other men aboard the ship.

"You seem very confident in your husband's abilities."

"He's not the kind of man people challenge." Hallie unlocked her front door with a press of her thumb to a red pad. "When Vicious gives an order, it's followed without question."

She wondered if Hallie was one of those people who followed orders given by Vicious. She had a sneaking suspicion the short, spunky woman was the general at home and Vicious was the one jumping to follow her orders.

One step into Hallie's home and Naya's jaw dropped. It wasn't the size difference that stunned her but the homey, inviting warmth of the space. Hallie's home was laid out almost identically to the one Naya now shared with Menace. The furniture and materials were all the same with only a few differences in upholstery colors and the paler, softer gray on the walls, but Hallie had done something extraordinary with the blank canvas of her home.

"Your home is beautiful." Naya admired the framed painting on the entryway wall. It was a simple design with the letters V and H intertwined and nestled in two feathers. There was something familiar about the look of it. "Where did you buy this?"

"I painted it." Hallie lovingly touched the frame. She gestured toward the open living area. "I've done all the artwork in our home."

Naya entered the living room and scanned the stunning pieces on the walls. "You're very talented."

"Thank you."

"And you sew!" She fingered one of the plush decorative pillows on the couch. The lilac hue complemented the silvery upholstery. She spotted the sewing basket on the floor. It was piled high with embroidery projects. A stack of completed pieces, baby clothes and bibs, sat on the cushion of the chair.

"You can order fabric and sewing supplies through the clothing store." Hallie gathered up the sewing supplies on the couch and moved them to the basket. "I was finishing up some sewing when the alarms sounded. A friend of mine is due any day."

Naya picked up one of the small bibs. "You're very good."

"I'm not nearly as good as my oldest sister but I do all right. Do you sew?"

Naya laughed. "No."

"Would you like to learn?"

"Not really," Naya admitted and hoped she wasn't hurting Hallie's feelings. Clearly this woman relished her homemaking duties.

Hallie surprised her by laughing. "I like honesty. Sewing isn't for everyone. You could always barter if you needed sewing services."

Naya perked up. "Barter? Now that's something I know how to do."

"Really?" Hallie motioned toward the kitchen. "Would you like something to drink? I've got tea and juice."

"I'll take tea if it isn't too much trouble."

"It's not."

Naya glanced into the large formal dining room. The embroidered tablecloth and centerpiece of candles and flowers were gorgeous. Hallie had even made chair covers to soften the harshness of the all-metal look. "How in the world do you keep houseplants and flowers alive up here?"

"A friend of ours brought me some of the hardiest houseplants available on Calyx. One of the biologists in the science department let Vicious buy a special growing light and some food for them. I move them under the light a few hours every evening and feed them once a week. So far, so good. Would you like one of the plants?"

"No way." Naya shook her head. "I have a tried-and-true brown thumb."

"I'm sure you're not that bad." Hallie showed her to the small table in the spacious kitchen. She brushed crumbs off the simple runner and caught them in her hand. "Sorry. Vicious seems to think kitchen elves clean up after him."

Naya smiled and slid into a chair. "He's, um, really intimi-dating."

Hallie laughed. "He's not as scary as he looks." She dumped the crumbs in the silver trash receptacle. "Well, okay, he can be that scary but never with me or any other woman for that matter. He only shows the *grrr* side when it's absolutely necessary."

"Is it necessary often?"

"Only when he's defending me or his men."

Naya rubbed her finger across the bright-white flowers embroidered on the runner. "You're happy here?"

"Very," Hallie confirmed and took down the tea sup-plies from a cabinet. "You're from Connor's Run, right?"

"I am."

"Well, I came from Harper's Well. My life with Vicious is heaven compared to the hell I endured there."

Naya didn't doubt that. "He makes you happy?"

"Yes." Hallie cast a quick smile her way before fidgeting with some strange machine built into the wall. "We love each other very much."

"Was it hard in the beginning?" Naya watched as the contraption whirred to life and spit steaming-hot water into mugs. "That's amazing!"

"You probably have one in your quarters. Most of the units in the officer housing section have the same built-ins." Hallie carried the tray with mugs and sweeteners to the table. "Sugar. Milk. Honey. Help yourself."

Naya sweetened her cup of tea with a drizzle of honey and gave it a stir. Hallie opened a sleek black door and retrieved a covered dish. "I did a breakfast casserole this morning. Would you like some?"

"I would. We didn't have time for breakfast before the alarms started."

"There will be another drill in a week or two, but it will be in the evening, which is just as annoying." Hallie dished out a portion and put the plate into another weird device. She tapped a keypad and it started to hum. "This machine heats food quickly. They sell frozen boxed dinners in the commissary that can be quickly prepared with this. I don't like them very much, but Vicious swears they're delicious."

Naya made a mental note to ask Menace about them. To a girl who couldn't cook, the prospect of putting a frozen box of food in that super oven sounded like a life-saver.

The machine dinged and Hallie removed the hot dish. She brought it to the table with utensils and a napkin. After grabbing a couple of cookies from a jar on the counter, Hallie came to the table. Naya poked her fork into the fluffy egg-and-bacon casserole. She spied bits of potato and specks of cheese. One bite proved that it was as delicious as it smelled. So Hallie could sew, paint, keep house and cook. Naya wanted to hate her but couldn't. That smile and gentle air about her were too disarming.

"To answer your question, it wasn't easy in the beginning. Vicious is basically the ideal Harcos male. What I mean by that is that he is maddeningly arrogant."

Hallie said it with a grin but Naya guessed she hadn't always found her husband's arrogance so amusing. "Menace has an arrogant streak in him as well. He seems to think that if he just says something will be one way, it will be."

Hallie rolled her eyes and laughed. "The whole I'm-going-to-make-you-happy thing, right?"

"Yes! What makes them think they can just catch us in a race, drag us back to their weird-ass ships and make us into happy little wives?"

"Tradition," Hallie answered simply. "They've been taking wives from their treatycontrolled territories via the Grabs for hundreds of years."

"It's a bad tradition. Can you imagine how many unhappy couples there are?"

"Not as many as you'd think," Hallie replied. "At least not in this sector. Our wives' group has access to the census data from the ships taking part in the Grab program on our planet. The divorce rate is less than ten percent."

Naya swallowed her mouthful of food. "Divorce?"

Hallie smiled knowingly. "They keep that part of the contracts quiet. I never saw it in mine, but it's there."

Even though Naya was starting to care for Menace, she wanted all the information she could get—just in case. "How does it work?"

Hallie didn't hesitate to give her the answers. Naya respected her all the more for it. "Well, first, you need to know that the first thirty days of a Grabbed bond are on shaky ground legally. For instance, if you leave your quarters without an escort, you're considered lost property. Whoever finds you first gets to keep you."

"What?" Outraged, Naya dropped her fork "That's ridiculous. What am I? A wallet?"

"It's an awful rule. A few months ago, something like that happened on the *Arctis*."

"*Arctis*?"

"It's one of the guard ships that flies with us. After the last Grab, a bride got away from her husband and was taken by a land corps soldier. It became this huge mess.

They deployed the SRU team from the *Valiant*."

"SRU team?"

"They're an elite group of soldiers who deal with so-called 'special' circumstances. Terrorist threats, hostage negotiations, escorts and other high-risk things like that."

"Oh." Naya breathed a little easier. "I thought maybe you meant they were secret police."

"No. The men on the SRU teams are good, upstanding men." She hesitated. "There is a unit that's sort of like the secret police but they're called the Shadow Force. I can't imagine you'd ever come into contact with them, so I wouldn't worry about it. They don't go after citizens like the secret police on Calyx. They're focused solely on the Splinter movement and terrorism."

"Good to know." Naya scooped up another forkful of her breakfast. "Being arrested three times in Connor's Run was enough for me."

Hallie's gaze snapped to her face. She smiled sadly. "You can add me to that club."

Before Naya could ask her why she'd been pinched, Hallie scooted back in her chair and stood. "Let me get you some of our pamphlets. We're having a new wives meeting later this week but you may as well take the information with you today."

Naya watched Hallie leave and tucked right back in to her breakfast. She couldn't remember the last time she'd eaten something so good. When Hallie returned, she slid a thin stack of pamphlets onto the table and sat down.

"Each pamphlet will give you information you'll need to make your transition to this new life successfully. The first one is about navigating the ship and using all the different devices in your home. The second is about your rights aboard the ship and in this new society. The procedure for filing for a separation is in there. The blue one outlines your access to medical care and explains the most common medications and procedures. The green one is all about shopping in the retail section as well as understanding the monetary system here. It's credits, by the way."

"Credits?"

Hallie nodded. "You'll get the hang of it." She lifted her wrist. "The chip they gave you is your method of payment. It's attached to Menace's bank account. The money is deducted automatically."

"That would have been handy back on Calyx," Naya murmured. "I wouldn't have had to chase down so many people who owed me money."

"You were in business?"

"I owned a pawnshop."

"How cool is that?" Hallie seemed impressed. "You're going to be a great addition to our wives club."

"I am?" Naya sipped her tea. "I'm not so sure about joining a social club."

"Oh, you have to!" Hallie practically pleaded with her. "It's so nice to get together with other women from our planet. We're so outnumbered by men here. Plus we're doing good work."

"How so?"

"We've created a domestic violence resource center. Next month, they're opening a new counseling division in the med bay for couples who need a little help adjusting or communicating. We're getting a distance learning program so those of us who want to finish our educations can do so. Some of the mothers in the group have started a playgroup and even have a babysitting pool that they use to give one another a day or night off every week."

Naya wasn't so sure about that babysitting stuff but she thought the idea of counseling was probably a good one. Finishing school had always been a dream. "I guess it wouldn't hurt to come to one meeting."

Hallie beamed. "You'll love it—and I make cookies!"

Naya laughed. "I'm sure you do."

Hallie held her mug in both hands and sat back in her chair. "What can I say? I'm a happy little homemaker. We all fill different roles in life. Who knows? Maybe you'll open the first wife-owned business on the ship."

Finished with her breakfast, Naya reached for the pamphlets. "Is that even possible?"

Hallie shrugged. "I don't see why not. There are vacant storefronts in the market. You wouldn't be able to run a pawnshop. I'm not sure the concept would work here. They don't do debt or credit here."

"I wasn't really thrilled with running a pawnshop in the first place," Naya admitted. "It was just the easiest business for me to get into at the time. The only way to make a business work is to find a need that isn't being filled in the current market."

"You mean like having access to comforts from home or clothes that fit and aren't ugly as homemade sin?" Hallie pinched the front of her boxy dress. "If you saw what kinds of alterations I have to make just get my clothes to fit!"

Naya sized up Hallie. "You must have a ton of fabric left over."

"I turned some of it into napkins or throw pillows The rest is in my scrap box." She made a face. "Vicious thinks it's silly for me to keep the scraps but old habits, you know?"

"Oh, I know." Naya's gaze fell to the top pamphlet. Surprise gripped her. The drawing on the front was all too familiar. "Who drew this?"

Hallie broke a cookie in half. "I did. Why?"

Naya's startled gaze jumped to her new friend. What had Danny said? The Artist had been Grabbed and lived happily on a ship. Could it be? Was Hallie the young woman she'd known only as the Artist? "I bet my aunt Ruthie Frances would love one of your paintings."

Hallie stiffened. Her shocked expression slowly faded. "I know Ruthie would."

Ruthie Frances. Red Feather. "Should we keep talking in code or do I just come right out and ask?"

"Ask me."

"You were part of the Red Feather. You drew passports."

"I did. And you?"

"I'm very good at smuggling."

Hallie's eyes widened briefly. "Wait! Are you Dankirk's contact in Connor's Run?"

Now it was Naya's turn to be surprised. "I was. You know Danny?"

"I spoke with him via my sister just the other day. He has a list of women who want out of Harper's Well. Dankirk helped my sister escape to the colonies. How are things now? Has the smuggling chain been busy?"

"There were riots in The City five weeks ago. The government clamped down pretty tightly."

"Riots?"

"Over food shortages," Naya explained. "We had people pouring into Connor's Run and Grogan's Mill. There were so many cargo ships from the Jesco colony making illegal flyovers and taking passengers that the colonies put up a barricade. The backlog for customs processing in Safe Harbor and Jesco is so bad that some of the illegal immigrants were dying in the cargo holds."

Hallie gasped in shock. "That's awful."

"The fees for those kinds of transports have gone up tremendously. The ships we work with like the *Shepherd* are still doing low-fee transports, but it's getting harder and harder to move people. Finding people to sponsor immigrants is almost impossible. The colonies have also stopped offering paperless entry for women who win the Grabs. I had to buy fake papers for Jennie and me. They weren't nearly as good as yours."

"Jennie?"

Sadness squeezed her chest. "She's my friend. Her number was pulled in the lottery so I bought my way onto the list. We had a pact that we'd both run together and get taken together if we couldn't escape."

"Is she here with you? I can put a call through to her quarters and have her over if you'd like to see her."

Naya gulped down the grief that swamped her. "No, she actually made it to the safe zone where her boyfriend was waiting."

"Oh," Hallie said quietly. She reached across the table and grabbed Naya's hand. "I'm sorry."

Naya looked at the friendly hand gripping hers. Hallie's kindness overwhelmed her. "Thank you."

"I know how hard it is to adjust to your new life. I'm not promising it's going to be sugar and sweetness. There are going to be bumps. You're probably going to want to thrash Menace a few times but you'll get through it. If you're meant to be together, that is. If you're not? You come to me. I'll make sure you get your separation papers and I'll help you find your way to the colonies and your friend."

Naya gawked at Hallie. "You'd do that for me? But Menace is your husband's friend. Wouldn't that make things difficult between you?"

"You let me worry about Vicious. You just worry about your relationship with Menace." Hallie pulled her hand back. "If you can make it work, I think you'll be very happy. Menace is a wonderful man. Vicious wouldn't count him among his closest friends if he wasn't loyal and honest."

Hallie hadn't said anything that Naya wasn't already thinking when it came to Menace. "I do like him. He's been patient and sweet with me. The sex is pretty awesome too."

Hallie actually blushed and dipped her gaze. "Yes, these Harcos men seem to be masters of seduction."

"Boy, that's no joke. I thought Menace was going to make me pass out last night."

Hallie laughed. "Yeah, I've, uh, been there quite a few times."

Naya knew enough about Hallie's hometown to guess that she was probably a virgin when she'd come onboard the *Valiant*. What a shock her first introduction to sex with her sky warrior must have been!

"Why don't we go dig through my closet and see if we can find you some shoes?" Hallie gathered up their dishes. "The first pair Vicious brought me was too big, but I bet they'll fit you just fine."

Naya followed her out of the kitchen. Once in the spacious master bedroom, she couldn't ignore the door to the couple's playroom. Naya didn't even want to imagine what a frightening man like Vicious did to poor Hallie in there.

Following her gaze, Hallie shot her an apologetic look. "I should probably warn you about the officers-only club. Menace will want to take you there."

"A club?"

"It's a place where officers and their wives and sometimes their single friends get together to play in public or the theme rooms."

Naya's gut clenched. "I'll pass."

"You might not be able to," Hallie replied, her voice muffled as she stepped into the oversized closet. A moment later she reappeared with a pair of simple black flats. "These aren't the most supportive shoes, but they'll do until Menace can get you something else."

Naya sat down on the bench at the end of Hallie's massive bed and slipped on the shoes. "Why wouldn't I be able to pass on the invite to the sex club thing?"

"Vicious and I had only been together a day when he came home with an invite to a private party given by General Thorn. I didn't want to go. I was terrified, honestly, but I knew that if we didn't go, Vicious might be snubbed by his superior. For officers, the promotion game is one that includes making appearances at a variety of functions. Vicious gave me the choice to say no, but I couldn't do it." Hallie sat down next to her.

"I ended up wearing a cat costume."

"Wait. What? A cat costume?"

Hallie giggled and clasped her face in her hands. "I know. How ridiculous, right? General Thorn has a fetish for cat-play games. There are actually groups of couples who get together here on the *Valiant* for puppy-and-cat play parties."

"I don't understand." Naya tried to process Hallie's information. "You dress up like a cat or a puppy and pretend you're one?"

"It's a little more intense than that for couples who are really into it but, yes, basically," Hallie said. "It doesn't do anything for me but I know a few women who enjoy it very much. They find extreme pleasure in giving total control to their husbands, their masters."

Naya shook her head and slipped on the shoes. "That's batshit crazy, Hallie."

"In this society, they believe everyone is entitled to their desires and their brand of kink. If you go to the officers' playroom, you'll probably see some strange things.

Well…strange to women like you and me," she clarified. "To these guys, it's as normal as breathing to see a woman tied up, flogged and taken in public by her husband and his two best friends."

Naya blinked a few times. She would never admit it aloud but there was something oddly alluring about Hallie's description. "I don't even know what to say to that."

"To each their own, I guess."

Naya took a few test strides in the shoes. They were a little roomy on the sides but they'd do. "Were you really angry when that party was over and Vicious brought you home?"

"No," Hallie said, her face flushed. "Actually I found it all rather arousing there at the end. Vicious showed me that there's no shame in exploring my sexuality. When I'm with him, when his hands are on me, I feel braver than ever and so incredibly secure."

Naya understood that. "I felt that with Menace this morning. It was…uncomfortable."

"I know what you mean," Hallie assured her. "This mix of pleasure and pain and dominance is confusing. Even now, I sometimes have nights where I struggle with giving up control to Vicious, but when I do? He always rewards my trust."

Naya caught the subtle emphasis Hallie used when she said *reward*. Oh yeah. One night with Menace and Naya understood all about rewarding trust.

A chime interrupted their conversation. "What's that?"

"The front door," Hallie explained. "Have you used your control console yet?"

Naya shook her head and Hallie gestured for her to follow. In the entryway, Hallie showed her a big green screen.
The word *visitor* flashed in white in the center.

"This alerts you when someone is at the door. You can
tap this corner square to see who it is. If you don't want to
answer for some reason or you're busy, your visitor will be
able to leave you a vid-message that you can watch at
another time."

Hallie tapped the upper corner and the screen changed
from green to a picture of a man. With his face down, only
his dark-brown hair was clearly visible.

"I haven't seen many of these guys with dark hair."

Hallie smiled. "Darker hair is common in the men who
have mothers who were taken in Grabs."

The man on-screen lifted his face. Naya winced at the
sight of such a scarred face. One eye had been totally
gouged out and was nothing but a puckered scar. A gash
like a lightning bolt marked that same side of his face.
"What happened to him?"

"Terror was attacked on a mission. Vicious had to sew
him back together." Hallie touched her arm. "Please don't
stare at him."

Naya glanced at the scarred man on the screen. "I
won't."

"Thank you." Hallie walked to the door.

"Is he like Vicious and Menace? You know, scary on
the outside but soft on the inside?"

Hallie shook her head and grabbed the door's handle.
"No, Naya. He's even scarier on the inside than he looks on
the outside."

With Hallie's frightening assessment ringing in her ears, Naya hung back and waited. Hallie stepped aside and Terror entered the apartment. His gaze moved to Naya and then back to Hallie again.

"I should have known your little welcoming committee would have reached Menace's new woman first," Terror said. "Have you finished interrogating her or do I need to drag her down to a holding cell to get her life story?"

Hallie dared to thump his arm. "Be nice, Terror."

Naya didn't find his teasing remark very funny. She warily watched Terror as he strode toward her. He had an air of mystery around him. The way he carried himself reminded her of the secret police who had terrorized her so many times. Her internal alarm pinged instantly. She knew the type. He might have Hallie fooled but this guy wasn't what he pretended to be.

Terror stopped a bit too close, purposely invading her personal space, and extended his hand. "I'm Terror, a good friend of Menace."

"Naya." She quickly shook his hand and tried to let go but he held tight. His fingertip rubbed her wrist, right where her pulse beat wildly. She wasn't amused and yanked her hand free from his.

Terror's one eye narrowed. "You're from Connor's Run." He wasn't asking. "I hear you ran a pawnshop down there. I can only imagine what kinds of interesting things came through your front door."

Naya's gut clenched but she schooled her features. This wasn't the first time she'd had to deal with some slick government type trying to get her to incriminate herself through friendly conversation. "I had a unicycle come through the front door once. That's about as interesting as it got."

"A unicycle?" Oblivious to Terror's subtly aggressive questioning, Hallie interjected herself in their conversation. "From the circus three years ago?"

Naya dragged her gaze to Hallie. "You remember that? Did you get to go?"

Hallie shook her head. "We didn't have the money but I got to see the animals and some of the performers from afar." She tugged on the sleeve of Terror's shirt. "Would you like some tea? I have cookies."

Terror nodded. "I'd like that. It will give Naya and me time to get to know one another a bit better."

Hallie hesitated. "You won't be rude?"

Terror laughed, the sound dry and harsh. "When have you ever known me to be rude?"

"Oh I don't know. How about last week when we had lunch on the observation deck?" Hallie arched a dark eyebrow. "If you make my guest uncomfortable in my home, I'll make sure that Vicious makes things very uncomfortable for you, Terror. Got it?"

He actually smiled at Hallie. "Yes."

Naya wanted to run after Hallie but didn't move. She wasn't about to show this frightening man one glimmer of weakness. He couldn't possibly know anything about her past. Even if he had somehow gotten his hands on her police reports, there wasn't anything concrete in them. She'd never been formally charged after her arrests.

"Let's sit." Terror gestured to the seating area. Naya

calmly made her way to the closest chair. Terror took a spot across from her, probably so he could watch her every move. "You must have been very scared when your number was pulled in the lottery."

"I'm not sure scared is the right word." Naya didn't miss the peculiarity of that question. He asked it almost as if he knew she hadn't been on the original roster.

"What word would you use? Excited? Determined?"

Now she knew something was up. "Resigned. Hopeful."

"Really?" He eyed her carefully. "You're lucky that you were Grabbed by Menace instead of the pilot, Flare. You caught yourself a very good man. Very well-connected," he added.

"You seem confused. I didn't do the catching. I was the one taken down and collared. Menace was just lucky enough to catch me."

"We'll see."

Naya fought the urge to tell Terror to go fuck himself. "I don't know what your deal is, Terror, but if you have something to say to me, just fucking say it already."

"Is everything okay?" Hallie appeared in the living room. She took one look at Terror and frowned. "What are you doing? Did you upset her?"

"I think there's been a misunderstanding," Terror smoothly replied. "You know I'm not very good at making pleasant conversation, Hallie. I think I may have accidentally offended Naya."

Naya couldn't believe how slick Terror was. She glanced at Hallie. The other woman looked supremely annoyed and not at all convinced. "Terror, I think you should—"

The front door opened and Menace's familiar voice met Naya's ears. She sagged with relief as he came into view with Vicious. She had to force her feet to stay still. She desperately wanted to jump out of her chair and run to him.

"Terror!" Menace grinned at the other man. "I didn't know you were back onboard."

"We got back last night." Terror gripped Menace's hand. They clapped each other on the back. "I was just talking to your lovely wife. She's quite a catch, Menace."

Naya wanted to shoot him the finger so badly but kept her hands folded in her lap.

Menace turned his gaze on her. It was a look of pure adoration that warmed her skin. "Yes, she is."

He held out his hand and Naya happily joined him. She was afraid to ask but had to know. "Is everything okay now?"

"Everything is fine, Naya."

Burrowed close to Menace's strength and heat, Naya wanted to believe him but one glance at Terror shattered her hope. She'd seen that look on the faces of the secret police investigators who had roused her out of bed in the middle of the night and thrown her in a cell for weeks on end.

Somehow Terror had caught a whiff of her past. Like a dog with a bone, he was never going to let go. He would unearth every misdeed she'd committed as a teenager. There was no escape now. The past had finally come back to haunt her.

Menace slid an arm around her shoulders and kissed the crown of her head. "Don't worry, sweetheart. No one is going to take you away from me." Oh how she wished that were true.

Chapter Ten

MENACE SNEAKED A glance at Naya as they waited for the elevator. She seemed uncommonly quiet and almost nervous. She clung to his arm and nibbled her plump lower lip.

"Stop that," Menace ordered softly and brushed his thumb over her sweet mouth. "You'll break the skin."

Her fingernails bit into his arm. "Sorry."

"Are you okay?" The elevator dinged and the doors parted. He put his hand on the small of her back and pushed her forward into the gleaming silver box.

"I'm fine."

"No, you're not. What is it?" He swiped the navigational screen and chose their floor.

"Nothing. I'm just tired. It's been a crazy morning."

He didn't care for the half-truths coming from her. Certain she wouldn't tell him the truth unless thrown off-kilter, Menace spun suddenly and trapped her smaller body in the corner of the elevator. Naya gasped and put her hands on his chest. Before she could tell him off, he captured her mouth in a slow, easy kiss. Naya whimpered and gripped his uniform shirt.

"Tell me the truth," Menace commanded and dragged his lips across her jaw.

"What's wrong?"

She swallowed hard. "Terror scares me."

Menace chortled. "He scares everyone, Naya."

"No, it's not that. I…." Her voice trailed off as she toyed with one of the buttons on his shirt. "I don't think he likes me."

"He doesn't like many people. Don't take it personally." Menace studied her face. He spotted the tense lines around her mouth. "Did he say something to you? Because he can be a real son of a bitch without realizing it."

"Yeah, I got that."

"Hey," Menace said gently and cupped her chin. "I don't care what Terror thinks.

Don't give him a second thought."

She smiled but it didn't reach her eyes. "All right."

Menace decided then and there that he was going to have a talk with Terror. Naya had had enough run-ins with the police on her planet to pick up on the vibes a guy like Terror, the top Shadow Force operative in the sector, would give off. Terror had investigated Hallie fully when Vicious had Grabbed her. Menace had no doubt Terror would do the same thing to Naya but she didn't need him giving her the third degree out of some misguided attempt to protect a friend.

"So what did you think of Hallie?" He touched the pamphlets sticking out of her shirt pocket.

This time Naya's smile was true. "I think she's incredibly sweet and a really nice person."

The elevator stopped and he took her hand to lead her to their quarters. "She's been good for Vicious and the ship.

She's an incredible force for someone so small."

"She wants me to join her wives club thing."

Menace tried to imagine Naya sitting around at Hallie's get-togethers to talk about whatever it was that women talked about at those things. He couldn't. "Are you?"

"I don't know. I'll go to the first one just because I have questions. I'll see how it goes."

Insecurity flared deep in his gut. Questions? He'd seen the pamphlets Hallie had given her. One of them he was already familiar with because it had caused quite a stir after the last Grab. Some men weren't thrilled by the fact that their women were informed of rights that were generally kept quiet, but Hallie and other wives had argued that giving new brides all the information would foster trust and communication between couples. He didn't disagree with that assertion but still couldn't shake the grip of fear that Naya would choose to file for separation rather than give their union a try.

"I can answer any questions you have, Naya. You don't need the wives club for that. Whatever you want to know, I'll tell you."

She touched his arm. "I know that. I meant questions only other wives can answer."

"Oh." Feeling sheepish, he grabbed her hand and gently pried apart her fingers. Holding her thumb, he pressed it to the biometric scanner. It beeped when it successfully read her thumbprint. "You're in the system now. You can control all the locks and consoles in our home and gain access to entry points throughout the ship."

Surprise rippled across her face. "But you said I'm on

restrictions."

Still clasping her hand, he tugged her into their quarters. "You are but as you just experienced, restrictions are lifted during an emergency or when you're with me or someone on my emergency contact list like Vicious or Hallie. When I decide to lift your blanket restrictions, there will be no delay in your ability to move about the ship freely."

"And when will that be?"

Menace shut the door to their home and listened to the reassuring *hiss* and *beep* of the locks engaging. Secure in their space, he backed her against the wall and crushed his mouth to hers in a possessive kiss. When he pulled away, she panted and clutched at his shirt. "When you've been a very, very good girl."

Grinning at his sexy teasing, Naya traced the heavy outline of the tattoo peeking out above his collar. "How do you suggest I go about proving that I can be a very, very good girl?"

"You can start by stripping out of those clothes."

Her eyebrows lifted with surprise. "Here?"

"Yes."

"But—"

"Now, Naya."

Her immediate response to his forceful tone pleased him. Her breaths deepened and she licked her lips. Menace suspected that Naya enjoyed being bossed around by him because she had been forced to maintain complete control for so long just to survive. Submitting to him seemed to feed some deep-seated need she'd only just realized she had. For Menace, the knowledge that he was the only man who had ever successfully ordered her around proved a heady thing indeed. It was a gift he would never take for granted.

Skin flushed, she peeled out of her ill-fitting garments and toed off the shoes Hallie had given her. Menace couldn't keep his hands off her. He palmed her lush breasts and let his hands ride her sinful curves. The feel of her satiny skin beneath his fingertips sent heat streaking through his lower belly. She mewled softly and rocked her hips.

Menace needed no other invitation. Dropping to his knees, he peppered her torso with kisses and licked a circle around her navel. She had been averse to the idea of a genital piercing, but he couldn't shake the idea of a shiny precious stone adorning that gentle dip in her belly. He nipped the area. "We should pierce this."

"What?" she asked breathlessly. "Pierce my bellybutton?"

"Yes."

"No."

He grinned up at her and nibbled a spot on her hip. "We'll discuss it later."

"Menace, I don't want—"

"Open your thighs for me." Cutting her off mid-argument really frustrated her. He tried not to laugh at the pissed-off look on her face. She was rather striking when her dark eyes flashed like that. "Don't make me ask again."

She glared at him but slid her feet wider apart. He grasped her inner thighs and tried to nuzzle his face against her sex. Her hands shot out to block him. With a quick shove, she pushed his face away. Shame burned her cheeks and made her voice waver.

"Don't do that, Menace."

Growling, he frowned up at her. "Put your hands behind your back. Now."

She blinked twice but followed his order. He brushed his thumbs up and down her slit. "This is my cunt, Naya. Your body belongs to me and I'll enjoy it whenever and however I please. Is that understood?"

She spluttered with indignation. "I'm not your toy, Menace!"

"No but you are my woman. Right now, I want to taste my woman."

She tried to squeeze her knees together but his firm grasp on her inner thighs prevented it. "Menace, it's not appropriate."

So they were back to that again. "Is this because we made love this morning?"

"Yes. You can't...you know...until I've showered again."

"Says who?"

"Um..."

"You worry too much." He kissed her mound. "Now hush and enjoy the feel of my tongue in your sweet cunt."

"Menace..." Her protest turned to a low moan as he swiped her pussy with his tongue. "Oh!"

Groaning with need, he delved into her pink folds. His tongue circled her clit. He made sure to let her know that she was absolutely delicious as he lapped at her. If it took a tongue-lashing every morning, he would break her of this idea that her body was unclean or shameful.

Her tense muscles relaxed. She lifted her hips and widened her feet even more. Smiling triumphantly, Menace grabbed her ankles and lifted her legs onto his shoulders. He cupped her ass and feasted on her pussy. As if overcome with ecstasy, Naya bounced her heels against his back and slapped her palms against the wall. She cried out his name again and again as she climaxed hard, her clit pulsing against his lips and tongue.

When he finally tore his mouth away from her, she sagged against the wall. He grinned up at her. The dreamy expression on her face told him he had completed his mission. He let her legs slip from his shoulders and rose to his full height. His cock was so hard he expected it to bust out of his pants any second.

As if reading his mind, Naya reached for his tactical pants. She jerked free the buttons and yanked down the zipper. With a rough shove, she pushed his clothing down his hips. Menace clasped her by the waist and lifted her off the ground. She wrapped her thighs around him and used the wall to brace her upper body. He plundered her mouth, kissing her fast and hard in the same way he intended to fuck her.

He groaned when she grabbed his dick and wiggled her hips. The throbbing head of his cock parted the folds of her wet pussy. As soon as she placed him against her entrance, he thrust forward, sheathing himself fully in her hot, slick depths. She cried out and threw her head back, baring her neck to him. He buried his face against her throat and held tight to her trim waist as he rocked in and out of her.

Naya's fingernails scratched at his scalp. She threaded her fingers through his short hair and panted against his cheek. "Menace," she moaned his name, the sound heavenly to his ears. "Menace! Oh! *Ah!*"

There was nothing easy or gentle about their mating. He claimed her with feral intensity. Their bodies slapped together as they chased release. Too busy holding her up to help her climax, Menace dragged his lips along her jawline. "Touch your clit, Naya. I want to feel your pussy milking me when you come."

She gasped at his brazen order but slipped her hand to the spot where their bodies joined. He changed the angle of his upper body to give her room. Their gazes met. The sight of her pink tongue swiping her upper lip spurred the memory of her mouth on his cock. He had to muscle down the overwhelming surge of lust that threatened to push him over the edge too soon.

Her sheath clenched him tighter and tighter. Naya's shallow breaths matched his. The moment she began to shudder, Menace let go and joined her in their shared climax. He thrust as deep as possible and jerked roughly as the bursts of bliss rocked him.

Cheek-to-cheek, they clung to each other. Menace planted his hands against the wall, bracing their bodies with his hips. He pressed his mouth to her neck. "You just get better and better."

She laughed and peppered ticklish kisses along his jaw. "Menace?"

"Yes, sweetheart?"

"I know I can ask for a separation…"

His stomach clenched painfully. Was she going to drop that bomb on him now? "But I want to give our relationship a try."

A rush of happiness threatened to topple him. He lifted his head and gazed down into her beautiful face. She wore an expression of uncertainty. Wanting her to know just how much he appreciated her offer, Menace smiled reassuringly and claimed her mouth in a sensual kiss.

She cupped his face and swept her thumbs across his cheeks. "I don't know about you but I could use a nap."

"I could use a little shut-eye." Menace tugged his pants up higher and slipped out of her slick heat. He wrapped his arms around her and pulled her away from the wall. Capturing her lips, he carried her away from the entryway. He let his hand drift down to her bare backside and gave her plump bottom a good smack. "But first I think I want another round with you."

Her eyes widened in shock. "Again? So soon?"

"What can I say?" He squeezed her ass before dumping her on the bed and crawling over her. "You drive me crazy."

"Menace, I don't know about—*oh*!"

Chuckling against her belly, Menace put a mental check in his column. He'd definitely won this round.

CURLED IN THE corner of Menace's surprisingly comfy couch, Naya fooled around with the strange touchscreen tablet. She had seen similar devices used by Josef when she visited his testing site with Jennie. This was the first time she had ever had a chance to play with one and get used to it. Menace had spent much of the afternoon helping her learn to use the various bits of technology in his—their—quarters.

She had meant what she said earlier about giving her new life with him a real try. After seeing the way he'd jumped to defend and keep her, Naya believed Menace when he said he wanted her and only her. She had been burned so many times in the past but Menace seemed to be proving himself different than all the people who had betrayed her.

Listening to Menace move around in the bedroom, she couldn't shake the nagging ache in the pit of her belly. She needed to tell him the real reason Terror had scared her. Menace was no fool. He had picked up on her anxiety and had seemed so ready to help her but she simply hadn't known how to tell him the truth. So far, he had accepted that she'd been arrested for theft and on suspicion of smuggling things like medicine but there was so much more to tell.

As a street kid struggling just to survive, she had done some truly terrible things. Things she doubted he would understand. Things that would probably get her arrested in his world. She had smuggled more than just medicine and tech. Her business had been seeded with the funds scraped together by her illicit activities for people who had absolutely nothing to do with the altruistic Red Feather.

"Naya?" Menace strode into the living area. "I'm going to head out for our premission briefing. I won't be back until morning."

Naya turned her upper body and got her first good look at Menace in full gear. The sight of him in all that harsh black and armed to the teeth chilled her. This was the boogeyman vision of her childhood. "Um…wow."

His jaw clenched. "I've scared you, haven't I?"

"A little," she reluctantly admitted. Her gaze moved over his terrifying black form. She had never seen one man wearing so many weapons. "You think you have enough firepower?"

His face relaxed and he laughed. "You sound like Vicious."

She gestured to the holsters strapped to his muscular thighs and the belt at his waist. "It's overkill. Don't you think? I mean, a vest, a belt, two thigh holsters and knives? Who the hell are you expecting down there?"

"I plan for the worst."

"Clearly."

Menace moved closer to the couch and brushed his fingertips along her face. He wore thick fingerless tactical gloves. The acrid scent of the fabric made her nose twitch.

"There's food in the refrigeration box and the pantry."

She grasped his hand and rubbed the underside of his bare wrist. "I'm not five, Menace. I pretty sure I can figure out how to make something to eat."

"Sorry. You're right." He bent down and kissed her long and hard, leaving her wanting and filled with need. "When I get back, we'll pick up right there."

His promise sent ripples of excitement through her core. "If you keep this up, I won't be able to walk by the end of the week."

Menace grinned. "Is that a dare?"

She snorted and smacked him. "You're incorrigible."

"And you're too sexy for your own good." Menace kissed the crown of her head. "You can use the tablet to control the entertainment center." He paused. "You might want to stay away from the nine-hundred range."

"Why?"

"It's pornography."

"Pornography? You mean…?"

He nodded. "Yes."

"I see."

"Have you ever seen pornography?"

Her ears grew hot. "Yes. I came across racy pics and magazines back in Connor's Run. They're sold in back alleys and bars. Teenage boys trade them as currency to buy cigarettes or whatever."

"But you've never seen a film?"

"Until this afternoon when you showed me that," she gestured to the big flat screen built into the living room wall, "I'd only ever seen short government films projected on white sheets in the town square."

"We'll have to watch one together."

"What?" Now her face was as hot as her ears. "No. I don't think so."

"I wasn't asking."

She pursed her lips. "You're a pervert."

"And you love it," he said with a laugh. He retreated to the entryway. "I'm locking the door. You won't be able to leave unless there's an emergency."

She tried not to dwell on the fact that he was basically keeping her prisoner. After what she had learned from Hallie about the lost property laws, Naya had no desire to explore the ship on her own. Another more troubling thought rushed to the forefront of her mind. "Can anyone else get in here?"

"Only Vicious," he said. "He's my emergency contact and yours. You'd have to let anyone else in the door."

"Good."

"What has you so worried?" Menace tilted his head. "Is it the pamphlets and all that business about the property laws and stealing wives? Because I can tell you right now, Naya, there isn't a man on this ship stupid enough to try to break into my home to steal you."

What about Terror, she wanted to ask. He definitely wasn't stupid, but Naya felt sure he was brazen enough to do it. Over lunch, she had cautiously pumped Menace for info on Terror. He had said the one-eyed soldier was a logistics clerk, but Naya had silently called bullshit on that. The secret police down on Calyx also had similarly innocuous titles. Janitors, sanitation workers, maintenance men—they were occupations no one gave much thought and men who were overlooked on the street. It was the perfect cover.

"Naya?" His gentle voice called to her.

"Yes?"

"Try to relax tonight. Enjoy the quiet time. Watch something silly or fun."

"I'll try."

He shot her one last sinfully sexy smile before walking out of view. She heard a few quick beeps before the door opened and closed. The loud locking mechanism made her feel fractionally more secure. Alone with her thoughts, Naya hugged her knees to her chest and tapped the screen of the entertainment console. Menace's suggestion to find an entertaining program seemed like a good one. Anything to rid her mind of the worry her run-in with Terror had caused.

But not even the melodramatic program on the screen could tear her thoughts away from the man who threatened her most. Oh, the two sisters fighting over the man who had proposed to one but gotten the other knocked up was interesting enough but those worries about Terror wouldn't leave her.

What could she do? Trust Menace with the secret that could send her to prison? She doubted there was anything he could do to help her even if he knew what she had done. Whether he would want to help her was the real question. The thought of being betrayed by Menace cut deeply. She had known him a very short time but already she was beginning to care for the green-eyed sky warrior.

Naya reached for the tablet again and found the information browser Menace had shown her earlier. She tapped at the screen and entered her search term. A few seconds later, dozens of results appeared. It was going to be a long night of reading.

Chapter Eleven

MENACE WORKED HIS jaws in a rhythmic motion, smashing the citrus-flavored gum between his teeth as they waited for the fixer Vicious had arranged via Hallie's contacts on the planet. It had been some time since he had been on a live mission off the *Valiant* but the old, well-honed instincts never really died. He had easily adjusted to the eerie yellow-green night vision projected by the tactical glasses he wore. Keeping the nose of his weapon down, he stayed on alert, ready to raise it and fire at the first sign of trouble.

The life-sign sensor on his wrist shot a signal to Cipher who waited back on the ship Zephyr had expertly and silently piloted into the small clearing outside Harper's Well. As the tech expert on the SRU team, Cipher monitored various streams of information including team positions, radar bursts of the surrounding vicinity and radio traffic from the *Guardian*, a small gunship currently in the airspace nearest them. The tech specialist was also a damn good shot and frighteningly good at improvising explosive devices on the fly.

Up and to his left, Venom had taken a sniper position. One of the top three shooters in the entire Harcos force, Venom was exactly the kind of man Menace wanted watching over them. He had seen Venom in action during the Sendarian siege eleven years earlier. The man had gone above and beyond the call of duty to keep the enemy away from the gated city and buy enough time for much needed supply drops to reach their pinned-down forces.

Twenty yards in front of him, Raze waited to make first contact. His relaxed posture hid the tension Menace was certain the SRU team leader felt. The most skilled negotiator Menace had ever met, Raze often fooled people with his easy smile and gentleness. At a moment's notice, Raze could become one of the most deadly soldiers imaginable.

"Two incoming life signs at the perimeter mark." Cipher's calm voice filled Menace's ear. The specialist spit out a positional reading and Menace adjusted his body accordingly. "Contact in ten, nine, eight…"

"Stop there," Raze loudly and clearly ordered. "Hands in the air. Face away from me."

Two members of the SRU team who Menace wasn't very familiar with came forward from their positions to secure the two and bring them forward. Cipher activated the small hovering lights they had set up earlier to illuminate the area. Menace pushed his night vision glasses on top of his head and blinked a few times to clear his vision.

His gaze fell to the young woman first. She had pale-blonde hair that hung to her waist and wore loose-fitting pants and a tunic. He pegged her age in the same range as Naya's. From this distance, she looked pretty. He hoped Flare would approve.

The man caught Menace's attention next. Though he looked short next to Raze, he was actually tall for a Calyx male. He held a bag in one hand. Menace thought it was the woman's at first but she gripped a brown one tightly.

"Menace." Raze's voice dinged in his ear. "Come on up."

Menace crossed the distance with quick, hard strides. At Raze's side, he nodded at the woman. "Ma'am, I'm Menace and I've been charged with escorting you safely to Flare."

She offered a meek smile. "Thank you."

He reached for her bag. "Let me take this for you." He pointed to the man's hand.

"Is that yours also?"

She shook her head. "No. It's for someone else."

"Someone else?" Menace's chest tightened. Was another woman hoping to hitch a ride?

"The name's Dankirk." The man offered his hand but Menace frowned at it. "Right," he said quietly and dropped his hand. "Look, a friend of mine was taken during the Connor's Run Grab. I'd like to get her bag to her."

Menace wavered. Most women usually brought a small bag to the Grabs and those bags were taken to the processing line so they could join their owners on their new ships and homes. Sometimes bags were lost or left behind. Naya hadn't had one with her but the woman who had packed that one probably missed it a great deal.

With a sigh, Menace reached for the bag. "What is the woman's name?"

The man, Dankirk, started to hand it over. "My friend's name is Naya."

There was no suppressing the jerk of surprise that

shook him. He held tight to the bag's handle. "Naya?"

"Have you met her? She's about this tall and has dark hair and brown skin."

"I've met her." Menace yanked the bag out of the man's hand and crooked two fingers at him. "You. With me. Now."

Dankirk didn't hesitate to follow but kept a safe distance. When they were in as much privacy as could be found in the clearing, Menace asked, "How do you know Naya?"

The man chortled. "I think the real question here is how the hell do *you* know her?"

"She's my wife. I Grabbed her."

The man's eyes widened. "You?"

"Yes." Menace narrowed his eyes. "You have a problem with that?"

"That depends," Dankirk replied. "Have you hit her? Are you going to hit her?"

"I've never harmed a woman in my life. I don't plan to start with my wife."

Dankirk studied him a moment. "She's very important to me. I need to know she's safe."

"She is."

"I want her to be happy. Fuck knows she never found happiness here."

Menace wondered if this was where Naya had learned her rather bad habit of cursing. "I plan to do everything in my power to make her happy."

"You better."

Menace wanted to chuckle at the man's empty threat

but the look on Dankirk's face stopped him. It was clear he felt something very strong for Naya. A painful sensation twisted his gut. What if this man had been waiting for Naya to reach the safe zone so he could whisk her away to the colonies? "Does she love you?"

The man laughed, the sound harsh and angst-ridden. "Not in the way you're thinking and not in the way I've always wanted. I'm sure you've figured this out, but she's not exactly the kind of girl who falls in love or trusts easily—and with good reason."

"Her family—"

"They're shits. Even her sainted father," Dankirk added. "I know she remembers Tom as being her hero, but he was the farthest thing from it to anyone else who knew him. With all his debts and shady dealings, he made it impossible for her to have a normal life after his death." Dankirk inhaled a sharp breath. "The best damn thing that ever happened to her was being Grabbed by you. Don't fuck that up for her. She's got a new life, a new start. She deserves it."

Taken aback by the intensity of the man's remarks, Menace remained quiet and let it all sink in. "I'll take care of her. You needn't worry."

"Do you promise?"

"She is precious to me. I give you my word that I will protect and care for her."

This time when Dankirk extended his hand, Menace grasped it. Dankirk slowly retreated. He waved at the woman Menace had been entrusted to ferry back to the *Valiant*. "Good luck, Penny. I'll make sure your mama knows you made it safely."

"Thanks, Danny."

Holding Naya's bag, Menace rejoined the small group and gestured for Penny to start walking. Menace flanked her while Raze and his two men led the way back to the waiting ship. Once he got the young woman safely buckled into her seat, he handed the bag to Venom. "Take this."

Venom's eyebrows shot up but he accepted the bag all the same. "What do you want me to do with your wife's bag?"

"Search it. I don't want any questions arising about the procedures followed to clear her things. Let Cipher scan it."

"Sure." Venom disappeared out of the seating area to the cargo section where Cipher had set up shop.

Menace dropped into his seat and tugged the various belts into place. Secured, he waited for the flashing light to turn solid green to indicate takeoff was imminent. He spotted movement out of the corner of his eye. Penny's fists were so tightly drawn her knuckles had gone white.

Worried she was going to stroke out from fear, he reached over and touched her arm. "Hey, it's going to be okay. There will be a few minutes of uncomfortable pressure as we zoom through the atmosphere. Before the gravity boosters kick in, there will be a few seconds of weightlessness." He grabbed the puke bag stuffed into the sleeve above her head. "If you need to vomit, use this."

"Th-thank y-you," she stammered. She took the bag with shaking fingers. Her teeth rattled together so hard he feared she might break one of them.

"Would you like a sedative? There's still time to administer an injection before we lift off from the surface."

"N-no," she said with a determined shake of her head. "I just need a mo-moment."

He held her wide-eyed, panicked gaze. "You'll be fine. Take some deep, calm breaths. I've heard some people like to close their eyes and count silently. That might help."

She shot him a grateful smile. "Thank you."

In the next instant, the light in the passenger area turned bright-green. The ship vibrated and gained speed. Next to him, Penny squeezed her eyes shut and gripped the puke bag. Across the aisle, Raze eyed her with some concern. Menace second-guessed his decision to offer the sedative. He should have just given it and asked forgiveness later.

When they reached outer space, she squeaked. He expected her to blow any second, but she got a hold of herself and managed not to lose it. Twenty minutes into their three-hour trek to the *Valiant*, she'd calmed enough to relax. Half an hour into it, she worked up the courage to speak.

"You were part of the Connor's Run Grab?"

Menace nodded. "Yes."

"You're happy with your wife?"

"Very."

"Danny told me all about the woman he was taking the bag to," she said with a gentle smile. "From what I gather, she's really amazing."

"Yes," Menace said softly. "She is."

Penny laughed. "I bet she wasn't afraid to climb on a ship like this and fly into space."

"No," Menace agreed. "I don't think she was afraid of the flight." He didn't mention that she was more terrified of him.

Penny seemed to understand. "It's not an easy thing, leaving behind everything you've known to make a new life with a strange man. Especially when that strange man belongs to the race that filled the grim tales of your childhood," she added. "You know, go to sleep or the sky warriors will snatch you away and make you their slave. Stay out of the woods or the Harcos will find you and take you to one of their ships where they'll use you as a guinea pig."

While Menace wondered how the hell his people's kindness toward the people of Calyx had been twisted into such gruesome tales, Raze asked, "What is a guinea pig?"

"It's a small animal that existed on Earth and was used in experiments by the scientists and doctors there. Our ancestors who fled the world of science experiments gone awry wrote about them."

Raze frowned. "We don't experiment on humans."

"You would say that, wouldn't you?" Her teasing smile made Raze chuckle.

"Yes, I guess I would." Raze unbuckled his harness and rose. "I'll be in the back with Cipher."

Still smiling, Penny opened her bag and took out a small square wrapped in white paper. "It's a sweet bread. Would you like a piece?"

Menace held up his hand. "No but thank you."

Penny nibbled silently and sipped from a metal bottle she had retrieved from her bag. Watching her eat left him feeling uncomfortably aware of the ways he had failed Naya on her trip to the *Valiant*. He hadn't even thought to offer her a drink or something to eat. After running and fighting him, she had probably needed both. No, he had been more concerned with getting her to be quiet and sit still.

Rubbing the back of his neck, Menace stretched out his legs. This experience with ferrying Penny to the *Valiant* was proving more pleasant than the transport ship ride he'd shared with Naya. There were no weeping brides and no sex-starved males tapping feet and drumming fingers on armrests.

"Are you friends with the man I'm joining?"

Menace glanced at Penny. "Not really."

"Oh." She looked surprised. "I thought—"

"I owed him a debt of honor. Picking you up and bringing you to him without incident is my way of settling that debt."

"Um…I guess that's nice."

Menace chuckled. "That's one way of describing it."

She returned her items to her bag and closed it up. He realized that she was fishing for information on her potential mate. "I believe our pilot, Zephyr, is familiar with your soon-to-be mate. Once we reach cruising speed, I can see if he'd be willing to speak with you about him."

"I'd like that."

An hour into their flight, Menace walked her to the front of the ship and showed her an empty seat behind the two pilot chairs. "Zeph, this is Penny." Fully aware of the pilot's Lothario reputation, he clapped the man on the arm. "Remember she's taken."

"Unlike you land corps boys, we sky corps men don't go around stealing other men's wives."

Menace let the zing about the *Arctis* bust-up slide. "I'll be in the cargo bay with Raze. Buzz me when she's done."

"Will do."

He found Raze and Venom sorting through the items packed into Naya's bag. He scanned the bench where they'd laid out her things. Clothing, a small notebook, a pair of boots, a belt…and a gun.

Venom must have seen the shock register on his face. "It was loaded but I've rendered it safe."

Menace picked up the small pistol. It had been a long time since a weapon like this had been in general circulation. His grandfather had used these in his first campaigns but they'd been phased out of the military by the time the old man had retired. Menace had a few of these old models in his personal collection and fired them for fun on occasion.

"I have to confiscate it." Venom gestured toward the weapon. "Normally I'd hand it over to you since that's your purview, but I thought you'd like to avoid a conflict of interest issue."

"Understood." He inspected Naya's sidearm. She'd kept it clean and ready for use. He spotted the T scratched into the metal. A little lower an N had been etched into it. Realizing the weapon had sentimental value, he said, "I'll petition to have it returned. I'm sure she'll want it back since it belonged to her father."

Raze flipped through the notebook. Photographs fell out and drifted to the floor. Menace knelt down and gathered them. They were pictures from her childhood. He couldn't help but smile at her gap-toothed grin and wild hair. She looked so happy, so carefree. What had happened to that little girl to make her into the wary, mistrusting woman he knew?

"I can't make heads or tails of this." Raze handed it to Cipher. "It's in code."

Cipher thumbed through it. "Yes, it is. What do you think, Menace? Do you want me to crack it?"

The idea of reading Naya's secret communications left him feeling uneasy. "No. She's just paranoid enough to code her day-to-day diary entries. What she's written in there is none of my business."

"Unless it is," Raze replied carefully. "That man is part of the Red Feather, their dissident group, and he called her his friend. If she was a member of that group and if this book details her work with them, I'm sure Terror will want to know."

Menace snatched the book from Raze's hand and stuffed the pictures inside. "The Red Feather is on the neutral list. They're not our enemies. I won't go digging through my wife's diary entries, entries she's gone to great lengths to keep secret, to give Terror more homework."

"It's going into my report, Menace. I have to cover my ass."

"Cover away," Menace said and began packing away her things. "The rest of the bag was cleared?"

"Yes," Venom confirmed. "The firearm?"

Menace handed it over. "Make sure it goes into the safe in the armory or the one in Vicious' office. If that's taken, I can't replace it for her."

"I will."

Menace trusted Venom to keep his word. His earpiece chirped and Zeph told him Penny was ready to take her seat again. With Naya's bag slung over his shoulder, Menace returned to the cockpit. Back in the passenger area with Penny, he made an effort to answer her questions and engage in her need for chitchat. He breathed a quiet sigh of relief when they finally docked.

After walking her through the immigration processing station, Menace escorted Penny to the infirmary. Flare had a private room in the orthopedic section. To Menace's surprise, Admiral Orion waited in the hallway outside Flare's temporary quarters. Menace snapped to attention and saluted the superior officer. "Admiral."

"Menace." He gave an at ease and smiled at Penny. "Welcome to the *Valiant*, ma'am."

"Thank you, sir." There was no mistaking the nervousness in her soft voice. "And it's Penny."

"That's a lovely name." He glanced at the closed door. "Well, Penny, I understand you were told of Flare's current condition."

She nodded. "His leg is badly injured. He'll need multiple surgeries and may walk with a limp."

"You're not averse to these issues? I only ask because, in our culture, an injured male isn't highly sought-after by brides."

Penny sucked in a shocked breath. "That's awful!" She lifted her chin. "I don't care if he's in a chair for the rest of his life. Those kinds of things don't matter to me." Then, a little calmer, she added, "My brother contracted the water sickness when he was seven. He hasn't been able to walk since then, but he runs a very successful mill and has a lovely wife and children. His life is very happy."

Menace decided then and there that Dankirk had a good eye for matchmaking. Vicious had spoken briefly with the man but left the selection of Flare's potential bride to him. He'd chosen well.

Orion looked relieved. "I'm glad to hear that you feel that way. Flare will walk again. It's just a matter of time and physical therapy. I know you were told there was a chance you might be going back to Prime with him, but a new medical station is expected to arrive within the next month. You'll move there while he undergoes his treatment. Once he's completed that, his situation will be reassessed. It's likely he'll be moved into a training position."

When Orion gestured to the door, Menace took a step back. His end of the bargain complete, he was ready to retreat to his quarters. Penny's hand on his arm stopped him. She smiled up at him. "Thank you, Menace."

He nodded stiffly and watched her enter the hospital room with Orion. He hoped Flare would be pleased with her. She seemed like a nice woman. They had a good chance of being happy together if they could work out their cultural differences.

As he traversed the ship, Menace couldn't shake the conversation he had shared with Dankirk. The man's words played on a loop in his head. Dankirk had said Naya didn't love him but it was clear her friend loved her. He seemed extremely protective of her. His assertion that being Grabbed was the best thing that could have ever happened to Naya still surprised Menace. There weren't many men on Calyx who supported the Grabs.

The memory of the notebook with its coded entries bothered him. Had he been wrong to take it back and keep it from Cipher? It felt so intrusive to go through her private things. They were only just establishing trust between them. If he sent her notebook back to Cipher and had him decode it, she would be furious. To her, it would be a betrayal.

He slipped inside their quarters as quietly as possible and dropped her bag on the entryway table. He had hoped to get into their bedroom and undress without waking her but she was too light a sleeper. The dimmed lights in their bedroom switched on and she appeared in the open doorway. He enjoyed the sight of her sleepy face and mussed hair. "Hey."

"You're back early."

"Zeph flies like a bat out of hell."

"The woman? She's okay?"

He nodded. "She's with Flare now. I think they're a good match."

Naya grinned. "Better than us?"

"I wouldn't go that far."

She started to say something else but her gaze fell on the entryway table. Shock slackened her face. "Where did you get that?"

He brushed his fingers across the well-worn leather. "A friend of yours."

"Friend? Jennie?" She sounded so hopeful.

He shook his head. "I met a man named Dankirk tonight."

"Danny was the fixer on the job tonight?"

"He was." Menace held her gaze. "I suppose I don't have to ask if you were a member of the Red Feather?"

"I was." She didn't even try to lie. "We—they're—just political dissidents. They bring medicine and technology to those who need and want it. They work to keep elections in The City as fair as possible. They help get sick people to hospitals in the colonies and aid in immigration efforts."

"Illegal immigration," he countered. "It's illegal to move people from your planet to the colonies without visas and proof of sponsorship from legal citizens of those colonized installations."

Naya crossed her arms. "Are we really going to have a political argument at four in the damn morning?"

"No." Menace sighed. "Here." He picked up the bag and held it out. "It's been searched and cleared."

She hesitated before walking toward him. "My pistol?"

He shook his head. "It's been confiscated. I'll petition to have it returned as soon as possible. If we get it back, it goes right into my gun safe, understood?"

"Yes." She took the bag and hugged it to her chest. "I never thought I'd see this again."

"Your friend seemed determined to get it back to you." Menace couldn't help himself. "Was he your lover?"

"What? Why would you ask me that?"

"Was he?"

"Why? Are you jealous?"

"Naya—"

"Yes, once," she answered angrily. "Danny and I had sex once. More than a year ago," she added. "It wasn't great but it wasn't awful. No, he didn't make me come. There! Are you satisfied with that answer, *master*?"

She spat the word so harshly that he flinched. Realizing he had been an absolute jackass, Menace wiped a hand down his face. "I'm sorry, Naya. I shouldn't have asked that."

"Why the hell do you even care, Menace? Didn't you tell me that the past is the past?"

"I did." Reluctantly he admitted, "Maybe I am jealous. That man knows you so well. He knows your secrets. He's spent a lifetime with you. How the hell do I compare with that?"

"You don't." She tossed the bag back onto the entryway table. When she slid her arms around his waist and leaned her head against his chest, Menace couldn't breathe. "We're building something new and different. What we had or didn't have with other people doesn't matter. This right here?" She squeezed him. "This is what matters."

His eyes closed briefly as the tension in his gut eased. Her correct assessment of the situation calmed him. Menace cupped her sweet face and captured her mouth in a tender kiss. Remembering his earlier promise, he swept her into his arms. "I'm pretty sure I said we were going to pick up right here."

She squirmed in his arms. "Maybe you could get undressed first. I've got the handle of a pistol jamming right into my butt."

Menace snorted. "I've got something I'd like to jam in

your—"

Naya clapped her hand over his mouth. With narrowed eyes, she warned, "Finish that sentence and you'll be sleeping on the couch."

Chuckling, Menace set her down in their bedroom and started to strip out of his tactical vest and holsters. "You're starting to sound like a wife."

"Keep it up, Menace. One good kick and you'll sound like a choirboy."

"Ouch," he said with a laugh. Pressing his thumb to the keypad of the gun safe installed in his closet, Menace unlocked and stored away his weapons. He removed his boots and shed his clothing.

Naked and already hard for Naya, he left the closet and found her sliding back into bed. The undershirt she had been wearing had been dropped on the floor. He would have to talk to her about neatness tomorrow. Desperate to get his hands on her again, he lifted the bedcovers and slipped in beside her. She came right to him.

When she tried to throw a leg over him to gain the more dominant role, he shook his head and pressed her fully onto her back. "Not tonight, sweetheart."

Pinned beneath him, she breathed excitedly but didn't fight him. She was getting used to being submissive to him. Her face flushed and her pupils seemed to dilate. The instant reaction she had to his dominance over her made his cock throb.

Menace captured both of her wrists in one hand and dragged them above her head.

He nuzzled her neck. "I'm going to give you a choice.

I'll cuff you to the headboard or I'll hold you down like this. Either way, I'm going to fuck you senseless."

Shuddery breaths breezed across his cheek. "Hold me down."

As need raced through him like a wildfire, Menace claimed her mouth in a possessive, demanding kiss. She arched under him. Still gripping her wrists in one hand, he used the other to caress her silky skin. Her dark nipples were tight peaks now. They begged to be licked and pinched and sucked.

By the time he'd finished tormenting her breasts with his mouth and fingers, Naya practically sobbed. He let his hand slide down her belly and forced her thighs wide open with his knee. His fingers explored her pussy. She was soaking wet in her desperation for him.

Rising up on his knees, Menace angled his body just so. His rock-hard cock found its target. He thrust forward into her welcoming slick heat. Naya cried out and tried to lift her arms but he held her wrists too firmly. The knowledge that she was completely at his mercy rippled through her. He felt it when her pussy clenched him.

"Now," Menace said with a teasing lilt, "let's see how much it takes for me to convince you that I am your master…"

Chapter Twelve

Four Weeks Later

"**I** DON'T UNDERSTAND why this is so complicated." Naya tried to suppress her frustration with the clerk in the clothing department but it was proving difficult. "I gave you the name of the warehouse on Calyx. How hard is it to import two cases of shirts and pants?"

The older Harcos male shot her a pissed-off look. He manned his computer console as if he were a sentry guarding state secrets. "I can't force them to trade with us. They won't meet our terms for import taxes and fees. Unless you want to pay the difference, those boxes aren't leaving Calyx."

"This is ridiculous." Naya rubbed her forehead and tried to think of a way to deal with the red tape. "Look, where I can get a copy of the trading agreements and tax fees and all that?"

The man pointed to the scanner on the corner of his desk. "Scan your chip. I'll have the relevant files sent to your personal tablet."

Naya waved her hand in front of the scanner until it beeped. "Thank you."

Annoyed, she left the store and made her way into the retail sector of the ship. Now that she and Menace had been together for more than thirty days, there was no issue of her being taken by another male. He had taken her off restrictions two weeks earlier as long as she had an escort, usually Hallie because no man on this ship would dare bother the wife of the general.

Naya glanced around the bustling shopping center. Her gaze fell on an empty storefront. The idea Hallie had seeded all those weeks ago about opening a store here had taken hold and sprouted. At the wives meeting earlier, Naya had confided her dream to Hallie. She planned to familiarize herself with the laws and rules before she made any concrete plans. Money would probably be an issue but she had a good chunk waiting for her in a bank on Safe Harbor. If it was enough and the laws were in her favor, she would talk to Menace and see what he thought about her idea.

There was no doubt in her mind that he would support her. Bit by bit, her sexy sky warrior had chipped away at the wall she had erected around herself. There had been arguments in the last month and there were times she really wanted to whack him upside the head with the nearest heavy object, but he truly was the most honest, loyal man she had ever met.

That he absolutely adored her, even when she was acting like a raging bitch, still left her feeling a bit uneasy. Her experience taught her to be wary of any man who thought that her waspish tongue was "cute". She tried to take their relationship day by day, but it was hard sometimes. She felt as if the ground was constantly shifting beneath her feet.

Crossing to the elevator bank, Naya caught movement out of the corner of her eye. At first she didn't even see him but then his one-eyed, scarred face registered. Her stomach coiled painfully. What the hell was he doing here?

Naya hastened her pace and squeezed into the already filled elevator. She dismissed the irritated glances of her fellow passengers. There was no way she was going to wait for the next car, not with Creeper McCreepypants giving her the stinkeye.

A week ago, Naya had overheard Menace talking to Vicious about Terror and his team leaving on a new mission. Her eavesdropping had confirmed her suspicion that Terror was no mere logistics clerk—and that he was incredibly dangerous to her. Knowing he was back onboard the *Valiant* made her knees knock together.

While Terror was away and no longer posing an immediate threat, Naya had been able to convince herself that Menace didn't need to know all the ugly details of her teenage years. She had done her research and learned that the things she had done were in a gray area when it came to the statute of limitations.

Menace kept telling her the past was the past and it couldn't be changed. He had overlooked her involvement in the Red Feather, but if he ever found out about the other things she had done? Naya's chest ached with the very real possibility that he would turn his back on her.

When she reached the floor where the armory was located, Naya stepped off the elevator. The guard at the doorway seemed surprised to see her but he scanned her wrist and waved her through to the office Menace occupied. She had come down here with him twice, both times only to grab something he needed from his desk.

No doubt he wouldn't be thrilled that she'd broken protocol to visit him while he worked, but the thought of making the long trek back to their private quarters with Terror hot on her heels made her sick. There were too many infrequently used corridors where the frightening Shadow Force soldier could snatch her.

She rounded a corner—and slammed into a very familiar chest. "*Oof!*"

"Naya?" Menace grasped her shoulders and set her back on her feet. "What are you doing here?"

"I just wanted to see you." She glanced over her shoulder to make sure she hadn't been followed.

Menace cupped her chin and peered down at her. An expression of concern colored his face. "Are you okay? You look scared."

Naya licked her lips. "I thought someone was following me."

He caressed her cheek with his knuckles. "Did you go to the med bay for your mandatory head check?"

She rolled her eyes. "I'm not crazy!"

"I didn't say you were. Space sickness is a very real threat, sweetheart. You've gone from spending every day of your life on solid ground to spending…what? Thirty-three days in space? It can affect your mind."

She huffed loudly. "I don't have space sickness. I thought Terror was following me."

Menace reeled back in surprise. "Terror? He's back on the ship?"

"I just saw him in the retail sector."

"He was probably trying to catch up with you to talk. I

know he's terrifying on the outside but he's a really great guy when you get to know him."

"I'll have to take your word for it."

Menace cracked a smile and checked his watch. "I'm off-duty in half an hour. You want to come back to my office and watch me finish inputting some data? We can grab dinner when I'm done."

Relieved that he would let her stay, she happily nodded. "I'd love that."

He slid his arm around her shoulders and led her to his office. The space was cramped and hot. Menace gestured to the chair in front of his desk but she ignored him, choosing instead to slide onto the empty space next to this work-station.

Chuckling, Menace dropped into his chair. "You are the prettiest damn paperweight I've ever seen."

"You could hire me on as your assistant. I could perch right here every day and brighten up the place." Naya crossed her legs, making sure to show off as much skin as possible. It wasn't often that she wore skirts back on Calyx but up here on the ship she'd rediscovered her childhood love of them.

Menace had discovered his love of the garments as well. His hand moved to her bare leg. He stroked her skin. "Temping offer, sweetheart, but I don't think I would get much work done."

"Probably not," Naya agreed, only too aware of his raging libido. She grasped his hand and returned it to his desk. "Finish your work so we can go home and play."

"We might not make it home," Menace grumbled and

picked up the stack of shiny silver cards on his desk. He scanned them one by one and tapped information into the empty fields on the big touchscreen monitor mounted on his desk.

"What are you doing?"

"I spent the morning certifying the first group of soldiers to use the new weapons we'll be receiving tomorrow. It's the newest version of a plasma gun. It's supposed to be ideal for urban warfare."

"I see." Naya didn't like the sound of that. If the men in this sector of Harcos operations were gearing up for urban warfare, it meant they had identified the locations of rumored terrorists on Calyx. She feared what that would mean for the innocent people down there who would inevitably be caught in the crossfire.

Menace paused his scanning and tapping and pointed to a small digital catalogue on top of a pile of similar weapons catalogues. "The specs are in there if you'd like to see them."

Naya picked up the lightweight catalog and swiped her finger over the touchscreen to activate the sales pitch. Images of explosions and terrifyingly large soldiers decimating enemy forces popped onto the screen. The bright-white bursts from the muzzles burned right through armor, clothing and skin. The gaping holes left in the bodies smoked and sizzled. Twenty seconds into the pitch, she'd seen enough and stopped it. "Gross."

He chuckled. "But effective."

"You realize that the people down on Calyx are farmers and millers and tradesmen. I mean, dentistry is considered magic to some of those people in the far-flung corners of our civilization. Do you really need a weapon like this?"

"It's not your people we're worried about, Naya. We know that the Harcos faction of insurgents, the Splinters, are here. That bombing four years ago in The City near our embassy had all the trademarks. There's no doubt they're trying to sow seeds of dissatisfaction down there to gain followers and fighters for their dwindling army."

"So what? You're going to hunt them down with those guns? What if you shoot the wrong people?"

Menace didn't glance up from his scanning and typing. "That's war, Naya. Collateral damage is acceptable."

Naya didn't think. She pulled back her fist and punched him hard on the shoulder. "How can you say that? Collateral damage? Those are people, Menace!"

He frowned and rubbed his shoulder. "That *hurt*."

"Oh, I'm sorry," she replied sarcastically. "That was collateral damage from my anger at your indifference."

Menace's jaw tightened. "What do you want me to say, Naya? That we never make mistakes? I'm no liar. Some-times innocent people are in the wrong place at the wrong time. I can't change that. I won't sit here and lie to you by promising you that these weapons will only be used against terrorists."

"Okay and what happens when these weapons get into the hands of those Splinter guys?"

"They won't."

His arrogance burned her already frayed nerves. "You can't know that, Menace. Hello! Your people have imposed a weapons ban on Calyx for centuries, yet we have weapons. You confiscated one from me, remember?"

"Oh, I remember all right."

"Then please listen to me. You are in the wilds of the galaxy out here. You cannot protect every shipment that comes your way." Naya stopped herself before she said something incriminating. This definitely wasn't the time to come clean to him, not here in his office. "Look, all I'm saying is that there have been things that came through the front doors of my pawnshop that were straight off your ships. You couldn't control pieces of tech. How the hell do you intend to control the flow of weapons, Menace?"

He sat back in his chair and studied her. Finally he spoke. "I don't disagree with your assessment, but that's not my department. I'm just the weapons specialist."

She sighed slowly and dropped her gaze. "People are going to die, Menace."

"They already are, Naya. That's why we have to stop these terrorists before they gain a real foothold on your planet. A handful of surgical strikes and we solve the problem."

She shook her head and stared at him. "That easy, huh?"

"That's what they tell people in my paygrade."

Signaling an end to their discussion, Menace returned to his work. Naya stifled the inner voice that urged her to just fucking tell him already. Their discussion had given her the perfect opening to just lay it all on the line. Fear stopped her. The idea that he would react with anger or disgust made it impossible for her to take the brave step of confessing her sins.

Menace worked diligently at her side. The hands that had brought her such pleasure and that cradled her close at night mesmerized her. She gazed at his handsome face. The thought of never again seeing his smiling face across the dinner table or feeling his lips gliding over her skin squashed whatever courage she'd been able to muster.

Refusing to ruin what she shared with Menace, Naya convinced herself that Terror couldn't possibly know what she'd done. There were no records. She'd only ever been arrested for petty crimes. Maybe Terror had his suspicions but he didn't have proof. She wasn't about to give it to him by unburdening her conscience on Menace. Some secrets had to be kept…whatever the cost.

NAYA HAD GONE awfully quiet as he worked. Menace scanned the last card and inputted the final pieces of data before logging off. He placed the cards back in their case and slipped it into the drawer of his desk where he kept the range records of every soldier on the ship. Touching her knee, Menace got her attention. "I have something I want you to see."

She rolled her eyes. "I think you showed me that this morning in the shower."

Menace chortled and shoved out of his chair. "No, not *that*." He held out his hand and tugged her off his desk. "I was going to give it to you later but you're here now so we may as well play with it."

"Now I know you're talking about sex. Is it another one of your weird toys?"

Menace frowned at her. "You make it sound like I'm a

sex-addicted pervert."

"Um…have you looked in the mirror lately?"

"Watch it," he warned. "There's enough soundproofing in the shooting range for me to toss you across my knee and swat that little ass of yours until it's bright-red."

Naya laughed and patted his chest. "Tease."

"You're awfully brave today, sweetheart." He led her into the shooting range and punched in the activation code that would alert the control rooms and police that any shots fired were for training purposes only. The last thing he wanted was an SRU team storming the range in the search for an active shooter.

"Take these." Menace pressed a pair of headphones and safety glasses into her hand. "You'll have to wear them."

She examined the protective equipment. "Why?"

"Because I'm rather fond of your beautiful eyes and I'm sure you like being able to hear," he replied. "Once we're in the shooting area," he gestured to the stations on the far end of the room, "you'll wear that gear or else you won't get to fire your weapon."

She perked up at that tidbit. "My weapon?"

Menace nodded. "Venom brought it down earlier. Vicious and Admiral Orion finally got around to stamping my permit. I know this is your firearm, but technically it's mine now. That means I'm responsible for it which means that after firing it today it goes right into the gun safe in our quarters."

"I understand."

"I'll bring you to the range as often as possible." Menace unlocked the armory gun safe. Unlike the small box in their closet, this safe was actually a room with walls covered in weapons. He kept at least two models of every weapon within the current Harcos arsenal in the safe, one for testing and the other for teaching.

Naya's small firearm was in a drawer near the door. He retrieved the unloaded weapon and removed four magazines from a nearby drawer. He didn't keep many of these old-school projectile rounds on the ship. They are so antiquated that only he and Venom had any proficiency with the projectile weapons.

"Before I give this to you, we need to discuss the safety procedures down here." Menace pocketed the magazines and carried the gun out of the safe. As he led Naya to a shooting station, he walked her through the rules and regulations of the range. To be sure she was paying attention, he made her repeat them and quizzed her on what to do if she had a jam or a misfire. Satisfied with her answers, he instructed her to put on her safety gear and handed over her weapon and one magazine.

Like an expert marksman, Naya checked the weapon. Holding it with the muzzle pointed downrange, she pulled back the slide along the top of the barrel twice to ensure the chamber was empty. Satisfied it was clear, she examined the magazine to be sure it had been loaded properly. She smacked the magazine into place, racked the slide again to force a round into the chamber and ran her finger over the safety to ensure it was locked.

"Fuck, Naya," Menace swore loudly. "That is the sexiest thing I've ever seen."

She laughed and shot him an amused grin. "Whatever

happened to your no bad language rule?"

"Yeah, that went right out the window the second you picked up that gun and showed it who was boss." Menace moved behind her and touched the target control built into the station's frame. "If your aim is as good as mine, it's all over, honey. I might have to take you right here."

Naya glanced over her shoulder. "You're joking."

Gripping her hips, Menace pressed his erection against her soft backside. "Does that feel like a joke?"

"No, but it sure feels like a violation of your range safety rules."

Laughing, Menace put on his safety glasses and headphones. He tapped her shoulder twice to let her know she was clear to fire. She flicked off the safety, took aim and fired her first round. She hit close to the center target, close enough to tell him that she knew exactly what she was doing with that gun. She popped off two more and moved closer to the highest target value.

When she'd emptied the first magazine and stopped to reload, Menace took the opportunity to adjust her stance. "You're a damn good shot but you could be even better."

To his surprise, she didn't give him her usual attitude when he tried to correct her.

"Show me."

Menace wasn't about to pass up the chance to teach her or to put his hands on her hips and arms. Ever the good student, Naya followed his instructions to the letter and vastly improved her accuracy and precision. By the end of the fourth magazine, he was already making plans to bring her back and let her try out different firearms in the arsenal.

Back in the gun safe, he reloaded the four magazines and tucked them into their drawers. He made quick adjustments to the inventory and did a final sweep of the range to make sure everything was cleared away and tidied. The layers of ballistics gel and magnets behind the projectile targets had caught the bullets fired by her. The spent casings were nabbed by the vacuum sensors on the floor of the shooting station.

"Thank you," she said as he closed down the range and locked the door. "This was actually a really sweet thing for you to do."

Menace tucked her unloaded firearm into his empty thigh holster. "I knew the moment I Grabbed you that you were the woman for me."

"Oh really?" Now she was laughing at him.

"Yes." He snatched her by the waist and dragged her into the small engineering access room just inside his office. "Any woman that thinks an afternoon at the gun range is sweet is a woman after my heart."

Giggling, Naya kissed him. "Why are we in a closet?"

"Why do you think?" The blinking lights from the ship's systems and the miles of communication conduits and cables glowed all around them.

"I think we're going to get into trouble. Aren't there cameras all over this ship?"

"Not in here," he answered. "There's too much interference from all this stuff to let them work properly. Now lift up your skirt and let me take off your panties."

"Menace!" she hissed. "We can't have sex in here."

"We can and we are." He dropped to his knees and shoved her skirt out of the way. If she wanted to play hard to get, he would just have to play harder. He gripped her inner thighs and forced them wide apart. The soles of her shoes whooshed as they slid across the slick floor. He grasped the fabric of her panties and pulled it out of the way.

"No, Menace! You can't—oh fuck!"

This was one time he didn't mind her exclamation. He sucked her clit right between his lips. Her hands flew to his head but she didn't try to force him away from her sex. Her capitulation only confirmed what he already knew. She couldn't resist him any more than he could resist her.

Intoxicated by his need for her, Menace lashed her pussy with his tongue. He coaxed her clit out from its hood and fluttered his tongue over the swelling bud. She moaned his name and scratched her nails over his scalp. The fiery sensation she evoked made his toes buzz. Loving her taste, he lapped at her pussy until she hovered right on the edge.

When he pulled his mouth from between her legs, she groaned in protest. He made quick work of freeing his cock and grasping the backs of her thighs. She placed her hands on a wide, strong bar that ran around the room and lifted her ass so he could jerk her panties down her legs. Balancing with one hand, she reached down and grabbed his dick. She pressed him into her wet entrance. He thrust forward and impaled her on his cock.

Gripping his shoulders now, she let him bear her weight and fuck her as if he were a wild man. Cheek-to-cheek, they panted and moaned. She clawed at his back and

whispered his name again and again. In their month together, he'd grown so attuned to her body and her needs. A
shift in the angle of his penetration and sinking his teeth
into her neck sent her over the edge with a screech of
pleasure. He surrendered to the sheer delight of her pussy
gripping and squeezing his cock. Balls-deep, he shuddered
and shot his seed.

She lovingly stroked the back of his head while they
both tried to recover from the intensity of their quickie.
Smiling, he licked the spot he'd marked with his teeth and
kissed it gently. Now seemed like a good time to tell her
about his plans for their evening. Sated and sleepy with
afterglow, she was less likely to whack him upside the head.

"We're going out tonight."

"Dinner, right?"

"Not exactly," he said carefully and pulled back enough
to meet her questioning gaze. "I'm taking you to the officers' club."

"You're *what*?"

"I'm taking you to the officers' club. We're going to
have some fun." Before she could argue, he put his finger to
her mouth. "This isn't up for discussion. We're going. You
will have a good time."

"Will I?" The tone of her voice warned him there
would be repercussions for his unilateral decision to take
her to the BDSM club.

"You don't scare me, sweetheart." He kissed her hard
and deep and then let her slide to the floor.

Naya righted her clothing. "Brave words from a man
who is bringing my sidearm back into our quarters."

He wanted to believe she was joking, but she was just feisty enough to be serious. "It's unloaded."

She brushed by him and opened the door. Tapping his chest, she smiled mischievously. "As if I'd let a little thing like that stop me."

Her breasts rubbed against his chest as she disappeared out of the closet. He stepped out after her and snatched her arm, hauling her tightly to his chest. He pushed loose waves of hair behind her ear and peered into her dark eyes. "Give this a chance, Naya."

She exhaled roughly. "You could have asked me first."

"I could have," he agreed, "but I wanted to surprise you."

"Yeah, well, mission accomplished."

"Don't be like that," he whispered and kissed her tenderly. "I arranged something especially for you."

Interest sparked in her eyes. "Oh?"

He let his hands travel the curve of her back to settle on her backside. He gave her bottom a little swat and she rose up on her toes. "Remember that film we watched last week?"

Her shallow breaths and the faint blush of embarrassment told him she did. "Um...yes."

The moment her riveted attention had snapped to the screen that evening in their quarters, he had recognized that he had finally uncovered her deepest, darkest fantasy. He still wasn't sure if she wanted to live that fantasy out in the flesh, so to speak.

Tonight he planned to get that answer.

Chapter Thirteen

NAYA NERVOUSLY ADJUSTED the cups of the black leather bra. She gazed at her reflection in the mirror and wondered how in the hell she was ever going to work up the courage to walk out that bathroom door. It was one thing to prance around halfnaked in their home, but quite another to go to a club dressed like this.

The leather bra pushed her breasts up and together, creating an obscene amount of cleavage. The tiny scrap of fabric that was supposed to be panties barely covered her privates and completely exposed her ass. Black stockings with a wide lace band hugged her legs. Bright-red pumps tilted her forward and made her legs look longer and leaner.

Menace had given her the new outfit with such excitement but she wasn't exactly thrilled by the idea of letting other men see her like this. She enjoyed looking sexy for him, but having strange guys ogling her? Not at the top of her list of ways she wanted to spend a Friday night.

"Do you need some help?" Menace's voice penetrated the door.

Naya picked up the strange black contraption that had come with the outfit. She still hadn't figured out how it worked. "Yes."

The door opened but Menace didn't come inside. She met his gaze in the mirror. He looked taken aback. She squirmed anxiously. "What?"

"Baby, you are *hot*." He crossed the distance between them in two long strides. His appreciative hands roamed her body. "So sexy."

She could say the same about him. He wore leather pants and a skintight black shirt that outlined all those hard muscles of his chest and arms. His tattoos looked even harsher on his tanned skin. The way he looked at her made her pussy throb. She showed him the strange leather belt with the dangling straps. "I don't know what this is."

"It's a garter belt." He took it from her hand and wrapped it around her waist. His strong fingers easily snapped the silver studs together in the back. Hands on her hips, he kissed his way down her back. She shivered under his sensual touch. Kneeling behind her, Menace rubbed her bare upper thighs. "These straps clip on to the tops of your stockings."

"Oh." She used the mirror to watch him fix the garter belt. She touched the metal rings placed at each hipbone. "What are these for?"

"Your cuffs." He rose slowly and put his hands on her shoulders. He dipped his nose into the high ponytail she'd fixed according to his instruction. "I'll keep your hands cuffed at your sides in the club."

"Why?"

He kissed her shoulder. "Because I want to."

She frowned. "So that's the way it's going to be to-night?"

He skimmed his lips across the sensitive patch of skin just below her earlobe. "Tonight is all about your pleasure. The moment we walk out of the bathroom you are going to give up complete control to me. You're going to trust me to take care of you."

Could she do that? Naya watched him slide his soft lips along her shoulder. His big hands spanned her bare belly as he gently stroked her skin. The answer came swiftly. *Yes.*

Stomach wobbling and mouth dry, she whispered, "I trust you to take care of me."

Menace's gaze snapped to the mirror. They stared at each other for a long moment before he straightened to his full height. Even in the high heels, she was dwarfed by him. When his fingers moved to the buckle on the white bride's collar, Naya experienced a tremor of uncertainty. Had she said the wrong thing? Why was he taking his collar off her?

"Easy," Menace urged as he removed the collar he'd used to claim her. He placed the white collar on the counter. "We'll put this in a keepsake box for you."

Naya touched her bare neck, the sensation strange after a month of wearing his collar. She'd gotten so used to its familiar embrace. She felt more naked without it than she did in the skimpy leather outfit.

He reached into the pocket of his leather pants and retrieved a bright-blue collar with a simple silver tag dangling from the front. "It's customary for a husband to gift his wife with a permanent collar. I was going to give you this one later tonight, but I think now is the right time. Don't you?"

His husky voice left her nearly breathless. To these

Harcos men, a permanent collar was as good as a wedding band. They put a lot of thought into picking the right one. Instead of the customary black, Menace had chosen her favorite color. The tag dangling from the front bore the initials of both of their first names. His initial was larger and in upper case while hers was smaller and in lower case, denoting who was the master in their relationship.

And he *was* her master. She'd balked at the very idea of ever allowing a man any dominance over her...until Menace. He hadn't forced her submission through pain or fear. He'd won her trust with kindness and pleasure and by proving that he would take care of and protect her.

When he finished fastening the collar in place, Naya fingered the stiff blue leather and toyed with the silver tag. Menace slid one arm around her waist and cupped her face, turning her into his seeking kiss. Their lips met, chastely and sweetly at first, sealing the moment that she had freely given her trust to him. His kiss grew more insistent and demanding but he didn't take it any further. He seemed to share her desire to draw the night out and enjoy the anticipation.

"I checked the chart," Menace said as he caressed her face. "We're still safe tonight."

She smiled and nodded. He had become almost obsessed with recording her morning fertility signs on the chart he had helped her create on their household tablet. Their application for contraception still hadn't been processed but he was keeping his word on letting her choose when or if they began a family. Their first month relying on her chart and a version of abstinence during the risky period had worked beautifully. Menace hadn't been willing to go without any kind of intimacy, so he had made sure to show her various creative ways to use their mouths and hands on each other. He pressed his lips to her forehead. "Ready?"

"As I'll ever be," she admitted.

Menace took her hand and led her out of the bathroom. In the bedroom, he paused long enough to put a pair of bright-blue cuffs on her wrists. The new cuffs were stamped with his name and had a soft white lining. Each one had a connection ring dangling from the underside so they could be hooked together with a chain or tethered separately. He hooked the cuffs to rings on either side of the wide leather belt around her hips.

Naya fought the surge of panic that gripped her. With her arms cuffed at her sides, she would be unable to defend herself. It was only Menace's reassuring body heat and the scent she had come to love so much that broke through her haze of panic. She trusted him to protect her. He would never allow anyone to harm her.

Tipping her chin, Menace asked, "What was that thought? You looked ready to bolt."

"I realized I wouldn't be able to lift my hands to protect myself."

"But?"

"But then I remembered that you promised to take care of me."

The grin curving his sexy mouth told her just how much her response pleased him. "I won't let anything happen to you tonight. If I somehow misread you, use your safeword."

"I will."

Menace placed his hand on the small of her back and gently pressed her forward. "We won't be spending much time on the main floor of the club. I've reserved a private room for us. Main floor protocol is much different than anything we've done together."

"How so?" Anxiety fluttered in her core.

"You are not allowed to wander without me. If you're caught without your master, a monitor will put you in the stocks and let any man who walks by take a swat at you with a paddle to teach you a lesson."

Naya gasped and stepped even closer to Menace. "You mean some other man could hit me?"

"Don't worry. I won't be letting you out of my sight." He rubbed her lower back before picking up an ankle-length gray jacket from the table in the entryway. He placed it around her shoulders and zipped the front. "We'll take this off after we check in at the club."

She glanced down at the hideous coat. It was ugly as hell but it would keep her modest on the trek to the club. "Thank you."

Menace gestured to the front door. She waited for him to open it and stepped into the hallway. While he locked the door, he gave more instructions. "Also remember not to address anyone, not even another wife, without first getting my permission. You will address other men as Sir. Understood?"

"Yes. What about you?"

He tapped the elevator button. "What do you call me?"

"Yes."

"Oh, I don't know. Master, my liege, light of my life—"

"Yeah, I got it." Naya rolled her eyes but couldn't squash the smile his playfulness inspired. They stepped into the waiting elevator and he punched in the access code for the private floor that housed the officers' club. "Anything else I should know?"

"I want you to stay open to possibilities tonight. Watch other couples. See if anything interests you. We haven't really discussed hard limits yet. There may be things you see tonight that you are absolutely never willing to try and that's all right. There may also be things that excite and arouse you." Menace used his body to box her into the corner and let his lips dance along her neck. "I want you to tell me about those things."

The elevator ride ended much too quickly. Before she knew it, Menace had checked them in, taken away her jacket and led her into the darkened interior of the club. It took her eyes a moment to adjust to the dimly lit space. Throbbing, thumping music blanketed the air. The huge open floor-plan hosted a bar with multiple seating areas.

Her first clue that she wasn't in a real bar was the sight of a bare-naked woman down on all fours and serving as a table for the two men kicked back in chairs near her. Two red cups rested on her flat back. How the woman managed to maintain her untenable position perplexed Naya. Judging by the red stripes on her ass and the pool of liquid next to her hand, she hadn't been successful.

Menace grabbed her lower arm, just above the cuff, and gave her a tug. She matched his pace as he took her deeper into the club. She got her first look at the public stations. Some of the equipment she'd seen or used in Menace's playroom. The spanking horse, for instance, or the restraint table, but that big scary X in the far corner made her belly flip-flop. The woman tied to it shrieked as her man lashed her back with a whip. People crowded around to watch him whipping her as if she were a brokendown mule.

Naya's feet faltered. What the hell kind of place was this?

"Look at me."

Menace's deep, strong voice cut through her panic. "It's consensual, Naya. She wants it. She wants to be whipped by her Master."

"How can you possibly know that?"

"The monitor," he said and pointed out the hulking man standing near the station. "Any man with a bright-orange armband is a monitor. They know when it's time to step in and stop something. The safeword for the entire club is red, but every master registers his woman's safe-word when we check in here. The same ID chips that keep track of you around the ship keep track of you here. See those watch-like devices they wear? Each one has a screen that informs them of the safewords of the couples closest to them."

Naya's gaze drifted from the monitor to the woman on the cross. She rose up on her toes in anticipation of every snapping bite of the whip. The muscles in her back and legs weren't tense with fear. For a woman getting the snot lashed out of her, she looked relaxed.

It struck Naya that this woman probably had reasons

for enjoying the pain of her husband's whip. Naya relished the feel of Menace pinning her in place or cuffing her so that she was totally submissive and at his mercy because it was a taste of the danger she'd managed to evade while living on the streets. Surrendering control to Menace, letting him take her, gave her a rush that she couldn't eloquently explain. It was primal and real.

"Come." Menace squeezed her arm and propelled her forward. "I see some familiar faces."

She wasn't so sure she wanted to run into any familiar faces dressed like this. Keeping close to his side, Naya allowed her gaze to roam the bustling club. The amount of skin and sex on display left her speechless.

Along one wall, there was some kind of game being played. Naked women wearing red devices between their thighs walked down lanes outlined in glowing white stripes while balancing balls on their hands. She saw one woman convulse with pleasure and drop her ball. Sweat slicked the woman's skin and her moans were high-pitched. Naya figured the device was some kind of vibrating toy. To receive her punishment for dropping the ball, the woman bent over and grabbed her ankles, presenting her bottom to anyone who wanted to take a peek. A man stepped forward and gave her one hot stripe across her backside with a cane.

Tearing her gaze away from the rigged game, Naya caught sight of an elevated seating area. It looked like an exclusive place. She was a bit surprised when Menace angled them through the crowd toward it. The monitor at the stairs took one look at Menace and waved him through. Apparently being high-ranking and well-liked had its privileges.

Up in the cozy room cordoned off by gauzy silver curtains, Naya saw a very familiar and very intimidating face. Leaning back in a comfortable chair, Vicious talked with another man. The dark-haired man sported a pilot's haircut with four stripes shaved into the right side of his head.

Her gaze fell to the spot next to Vicious' chair. Even with her forehead touching the floor and her naked bottom in the air, there was no mistaking the petite frame of Hallie's body. Shock gripped Naya like a vise. She'd never imagined her extremely modest friend baring that much of her body in public.

The shiny white fabric of her tiny skirt had been flipped up to give Vicious total access. As he talked, Vicious slid two fingers in and out of Hallie as if it were the most natural thing in the world to penetrate his wife while talking shop. How her friend managed not to squirm or squeal, Naya would never know. Apparently Vicious had trained her well.

It occurred to Naya that the depth of Hallie's love and commitment to her husband must have been limitless. If Menace ever asked her to do such a thing, she'd use her safeword and then promptly knee him right in the nuts.

She glanced at Menace and found his amused smile incredibly aggravating. He tugged her along to an empty chair.

Vicious noticed him then and smiled. "Menace! Good to see you and your beautiful wife."

"And you," Menace said before taking the empty spot. He gestured to the floor.

"Kneel."

Naya narrowed her eyes but shot him a sickly sweet smile. "Of course, *my liege.*"

Across the seating area, Vicious laughed. "When you get home, I'd cuff her to the bed if I were you. I'd hate for you to wake up with a pillow over your face in retribution for whatever you plan to do to her tonight."

Menace gave her hair a tug. It wasn't enough to cause pain but enough to get her attention. "I'll take it under advisement."

Vicious had described what he considered to be a punishment, but Naya's nipples tightened at the very thought of being cuffed all night. Menace would take advantage of her limited motion and leave her so limp and breathless she would wake with shaky legs.

The general tilted his head as if studying her. "Or maybe not."

Menace chuckled and stroked her back. "When you're finished with Hallie's punishment, I'd like to request permission for my wife to speak with yours. It's her first time at the club and she's feeling skittish."

"Oh, this isn't punishment." Vicious worked his hand a bit faster. "This is foreplay. Hallie's been such a good wife this week I decided to reward her with her favorite things."

Favorite things? Hallie, sweet and innocent-looking Hallie, *liked* to be taken in public? Naya couldn't wrap her mind around it.

As the pilot engaged Menace in friendly conversation, Naya dared to lift her gaze to Vicious again. All of his attention remained on Hallie's naked bottom. When he pulled his fingers from her body, there was no ignoring the glistening nectar coating them. By the looks of it, Hallie was enjoying her precarious position very, very much.

Vicious reached down and grasped Hallie by the waist. She was so light he didn't strain when he lifted her off the ground and onto his lap. The massive, intimidating general cupped her face with such gentleness and spoke so softly only Hallie could hear what he said. He teased his mouth over hers once, twice, before finally claiming her lips.

Watching Vicious kiss Hallie was one of the most erotic things Naya had ever seen. She finally understood why so many of the other wives gossiped about Vicious and Hallie's love life. The man oozed such raw sexuality and complete control that it mesmerized her.

Menace's lips ghosted across her ear. "Jealous?"

She glanced back at him and saw the teasing smile on his face. "No," she answered honestly. "Intrigued? Yes. Jealous of another woman's husband? Never."

Menace rubbed the back of her neck and kissed her temple. "Good answer."

She snorted. "Whatever you say, Master."

It was another minute or two before Vicious finished kissing Hallie. He whispered something in her ear and then let her climb off his lap. To Naya's astonishment, Hallie turned, bent over and lifted her skirt once again. Vicious smacked her backside twice, the pops so loud that Naya flinched. Hallie actually had a grin on her face when she straightened and smoothed down the shiny white fabric of her miniskirt.

Would tonight's surprises ever end?

As Hallie walked toward her, Naya caught her first look at the tattoo now exposed on Hallie's left side. It curved along her hip and rib cage toward her breast. From what Naya could see, it had many of the same elements of the painting hanging in the couple's entryway. Remembering the way Menace had explained the Harcos tradition of honoring one's family with tattoos on the left side of the body, the side closest to the heart, Naya realized that some wives did this too.

Hallie gestured to a small silver mat on the other end of the seating area. Naya looked to Menace who nodded his permission. Knowing she was a bit off balance because of her cuffed arms, he grabbed her waist and helped her stand. "Thank you, Master."

His only reply was to caress her thigh and give her a little pinch. She yelped but didn't stick around to let him swat her. That big hand of his had given her a few good whacks last week. She'd felt the sting for two days and wasn't in any rush to relive that experience.

Sitting cross-legged in front of Hallie, Naya stared at her friend. Hallie blushed and nervously fingered the end of a braid. She'd parted her hair in the middle and braided each side, adorning the ends with hot-pink ribbons. Hallie spoke first. "So…um…"

"Yeah," Naya said with a nervous laugh.

"All I can say is that seven months ago, I was where you are now. All of this terrified me. Vicious showed me so much patience. He made sure I felt secure and safe while we explored the different aspects of this part of their culture."

"And now you like, *you know*, in public?"

"Sort of," Hallie said. Dropping her gaze, she explained, "It's the embarrassment of having other people watching my husband take me that makes me climax the hardest. I think, maybe, it's because I was publicly humiliated as a criminal. Somehow that experience got hardwired into my brain in a really weird way. When I'm with Vicious and his hands are on me that embarrassment changes to something so powerful. I can't…I can't really describe it."

Naya swallowed hard. "I think I understand."

Hallie touched Naya's knee. "You trust Menace, right?"

"I do."

"So trust him to guide you through this," Hallie suggested wisely. "If things go pear-shaped, you just whip out that safeword and reassess."

Naya could feel Menace watching her but didn't dare glance back at him. She scooted a bit closer to Hallie. "I think he's going to make one of my fantasies come true tonight."

Hallie's eyes widened. Excitement flashed across her face. "Ooh! What is it?"

Overcome with embarrassment, Naya couldn't bring herself to tell Hallie. "It's just something I saw in one of those dirty movies."

"Aha! The 900 range? Yeah." Hallie rolled her eyes. "Vicious calls them the learning channels. Some of the things he's persuaded me to watch on there!" She started giggling. "I mean, *really*?"

"There seems to be a sort of normal level of kink and then another level of frightening stuff that gives me the creeps."

"But what you saw in this movie didn't scare you?"

Naya shook her head. "It excited me. A lot."

"So why do you look so worried? Menace obviously cares for you a great deal. He wants you to feel empowered and sexy. He won't let anything happen to you that you don't want."

Naya wished she could bring herself to confess what had excited her so much. Then Hallie would understand why Naya was so nervous. She remembered Hallie's advice and found some reassurance in that. "Safeword, right?"

Hallie nodded. "Safeword."

A moment later, Hallie reached out and swept her fingers across the blue collar now hugging Naya's neck. "It's really beautiful."

Naya touched the collar again. "It is."

"Blue is your favorite color?"

"Yes, and it's the safeword Menace gave me."

"How sweet," Hallie said and smiled genuinely. "Your collar is a constant reminder of who you belong to and how safe you are with him."

The full gravity of Menace's choice of collar hadn't hit her until just then. The reality of just how much Menace cared for her hit Naya right in the gut. Her feelings toward him became so clear. A certain word danced in the forefront of her mind but she didn't dare use it. She'd already made herself so vulnerable by trusting him completely. To admit that what she felt for him was something so powerful was too much, too fast for her.

"Kitten."

Vicious' voice cut through the music and conversation. Naya watched as Hallie turned her attention toward the general. He held up one finger. Hallie obviously understood the signal because she nodded. "That's my cue to wrap it up."

"Oh." Naya felt so calm and at ease talking with Hallie. Once she was gone, Naya would be completely at the mercy of Menace's plans.

Hallie grasped her hand and gave it a squeeze. "Come see me tomorrow. We'll do a brunch and talk. How does ten o'clock sound?"

"Perfect."

"Great." Hallie hugged her and then jumped to her feet. She made her way to Vicious and stood dutifully next to his chair while he finished his conversation with Menace. When he was done, Vicious wrapped an arm around Hallie's tiny waist and lifted her right onto his shoulder as he stood. He clamped his hand on her bare backside and left the area with Hallie dangling over his back. She wore a dopey grin and shot Naya two thumbs up for encouragement and luck.

Shaking her head at her friend's silliness, Naya rose slowly from her cross-legged position and rejoined Menace. She started to kneel but he stopped her. Menace slid his arm around her waist and gently petted the spot above her bellybutton. He pointed to the dark-haired man sitting across from them. "Say hello to Hazard."

Naya eyed the tall Harcos warrior. He had a kind face. "Hello, Sir."

"Hello, ma'am."

Ma'am? That wasn't at all what she expected. His easy-going smile settled her nerves.

"Hazard is an old and dear friend of mine. He doesn't get to spend much time in this area but he's on a one-week layover on the *Valiant*. Hazard has agreed to help me make your fantasy a reality tonight."

Naya stiffened as the implication hit home. Last week, when Menace had been flipping through the various channels available in the 900 range, he'd landed on a prison scene where one woman was being taken by five guards.

At first, she'd experienced utter revulsion at the very idea, but then something primal had flicked on deep inside her. Living on the streets as a child, her greatest fears had been kidnapping, arrest, interrogation and sexual assault. Like Hallie, Naya's body seemed to have confused the signals between fear and arousal. The things that terrified her most seemed to arouse her the most.

She gulped and glanced at Menace. "You want your friend to… With us?"

Menace's fingertips stroked the swells of her breasts. "Possibly."

She relaxed a little. It was clear Menace wasn't going to just let Hazard have free access to her body.

"This is fantasy, Naya. It's a chance for you to explore the things that arouse you and frighten you in a safe environment." He grasped the front of her collar and tugged her face down until their lips were almost touching. The controlling gesture made her belly swoop with excitement. "Are you ready?"

Her eyes closed briefly. Arousal and fear swamped her,

the waves of strong emotion drowning her. When she opened her eyes, Menace's steady gaze warmed her skin. There was only one thing to say. "Yes."

Chapter Fourteen

MENACE KEPT A close watch on Naya via the monitor attached to the private playroom door. She sat on a metal bench in a room designed to look exactly like a hybrid prison cell and interrogation room. He'd left her arms cuffed at her sides to ratchet up her anxiety. He wanted her apprehensive and a bit scared but never terrified.

"Here." Hazard tossed him a gray shirt emblazoned with the guard insignia from the Kovark prison system.

"Is this real?"

The dark-haired pilot nodded and slipped into his shirt. Instead of simple guard insignia, Hazard's shirt bore the marks of a warden. "I grabbed a few of these the last time I was on a long-range prisoner transport. I try to pick up things I know you boys out on these installations can't get your hands on easily. These shirts are better than credits when it comes to trades with other pilots and soldiers. You wouldn't believe how many of the guys here on the *Valiant* want them. This fantasy of your little wifey in there is a common one."

"That doesn't surprise me." Menace jammed his arms through the shirt and zipped up the front. He supposed it was good that Hazard had found some perks to his punishment duty of flying the long treks between outposts. "How much longer do you think they'll keep you on long-range duty?"

Hazard *harrumphed.* "At least seven months," he answered. "I won't have another duty review until then. After that stunt I pulled, I wouldn't be surprised if Orion kept me on this shit duty for another year just to teach me a lesson."

"You're lucky the admiral didn't bust you down more than one rank."

"He also took most of my damn Grab points."

Menace winced with sympathy. "To be fair, you could have gotten a prison sentence. You disobeyed a direct order and lost a ship in the process."

"I also rescued three of our men from enemy hands. Technically I brought the ship back in one piece. It just, you know, fractured and burst into flames when we docked." Menace snorted. "Twenty-plus years in the service and you're still a hothead."

"Spare me, Menace. How many scrapes did the two of us barely survive when I was your squadron's pilot? I've lost track of the number of times we were disciplined."

"That was a long time ago," Menace replied. "I have a wife now. Those days are long gone."

"Sure they are." Hazard smiled and clapped him on the shoulder. "You ready to do this thing?"

Menace nodded and gripped Hazard's wrist. His touch was firm but nonthreatening. "Naya means more to me than you can possibly understand. I'm giving you a hell of a lot of leeway with her, but one wrong move and you'll have to learn to work the flight controls with your feet."

Hazard became serious. "You have my word of honor. I'm here only to help a friend give his wife pleasure. I go only as far as you allow and she desires."

"Good." Menace stepped back and gestured to the door. "After you, Warden."

With a waggle of his eyebrows and an enthusiastic grin, Hazard shoved the door wide open and stormed inside. Menace came in half a second behind him and kicked the door shut. Naya jumped on the bench. Eyes wide, she quickly assessed the situation and realized Menace wasn't in charge. Her uptick in breathing told Menace all he needed to know. She was off-kilter and perfectly primed for the wild ride he had in store for her.

"Prisoner A114, on your feet!"

Startled by Hazard's shout, Naya leapt off the bench. Her gaze jumped from Hazard's face to his own. He kept his features schooled. If she wanted to stop, she had her safeword. In the same way she trusted him to keep her safe, he trusted her to know when to use her out.

"Guard, strip her."

Menace grinned evilly at Hazard's order. He crossed to the back wall where Naya stood. Behind him, Hazard picked up the gunmetal-gray case that contained all the various props and interrogation tools Menace had chosen for the scene. He threw it onto the table in the center of the room. Naya flinched as the metal case bounced on the flat surface.

"Turn around," Menace barked. Though he had taken his time securing her garter belt and cuffs earlier in the evening, he worked quickly and efficiently this time, showing her no gentleness. For her to give in to the fantasy, every detail had to be right. No guard in Kovark would show a prisoner even an ounce of kindness.

Naya's cuffed wrists dangled at her sides. Naked and flushed, she breathed hard. Menace recognized the mix of shame and arousal that stained her skin. To a dominant man, there was no more beautiful color in the world than that particular shade.

Hazard unlocked the case and retrieved two medical gloves and a tube of lubricant. "Search her. The last one we interrogated had a sheathed shiv hidden on her."

Naya's gasp of outrage echoed in the room. She shot Menace a look but he pretended not to see it. If she wanted to stop, she knew what to do. He suspected she was caught in that place where she wasn't sure if she was brave enough to face uncertainty. He didn't doubt her for a moment. Her courage and curiosity would propel her forward.

Menace made sure to snap the gloves against his wrist just to add to the tension in the room. "Bend over and grab your ankles."

"I will not!"

Hazard took a step around the table. "Do I need to come over there and secure the prisoner, Guard Menace?"

Naya took a second to gauge Hazard's sincerity before snapping forward at the waist.

"Face the back wall," Hazard ordered. "I need to supervise."

She lifted her head just enough to glare at Hazard but did as instructed. Menace used the toe of his boot to force her feet wider apart. Her pretty pink pussy and ass were on clear display now. He didn't blame Hazard for wanting to see her. With her honey-brown skin and dark hair, she was something of an anomaly. There was only one other world where they'd found brides like her and they were hard to come by.

Kneeling beside her, Menace used his gloved fingers to part the folds of her sex. She opened like a hothouse flower, her dewy skin beckoning his searching digits. He needed no lube to check her. The slick nectar coating her skin assured him that even though she found this experience disconcerting, she also found it incredibly arousing.

Naya inhaled a short, loud breath when he penetrated her with one finger. He let his thumb brush across her clit three times but no more. He wanted her on edge. When he flipped the lid on the tube of lubricant, her pussy fluttered around his finger. She knew what was coming. Still, he decided to torment her a little longer by adding a second digit to the first. He plunged them in and out of her wet channel at a slow pace. Her toes curled against the floor and he stopped. She had gotten enough stimulation to stay aroused.

He smeared the clear gel on her rosebud and probed her with one gloved fingertip. Her back passage gripped him tightly. They had played around with small- and medium-sized plugs so he knew she could take more than just his finger but he didn't push it.

Finished checking her, he stood and stripped off his gloves. "She's safe."

"Stand up, prisoner. Face me."

While Naya hurried to follow Hazard's orders, Menace

dropped the gloves in a receptacle in the corner and took a position behind her. He wanted her sole focus on Hazard and planned to hide from her line of sight to keep her unsettled and gripped by the fantasy.

"Hands behind your head. Widen your stance. Wider!" Hazard pulled a thin cane from the case and tested it with a bend. He swung it through the air twice, the *whooshing* sound sending Naya back a tiny step. Although Menace was fully aware Naya had no love for them, he'd chosen a cane as part of the interrogation implements because he knew the effect on her. Hazard had promised never to let the cane mark her skin—but she didn't know that.

"Eyes forward, prisoner. Don't be looking to Guard Menace to save you. Two of the men wounded in your breakout scheme were his friends."

Naya squeaked when the tip of the cane touched her collarbone and moved down between her breasts. Hazard rested the top of it on her left breast. "So you really thought you could escape from Kovark?"

Voice shuddery, she said, "I don't know what you're talking about, Sir."

"Don't play dumb with me." Hazard ran the cane's tip around her nipple and then down her belly. He tapped it along the curve of her waist and hip, not hard enough to mark her but with enough pressure to make her fingers curl into her pubic hair. "The moment you stepped off the transport ship and into central processing I knew you were going to be a problem for my prison."

"Warden, I—"

"Silence," Hazard hissed harshly. "I don't want your

lies." He walked around behind her, flashing Menace a wink the second he was out of her vision range, and gave her backside the lightest swat. Even with that bare kiss of the cane, she yelped and lifted onto her toes.

"Sir, please—"

"Enough," Hazard growled. "I have eyes and ears all over this prison. Do you understand what that means? There are no prisoner secrets in this place."

"Y-yes, Sir."

Hazard stepped back in front of her and placed the cane against her nipple again. "Now tell me the names of your escape crew."

Menace watched the subtle shift in Naya's body language. Her fear was palpable but her shoulders had straightened. *Shit.* She was going to play this as the tough girl from Connor's Run.

"Warden, if you have eyes and ears all over this prison, you must already know those names."

"Oh we're going to the play the smart-ass card?" Hazard lowered the cane and snapped his fingers. "Guard, show the prisoner what happens to smart-asses."

"Happy to, Warden." Menace snatched her right off the floor and carried her to the bench along the back wall. He sat down and draped her across his thighs. She gasped and put her hands back to stop the inevitable spanking. "Hands on the floor or I'll ask the warden for the use of his cane."

She whimpered but did exactly as told. Fingertips on the cold floor, Naya dropped her head and went limp across his lap. Over the last few weeks together, she had taken his lessons to heart. He had made sure she understood that it was in her best interest to remain as relaxed as possible.

With her small body supported by his thighs, Menace swept his calloused palms up and down her plump ass. Soon her brown skin would darken with heat. His cock throbbed to life. This fantasy had been put together to make her scream with pleasure, but Menace was finding it incredibly arousing himself.

"Oh!" Naya cried out as his hand cracked her backside. "No! No! No!"

She wiggled on his lap, the movement making her ass cheeks jiggle. Her soft belly rubbed against the head of his cock. He had to push down the surge of excitement that rocked him and concentrate on her tone and breathing. She was saying no but meant yes. There was a fine line he had to walk.

His hand bounced from cheek to cheek. He kept the power behind each strike enough to make her cry but never enough to harm her. She would have a red, sore ass by the end of it but no lasting damage.

"Please, Sir! Please! No more! No! *Oh!*"

Her begging cries were music to his mean Master ears. If they'd been back in their quarters, he would have tossed her on the nearest table, pushed her thighs wide open and attacked her pussy to show her that every bit of pain came with even more pleasure. But he wasn't in charge now and this scene was just getting started.

Menace glanced at Hazard and gave a small nod. Understanding their silent communication, Hazard announced, "I think she's had enough, Guard Menace."

"Yes, Warden." Menace stood her up and fought the urge to wipe away the tears on her cheeks. No guard would do such a tender thing, but a husband definitely would.

"Stand up straight. Hands behind your back." Hazard tossed the cane back onto the interrogation table. "Let's try this again. Give me the names of your coconspirators."

Naya sniffled but shook her head. "Never."

Hazard retrieved a leather strap looped onto a handle. It was the kind of impact implement that would leave welts on a submissive's backside. "You realize we can beat your ass all night?"

She hesitated a moment before finally declaring, "I'm not afraid of you."

Hazard studied her. "No, I don't think you are. Guard?"

Menace stepped forward so she could see him and he could read her face better. "Yes, Warden?"

"Take the prisoner to administrative segregation. Make sure the other women see her getting a special cell. Have the mess send her a hot meal."

Fully into the fantasy now, Naya exclaimed, "You can't do that! They'll think I'm a snitch. I'll be on their hit list."

Hazard toyed with the thick leather loop of the strap. "That's not my problem anymore, Prisoner A114. I tried to give you an out but you wouldn't take it."

"I won't squeal on my friends."

Hazard moved so fast Naya took an instinctive step back. Stopping mere inches from her, the other man dragged the wide leather strap down the front of her body. He stopped when the strap was pressed against her mound.

"Maybe we'll see how loudly you squeal while riding our cocks."

Her eyes widened. "S-sir?"

Turning on the charm, Hazard said, "This is a lonely, isolated system, honey. A man has needs. It would be nice to ease them with a willing woman."

She gulped. Her frantic gaze skipped from Hazard's face to his. Menace stayed in the role he'd written for himself but her face softened at the sight of him. Looking reassured, she whispered, "And if I say yes?"

"When we're done with you, we throw you back in gen pop. You get to keep your honor and loyalty to your friends. We get to sink our cocks into some hot, tight pussy."

Menace had to give Hazard props for inhabiting the role of a sick, twisted warden rather well. For such a laid-back prankster, Hazard could be a real dickhead when the circumstances called for it.

Naya still hadn't given her answer. Hazard pinched her nipple and twisted it hard enough that she rose onto tiptoes and squeaked in protest. He laughed and released her tortured nipple. "I'd say that's a yes. Guard? String her up."

NAYA HAD NEVER been so wet. The evidence of her arousal seeped from her body and stained her inner thighs. The slick fluid cooled as the frigid air in the room hit her skin. No doubt her evil husband had kicked on the air-conditioning to keep her as uncomfortable as possible.

Speaking of her evil husband…

Menace grabbed her by the waist and hauled her over

to the wall of cell bars. The room they'd brought her into had struck a quiver of fear in her belly. She'd been in places all too similar to this one and it had been anything but a fantasy.

His familiar scent enveloped her and eased some of the rawness of her anxious nerves. In that guard getup he looked more, well, *menacing* than usual. She hadn't been sure what to expect when Menace and his friend had entered the room. She'd thought it would be kind of silly and hard to buy the fantasy they were trying to create but she'd been utterly wrong. That spanking had been real enough! Her ass still tingled from it.

Hazard played the role of warden with frightening accuracy. There had been a moment there when she'd actually believed he was going to cane her. That awfullooking leather strap attached to a handle scared the living daylights out of her. One swat with that thing and she would have spilled state secrets to get away.

Without his usual finesse or gentleness, Menace hooked her wrist cuffs to the bars. Arms overhead, she had extremely limited motion. He put pressure on her shoulders and guided her into a squatting position. The rings attached to her cuffs slid down the bars until they hit a horizontal support.

Rocking on her feet, Naya realized he'd put her into a stress position. She glared up at Menace but the bastard had the gall to grin. He looked ridiculously amused by her predicament. Of course, he wouldn't know that she'd actually been interrogated in a similar position once. The memories his action spurred weren't good ones and threatened to intrude upon the sultry fantasy. She pushed them down and locked them away, refusing to let something so ugly ruin something so amazing.

But she swore then and there that the next time the opportunity presented itself she was going to cuff Menace to their bed and torment him for an entire night. Knowing her kinky sky warrior, he would probably love every minute of it.

The sound of jingling metal drew her gaze. Hazard held a thin metal chain in his hand. Clips dangled from multiple ends of it. She recognized it as some kind of nipple clamp toy but wasn't sure where all the extra clamps went. One clip in particular looked different from the others. It resembled an oversized hairpin.

Hazard squatted down in front of her, his position mimicking her own. "Since I can't be sure you won't bite my guard, I'm going to give you a little incentive to behave."

Naya gasped when the first clamp bit her nipple. He wasn't like Menace, who normally teased her breasts with his mouth and fingers to prepare her. Hazard attached the second clip and she winced. The uncomfortable weight pulled on her nipples. The three clamps dangling from the main chain whacked against her belly and thighs. The realization of where those other clamps were going hit her like a ton of bricks.

"Oh no! No! No! No!" she spluttered like a fool as Hazard laughed and clipped the first clamp on her labia. She hissed at the sudden bite but tried not to jerk. She knew that straightening her torso would only pull the chain between her nipples and privates taut.

"Listen to this crybaby." Hazard chuckled meanly and put the second clamp on the other side of her pussy. His unfamiliar fingers glided through her wetness. She held a shocked breath as a man who wasn't her husband penetrated her. He showed such gentleness as he probed her sex. She realized then that even though he had assumed the role of prick in this fantasy, Hazard wasn't out to hurt her.

Having another man's fingers buried in her pussy left Naya reeling. She wavered between a deep sense of wrong and a quiver of excitement. Menace's reassuring presence somehow made it all okay. He'd arranged this evening for her. Presumably he'd given Hazard certain parameters and touching her so intimately was clearly within them.

Naya locked gazes with Menace. His nostrils flared and his neck showed the bright flush that betrayed his arousal. There was no missing the outline of his massive cock in his tight pants. He liked watching Hazard touching her as much as she enjoyed the other man's searching touch.

"Our prisoner is a very dirty girl," Hazard finally remarked. His fingertips drifted to her clit. He circled the swelling bud slowly and forced her gaze to meet his. "I think we're all going to have a very good time. Don't you, Guard?"

"Absolutely, Warden."

Hazard's fingers moved to either side of her pulsing clit. It felt as if he were pushing her labia away from it. "Hold still or else."

Naya had barely registered his instructions before she felt the intense pressure of something metal squeezing her clit. It wasn't the same bite as the other clamps. Hazard readjusted the grip of the clamp by prying apart the metal sides a bit. It was still squeezing her clit but the pressure was much more bearable.

Glancing between her open thighs, Naya couldn't believe how strange her clit looked. Pinched by the clip, her clitoris looked bigger and more swollen than ever. It felt different. The usual throbbing seemed almost muted. Her experience with nipple clamps told her that sensation wouldn't last long.

Hazard gave the connecting chain a tiny tug. Naya groaned as the pinching discomfort sharpened. Hazard swept his hand down her belly. "Be a good girl and give Guard Menace exactly what he wants…or else."

Naya didn't need the subtle threat of pain to give Menace exactly what he wanted. Breasts aching and pussy clenching with need, she watched him saunter toward her. He unbuckled his belt and unzipped his pants as he walked. She wet her lips in anticipation of tasting his steely heat.

He stopped inches from her face. She had to lift up on her toes to put her mouth at the right level. Menace brushed his knuckles across her cheek before unleashing his rock-hard cock. He stroked the length of his impressive erection and traced her pout with the blunt tip. His pre-cum slicked her lips. She gathered the clear fluid with her tongue and gazed up at Menace with the kind of adoration that she could muster only for him.

"Open your mouth," he ordered gruffly. He pressed his cock between her lips. She happily welcomed his velvety flesh. He thrust forward and retreated at a leisurely pace.

His thick shaft stretched her lips. She burned with the need to feel her pussy stretched by him.

Certain Menace was enjoying this shared fantasy as much as she was, Naya endeavored to make this blowjob one he would never forget. She relaxed her jaw and let him go deep. The head of his cock lingered in the back of her throat before gliding back. She swirled her tongue around the tip and sucked him hard. Her tongue moved down the length of him. He fisted his stiff erection while her tongue fluttered along his sac. He was so incredibly sensitive there and loved it when she treated him to a little oral attention in that spot.

Menace groaned before plunging forward again, taking her just as deeply. Her poor clamped clit pulsed mercilessly! What she wouldn't give to be able to reach down and touch herself. As if reading her mind, Hazard put his hands on her body again.

Kneeling next to her, he palmed her breasts and let his fingertips graze her pinched nipples. He circled her navel before his hand moved even lower. The moment he ghosted his fingertips over her throbbing clit, Naya moaned. Menace's cock palpably pulsed in her mouth. The knowledge that another man was touching his wife's clit seemed to make Menace even more aroused.

"Guard, I think it's time we move this party to the interrogation table."

"Agreed, Warden." Seemingly enflamed by lust, Menace reached down and unhooked her cuffs. He picked her up and carried her over to the table. The metal tabletop was so cold against her blazing skin. The dimensions of the table were shorter and thinner than anything she'd seen aboard the *Valiant*. When Menace walked to one end and Hazard the other, Naya understood why.

"Warden, I believe it's customary for you to have first dibs." Menace grasped her cuffed wrists in one hand and held them down. He gestured to her body. "After you, sir."

Surprise flashed across Hazard's face. Whatever negotiations the men had made prior to this scene, apparently this hadn't been part of them. She sensed the control in the room had shifted completely to Menace. He'd been pulling the strings all along but from behind the curtain, so to speak. Now he was the one giving orders—and it thrilled her.

Hazard stroked her naked skin. He touched her with such sensual softness. He seemed to cherish the opportunity he'd been given. Placing a knee on the table, he pushed up off the floor and hovered over her. His body wasn't nearly as big or wide as Menace's but he still gave off an incredible amount of heat. He removed the nipple clamps and instantly dropped his mouth to her puffy, red peaks. His tongue laved her puckered skin. He suckled gently, soothing the hurt he'd created.

As Hazard kissed his way down her body and slipped off the table, Naya met Menace's unwavering stare. Even upside down, he commanded her attention. She stared into his bright-green eyes and lost whatever inhibitions remained. The burning desire reflected in his gaze seared her bare skin.

The labia clamps were both removed at the same time. Naya cried out and bucked her hips. Hazard massaged her sore lips and penetrated her with two thick fingers. She knew what was coming and steeled herself for the inevitable pain. Menace crushed his mouth to hers, the angle of his kiss so strange.

Down below, Hazard carefully unclamped the clip squeezing her clit. She groaned into Menace's mouth. She let his wonderfully talented tongue distract her from the discomfort. Suddenly Hazard's firm tongue flicked her clit. She inhaled so sharply and jerked so hard that Menace had to grasp her shoulders to keep her from flying off the table. Tearing her mouth from Menace, she cried, "Oh! *Oh!*"

Hazard licked her swollen clit. Three, four, five licks— and she climaxed. Howling as if she were some wild thing, Naya shrieked as her body finally found release. Pleasure racked her with intense spasms.

As her orgasm began to fade, Hazard changed his tactic. He lapped at her clit while fucking her with his fingers. She whimpered and hovered on the verge of another climax. He didn't rush to send her over the edge. No, he took his time licking and sucking and nibbling her clitoris until Naya practically sobbed.

Hazard savored her pussy as if it were a treat he rarely encountered. Maybe it was. He didn't have a woman of his own. She didn't even know where the closest sky brothel was. The idea that her pussy was the first one he'd tasted and tormented in some time made her dizzy with excitement.

Menace claimed her mouth again, this time standing to her side. His strong hands clamped her wrists in place, holding her down and activating those deep-seated fears of being taken and forced. Her husband's tongue thrust in and out of her mouth. He teased her with the promise of what was to come.

Two wicked mouths worked her into a frenzied state. Her hips rocked and her toes curled against the table. Eyes closed, she reveled in the absolute debauchery of the moment. Bursts of bliss shook her core. She moaned against Menace's lips as wave after wave of pure joy washed over her.

Still panting and shaking, Naya felt Menace's grip falter. He let go of her wrists and made a quick trade with Hazard. Gripping her thighs, Menace dragged her butt right to the edge of the table and thrust forward roughly. She gasped as his long cock breached and filled her. The table shuddered and jumped as Menace fucked her fast and hard.

She caught sight of Hazard stroking himself to the sight of their coupling. The yearning on his face made her chest ache. She knew that kind of loneliness. Wanting him to feel part of this, Naya reached for the pilot and silently urged him closer. He hesitated and shot a glance at Menace. Whatever look he received in return convinced Hazard it was okay.

She fondled his cock, the stiff length so different in feel and size to Menace's. She caressed his shaft and tugged him closer. Craning her neck, she swiped the tip of him with her tongue. His loud gasp ricocheted off the walls and ceiling. It became crystal clear to her that this man had agreed to help her live out her wildest fantasy without ever expecting anything in return.

With one cock in her pussy and another in her mouth, Naya embraced the wickedness of her naughty fantasy. Taken by two ferociously sexy men, she vibrated with absolute ecstasy. Menace pressed her knees toward her chest, tightening her passage even more and changing the angle of his penetration just enough to make her scream around Hazard's fat cock.

It was Hazard who found release first. He pulled free from her mouth and stroked himself to completion, his semen pooling on the tabletop. Menace used both thumbs to stimulate her clit. The up-and-down motion made her squeal with delight. Her pussy clenched his cock a split second before she rocketed to the moons. Head thrown back, she shouted his name again and again. "Menace! *Menace!*"

"Naya!" With one final, powerful thrust that sent the table skittering across the floor, Menace filled her with his seed. He slumped forward against her, his big, hot body warming hers. Naya cupped the back of his head and peppered loving kisses along his jaw.

Dazed by the experience she had shared with these two men, Naya shook with the awesomeness of it. Menace pulled free so gently and tucked himself into his pants before gathering her in his arms and carrying her to the bench. Hazard followed with a blanket he'd produced from heaven only knew where. He draped it around her shoulders and helped Menace tuck it tightly around her naked body.

While she enjoyed her husband's heat and strength, Naya closed her eyes and tried not to overthink what had just happened. It was a gift from the man who cared for her so deeply. Best not to look this gift horse in the mouth, she decided.

She heard Hazard cleaning up the room. He brought Menace a pack of moist towelettes and a package of over-sized paper towels similar to the ones in the med kit in their quarters. Menace placed them on the bench and shook Hazard's hand. The pilot laughed. "The pleasure was mine, Menace."

"The shirt?"

"Bring it by the bachelor quarters tomorrow. I'm bunking with Zeph until my next flight out of here."

"All right."

Hazard pushed the blanket aside to reveal her face. Naya's ears grew hot as the realization of what she'd done hit her. Hazard smiled tenderly and brushed a soft kiss against her forehead. "Thank you, ma'am. I won't forget this gift."

Naya wasn't sure what to say to that. Hazard didn't seem to require a reply. With the metal case in hand, he waved and left the private playroom. Alone with Menace, she snuggled closer.

"Are you all right?" His rumbling voice held such concern. "It wasn't too much?"

"I'm fine. Great actually," she added with a relaxed laugh. "I had no idea it could be like that."

"It can be like that again, but not very often. It was…more difficult than I'd anticipated to watch another man touching you. Even a friend," he amended. "Knowing that it gave you pleasure eased my jealousy some, but my possessiveness toward you is even greater than I'd realized."

"It's the same for me," Naya admitted. "I mean, I liked the way Hazard touched me but I liked it more because I knew it pleased you and it aroused you. Until I saw that you approved, I couldn't shake how wrong it was."

Menace embraced her more tightly. "Because you're mine."

"Yes," she agreed. "Because I'm yours."

"Naya?"

"Yes, Menace?"

Silence stretched between them. He seemed to be struggling to find the right words. Finally he exhaled and said, "Are you ready to get dressed and return to our quarters?"

Hope deflated within her. For the briefest of moments, she'd believed he was going to say *it*. A pang of sadness stabbed her gut at the realization that she wasn't going to hear that four-letter word tonight. Part of her wondered if it wouldn't be easier to be the first to blurt it out but she'd never said it to any man. The fear of saying it to Menace when he wasn't ready to return the sentiment absolutely killed her. No, he had to go first.

Refusing to let her issues cloud the wonder of the experience they'd shared, Naya forced her troubling thoughts aside. She wrapped her arms around Menace's shoulders and teased her lips across his. They shared a sensual, easy kiss. She grinned and whispered, "Take me home, Master."

Chapter Fifteen

MENACE COULDN'T IMAGINE a better way to wake up than with Naya bouncing on his lap and his cock buried in her snug pussy. Her rapturous sighs and soft moans filled him with such pleasure. He cupped her lush breasts and enjoyed the weight of them in his hands. She was an absolute vision with her wild hair and smoky eyes. The sight of his blue collar around her neck made his chest burn. *Mine.*

Gripping her collar, he tugged her down for a demanding kiss. She whimpered against his lips. He plundered her mouth, leaving her shaking and clutching at his arms. Hands on her hips now, Menace planted his feet on the bed and pounded into her silky, wet heat. Growling, he thrust into her harder and faster. He chased his own climax but needed to feel her come first.

Mouth open, she let loose an unending series of cries. "Ah! Ah! *Ah!*"

Another sound, this one annoying and insistent, interrupted the perfect soundtrack of his woman enjoying a ride on his cock. The doorbell chime drew Naya's attention. He cursed silently and touched her cheek, forcing her gaze to him. "Ignore it."

"But—"

"They can leave us a message." Menace thrust up into her and she whimpered. "Ignore it."

They tuned out the merciless chime and focused solely on each other. Menace watched her face and listened to her breathing pattern. Her eyes widened slightly and her breaths grew shallow and fast. Wetter and tighter, Naya gripped his cock with her pussy. She shifted forward and lowered her upper body. Her clit came into constant contact with his pelvis. She rubbed herself against him until she exploded.

He lost control when she shrieked his name. Slamming deep into her, Menace jerked with blissful spasms. The muscles of his abdomen and thighs blazed but he didn't care. The early-morning workout was more than worth it.

Cradled in his arms, Naya breathed heavily and drew on his chest. The sensation of her fingertip scribbling on his skin brought to mind an appointment he needed to make with one of the tattoo artists. It was time to have their family crest designed and applied to his body.

Certain it was the right moment to finally tell Naya what he truly felt for her, Menace caressed her face and coaxed her mouth to meet his. He threaded his fingers through her hair and kissed her tenderly. She tilted her head and studied him. "What is it?"

Her softly spoken words bolstered his courage. He suspected that she expected him to go first in declaring his love for her. After the way she'd been let down in her past, he understood why. "Naya, I—"

The doorbell chime ruined the moment. Just as insistent as earlier, someone tapped the keypad over and over. Infuriated by the interruption, Menace exhaled roughly. He gently rolled Naya onto her back and kissed her. "Hold that thought."

She smiled and smacked his bare ass. "Holding."

Laughing, he grabbed the pants he'd discarded so quickly last night and hopped into them. With one final look at Naya's gorgeous, naked curves, Menace left their bedroom. He strode to the door, tapped the Unlock button on the keypad and yanked it open the second the locks released. "What?"

Terror's face greeted him. Menace instantly noticed the tightness to his friend's expression. He'd known Terror long enough to read him easier than most. Something bad had happened.

Terror's one-eyed gaze moved over Menace's sweaty, half-dressed form. "I hope you enjoyed that. It's probably going to be the last fuck you ever have with her."

Shock tore through Menace. Anger followed quickly. "How dare you—"

"Spare me." Terror threw his arm out, hitting Menace right in the throat and knocking him off balance. He shoved his way inside and pushed Menace into the wall. "Where the hell is she?"

Enraged by his friend's treatment, Menace slammed both hands into Terror's chest and forced him against the opposite wall. "What is wrong with you? You can't barge into my home and demand to see my wife."

"Actually I can." Terror snapped his fingers and more soldiers, all of them decked out in full gear and carrying weapons at the ready, poured into his hallway. Menace gaped at the sight of Raze and Venom. Both men looked unhappy to be there.

Raze stepped between them. He put up a hand to stop Terror from advancing and glanced at Menace. "Let's give them five minutes to get dressed."

"I'll supervise," Venom offered. "We want them to cooperate."

Cooperate? Menace's gut twisted with fear. What the fuck was happening?

Terror exhaled roughly. "Fine. Five minutes, but if I hear either of them talking, they're both getting hoods."

Cold with dread, Menace stared at Terror. This was the version of his friend he'd hoped never to meet. This version of Terror could make a person disappear. This version of Terror was more dangerous than anything else in the entire arsenal of the Harcos forces.

"Come on." Venom grasped his upper arm and jerked him forward. "Move, Menace."

They entered the bedroom. Naya stood next to the bed, eyes wide in panic, and gripped the top sheet to her shield her body. He started to speak, but Venom's grip tightened.

Venom shook his head and addressed Naya. "Ma'am, you have five minutes to shower and dress. If you say one word, I'll be forced to separate the two of you."

Menace watched her expression morph from one of pure fear to one of resignation. She hurried to the closet, grabbed her clothing and rushed into the bathroom. Menace followed her lead. He shot Venom a glance as the other man trailed him into the bathroom. He'd spent enough time living in close quarters on the front lines to have no issue going about his morning bathroom ritual with another man watching. Naya was a different story.

She didn't meet his eye as she jumped in and out of the shower or when she toweled off and slipped into her clothing. Her usual modesty and embarrassment fled. Fear had activated those survival instincts that had kept her alive and safe so long in Connor's Run. He hoped she could stay calm and cool while they dealt with whatever the hell this was.

Rinsing off in the shower, Menace let his brain spit out various scenarios. Each seemed more unlikely than the first. Obviously something screwy was going on here. He didn't believe for one moment that Terror actually believed he was guilty of anything. They'd known each other since they were children. Their bond and trust was much too deep for that. But Naya…

Menace spotted her waiting near the door. Even with that brave expression and her squared shoulders, she was still afraid. Lingering in the bathroom and near him made her feel secure. His chest ached at the realization she wouldn't have him to lean on when they were taken from their quarters.

As he dressed, he remembered her fear of Terror. He'd written it off as the usual feminine fright. Had he been wrong? Was Terror really after Naya? Why? What in the world could she possibly know that would make him this upset?

Those answers would come soon enough. Venom stepped between them, preventing Menace from even touching Naya, and walked the two of them out of the bathroom. Menace's jaw dropped as he saw how quickly Terror's team of Shadow Force operatives had tossed their quarters. The mess would take hours to clean and they were still dumping drawers. Terror stabbed the mattress with the gnarly knife he carried and ripped the protective covering. What he thought he would find hidden in there, Menace could only guess.

"Found it, sir!" A young operative Menace had never met held up Naya's red notebook. Triumphant, he brought it to Terror who thumbed through the encoded pages.

He glanced at Naya, narrowing his one eye, and then slapped the book against the young man's chest. "Get this to Cipher."

"Yes, sir." The operative scurried from the room.

Standing near the doorway, Raze kept his weapon lowered. He met Menace's questioning gaze and gave the tiniest, almost imperceptible shake of his head. Whatever was going on here, neither Raze nor Venom wanted any part of it. Menace suspected both men had demanded they take part in Terror's witch hunt to safeguard him and Naya. At least with Raze and Venom present there would be witnesses if this thing went even further south.

Terror approached Naya. Menace stepped between them, refusing to allow his friend to intimidate his wife. Terror gave him a hard look. "I'm trying to protect you, Menace, but if you make things difficult for me, all bets are off."

"Protect me? You just searched my home without a warrant."

"I don't need one. When I want something done, I just

snap my fingers," he snapped, "and all sorts of men rush to get it done."

For the first time in his life, Menace was afraid of Terror. Not because Terror would hurt him. He wasn't afraid to face whatever pain the man had in store. No, he was terrified for Naya and the possibility of her having to deal with an unrestrained Terror.

"I want her cuffed." Terror spoke to Venom. "Take her down to central holding. Put her in an interrogation room." He eyed Menace. "If you make one fucking peep about her being in cuffs or going into interrogation without you, I will have her sent to the *Arctis* for questioning. Understood?"

"Loud and clear." Menace set his jaw. On board the *Valiant*, Naya had Vicious' protection. No matter what Terror accused her of, Vicious would never allow Terror to harm her or unleash Torment, his master interrogator. As long as she stayed on the *Valiant*, Menace could be reasonably assured of her safety. He hoped they would give him enough time to find a lawyer and fight whatever charges they were bringing before Terror did anything rash.

Venom removed his cuffs from his vest. As if getting arrested were the most natural thing in the world, Naya relaxed her shoulders and dropped her hands behind her back. Venom affixed the metal cuffs and took hold of her upper arm. "Move."

Menace watched Venom lead her out of their bedroom. At the doorway, she cast a lingering glance over her shoulder. The tears glistening in her dark eyes made him sick. He felt useless and impotent.

With a heavy sigh, Menace put his hands behind his back. "Cuff me. Let's get this over with."

For the first time that morning, Terror showed genuine regret. He looked pained and put a friendly hand on Menace's arm. "I'm sorry this is happening. You deserved so much better."

Puzzled by Terror's remarks, Menace allowed Raze to cuff and perp-walk him out of his destroyed home. In a sign of friendship and respect, Terror made use of the hidden access points and elevators to take him down to the on-ship jail. Menace breathed easier at the knowledge that none of his colleagues or neighbors had seen him in cuffs. It made the humiliation a little easier to bear.

They took him to a room between interrogation cells. Inside the dim room, Vicious waited with Torment and Pierce, Terror's Shadow Force cohorts. Stone-faced and always cool, Torment showed only the barest hint of recognition as Menace entered the room. Pierce, on the other hand, had a bruised and battered face and a hand and an arm wrapped in gauze. He'd been through the wringer and very recently.

Vicious cursed loudly. "Terror, get him out of those cuffs now."

Terror stood his ground. "It's procedure, Vee. Menace is under arrest for aiding and abetting the enemy."

Menace's stomach dropped as though it were a runaway elevator. "*What?*"

Pierce gestured to his face. "The gun shipment that I was on last night was attacked. We took heavy fire. Eleven men were killed and seventeen were wounded. We barely made it to the escape pods. The Splinter ships grabbed the cargo boxes from the debris field and fled."

Terror stepped forward and tapped the frame of the one-way mirror to activate it. Menace's gut clenched at the sight of Naya sitting alone in a cold interrogation cell. Last night, he'd helped her live out a fantasy in a cell like this one. Now she was living a nightmare. She kept her gaze fixed forward and her features schooled. If she was afraid, she wasn't going to let anyone else know it.

But he recognized the subtle signs. As her husband, he'd learned to read her like a book. Menace glanced at Torment. With his infamous interrogation skills, that man would have no problem recognizing her signs either. With that knowledge, Torment could do terrible things.

"I know that Naya was in your office yesterday," Terror said. "I know that you talked to her about the new weapons we're acquiring. Later she was captured on video entering an access closet. I believe she used the access to the ship's systems to upload and broadcast a signal to her Splinter counterparts."

Agog, Menace asked, "Do you have my office bugged?" He slashed his hand through the air. "And that's not what happened. I took her into that closet. The camera in my office doesn't have a full view of that side of the room."

Terror's gaze grew suspicious. "Why?"

"Why do you think, Ter? It's a dark closet without security cameras."

Pierce snorted with amusement. "I think you just bought yourself a disciplinary action from your commanding officer."

Terror wasn't going to let the honest explanation slide. "If you were distracted by having pussy on the brain, it's no surprise that she managed to work you for intel."

Menace took a step toward Terror. "You better watch it. I may be cuffed but I can still kick your ass."

"She's a mole, Menace!" Terror shouted in anger. "Don't be so fucking blind. She used you."

Menace gawked at Terror. "That's crazy. She's no mole."

"I already know that she worked very closely with the Red Feather," Terror countered. "It's one step from political dissidence to terrorism."

Behind them, Vicious cleared his throat. "I wouldn't go that far, Terror. The Red Feather has done a lot of good. They've worked with us quite a bit in the last few months and provided a great deal of intel and aid."

"Naya's cover as some simple girl from Connor's Run who ran a pawnshop and does good works for the Red Feather doesn't jibe with the truth, Vee." Terror held out his hand and Torment slapped an oversized and overfilled brown folder into it. "I got her police records. This woman is no stranger to trouble."

The folder hit the countertop jutting out from beneath the one-way mirror. Terror started whipping out paper arrest records and photographs. "She has two arrests for theft as a child. She was picked up for smuggling medicine and technology as a teenager but managed to escape before she could be booked or processed. I suspect her Red Feather friends bounced her from the police station and helped her disappear."

Menace stared at the arrest photographs of Naya. Painfully thin and with hair cut as short as a boy's, the adolescent Naya wore ill-fitting men's clothing. It occurred to him that she'd probably taken on a boy's persona while living on the streets to protect herself from kidnapping or rape. The expression of defiance on her face didn't surprise him.

Terror didn't stop there. "She was suspected of being part of a gunrunning ring out of The City. They tried to sweep her up in their stings, but she managed to evade them four times. The fifth time she wasn't so lucky."

A booking photo of an older Naya, maybe eighteen or nineteen, hit the counter. A black eye and split lip marred her beautiful face. She wore only a man's tank top and low-cut panties in the photograph. By the look of her mussed hair, she'd been roused from bed and hauled in for questioning. Bruises were already forming on her upper arms and neck. He shuddered to think what kind of violent pigs had put their hands on her.

"She told me all this." Menace lifted his gaze to Terror's face. "Not the part about the guns but the rest of it." He didn't add how much it hurt him that she'd kept this vital piece of information from him.

"And did she tell you about her family? About her brother and her mother?"

Menace nodded. "Her mother ran off when she was six. Her brother abandoned her when she was a teenager."

Terror laughed with disbelief. "Well I guess that's one way of putting it, huh?"

"What the hell is that supposed to mean?"

"It means she lied to you, Menace." Terror retrieved two photographs and rap sheets. The similarities between the older woman and younger man and Naya were striking. "This is Naya's mother, Amallie. She's now the most notorious gunrunner in this sector and lives in The City, not sixty miles from Naya's shop in Connor's Run. Her late husband was the leader of the Sixer gang, a violent group of thugs who work with the Splinters. This is Nattie, her older brother. Our most recent intel says he's become a drug-addicted loser but he still provides muscle for his mama."

Menace didn't know what to say. Numbness spread through his body. That night in his kitchen when Naya had spoken of her family, the pain on her face and in her voice had been so real. Was she really that good an actress? More importantly, was he really that stupid? Could he have been such an easy mark?

"The files from the secret police tell us that Naya started off doing small jobs for the Red Feather to eat and survive on the streets. When she was thirteen or fourteen, she started getting jobs from the Sixers to run guns. They were small shipments at first, but she was very good. Soon she was making a great deal of money. How else do you think a homeless orphan girl got her hands on the cash necessary to fund a pawnshop at eighteen?"

Menace didn't have an answer. He remembered their conversation about the gun shipment. What had she said? They couldn't ensure the safety of every shipment? Was that her coded way of telling him that her people were going to steal the weapons?

Betrayal surged through him. The burning pain of it

threatened to choke the life right out of him. He'd bought her sob story hook, line and sinker. He'd believed that she was the one. When Flare had wanted to take her away from him, he had fought for her. After showing her nothing but kindness and love and patience, she had lied to him.

Terror put both hands on his shoulders. "I have to question her. Legally she's still your property and I have to ask permission. I'm telling you right now that I won't hesitate to go above Vee's head to get that permission granted. Please," Terror said gently, "give me permission. Let me help you. I can't keep you out of prison, but I can save your life if you give her up. Show some cooperation."

Menace reeled with the awfulness of it all. There was no choice here. Even if he said no, even if he tried to protect the woman he'd grown to love so deeply, Terror would make one subspace satellite call and get permission to do whatever he wanted to Naya. If he said yes, maybe he could spare her some ugliness.

"I won't allow Torment to put his hands on her," Vicious said quietly. "She may be a terrorist, but I won't allow a woman to be tortured on this ship."

Staring at her, Menace couldn't believe she'd fooled him so easily. Had anything they'd shared been real? Was it all a ruse? He didn't think so. She couldn't fake their connection. She couldn't fake the depth of affection they shared when they made love.

But his love for her couldn't overcome the awful truth. Knowingly or unknowingly, he'd fed information to a mole, and men, his brothers-in-arms, had been killed. The guilt of that would eat away at him until he drew his last breath.

"Interrogate her."

Terror let loose a relieved a breath. He clapped Menace's shoulder. "I'm sorry it went this way, Menace. I never wanted—"

"I know." Deep down inside, he hoped she had a good reason for betraying him. It wouldn't make it any easier to swallow but maybe he could learn to understand it. Menace kept his gaze fixed on Naya, trying to remember every detail of the face that had ensnared him. There was no doubt in his mind. Once he left this room, he would never see his wife again.

"Take him to another room and get his statement, Torment. When you're done, transfer custody to the general."

Torment grabbed his arm. "This way, Menace. I'll make this quick and painless."

Menace didn't appreciate the gallows humor. Head hung with shame, he refused to meet Vicious' compassionate gaze. He'd put every soldier and airman in this sector at risk. Compassion wasn't something he deserved or even wanted.

Vicious grasped his shoulder and gave it a reassuring squeeze. "It will be all right, Menace."

But it wouldn't be.

Chapter Sixteen

NAYA GLANCED AT the door again. Her legs ached from being seated so long. She'd tried bouncing her feet up and down to maintain blood flow, but that only made her ankles and arches burn. She needed to use the restroom and her mouth was incredibly dry. Her stomach rumbled with hunger and reminded her about the brunch date with Hallie she'd missed.

The room's stark white walls and painfully bright lights made her slightly dizzy. A sensation of claustrophobia crept into her chest. She inhaled slowly and folded her arms on the table. She leaned forward and rested her cheek on them. *Breathe. Just breathe.*

How long had it been since she was separated from Menace? Three hours? Four? She couldn't tell. It definitely felt that long. Was he in trouble? She prayed that he would be spared. Whatever she'd done in her past, it had nothing to do with Menace.

Eyes closed, she fought the urge to laugh at the irony of her situation. Just last night she'd been "interrogated" senseless. Now she shivered with fear at the very real prospect of her fantasy becoming a true nightmare.

The door suddenly hissed and beeped as the locks disengaged. Her stomach lurched but she muscled down the urge to puke. She had to keep it together. Menace would find a way to save her. She may not have trusted him enough to tell all her secrets to him, but he had to know how much she loved him. He was going to be angry when he learned about what she'd done all those years ago, but he would find a way to protect her. He wasn't her mother or her brother or any of the other people who had let her down. He was Menace—and he loved her. She believed that with every fiber of her being.

With all the swagger of a man who was untouchable, Terror entered the interrogation cell. Another man flanked him, this one sporting a battered face and injured arm. He took up a position near the door. Terror strode toward her. He had a brown folder clamped under one arm and a tablet in the other hand. The folder she recognized. She'd seen the same ones down in The City and Connor's Run when she'd been arrested.

"Sorry to keep you waiting," Terror said and dropped into the chair across from her. He placed the folder and tablet on the table. "Interrogating Menace took longer than I'd anticipated."

His words hit her like a punch to the gut. She didn't dare let her expression change. She pushed down the fear she felt for Menace and tried to keep a handle on her emotions. Menace and Terror were friends. He wouldn't put his friend through an interrogation. *He's playing you.*

"That's Pierce. He's one of my agents." Terror reached into his pocket and produced a small piece of candy. He took his time unwrapping and popping it into his mouth. Totally relaxed, he leaned back in his chair. "I'm sure you've figured it out by now but I'm not exactly a logistics clerk."

"No! Really? I'm shocked." Past experience told her the smart-ass routine was a quick way to catch a boot to the face or worse but she couldn't help herself. Sarcasm had always been her default setting in times of fear.

"I'm sure you read me as easily as I read you. Pawn-shop girl from Connor's Run?" He snorted. "I hardly think so."

Terror's remark sent a quiver of doubt through her. What, exactly, did Terror think her guilty of doing?

"Your radar seems to have a glitch, Terror. I really am just a pawnshop girl from Connor's Run."

He crunched the candy between his teeth. His unwavering stare unnerved her. "This doesn't have to end badly, Naya. You can come clean right now and I can pull some strings at your sentencing. Cooperate and I'll show my gratitude."

Sentencing? Naya's heartbeat sped up but she tried to regain control of her body.

"Tell me about the Grab."

She blinked. "What?"

"Tell me about the Grab."

"It was cool that morning. I was wearing shorts. I had my hair in a ponytail. I ran with my friend Jennie. There were lots of birds. It was sort of overcast." She rattled on at the mouth. "Have I told you enough?"

Terror clicked his teeth and sat forward. She fought the urge to shrink back in her chair. Showing him weakness would give him an easy victory.

"I know you weren't on the original list. Your number wasn't pulled in the lottery. You bought your way onto the list. Why?"

Was that illegal? Had they hauled her in here because she'd broken some rule? "My best friend Jennie had her number pulled. We made promises when we were kids that we'd run together. We didn't want to be separated."

Terror didn't say anything. He just stared at her. Was he trying to read her face? Probably.

"Why Menace?"

She frowned. "What do you mean?"

"Why did you choose Menace as your mark?"

"My mark?" Naya glanced at Pierce. The roughed-up man still stood guard at the door. His intense gaze unsettled her. "Menace picked me. *He* Grabbed *me*."

"After you deliberately injured Flare and used your friend to lure Menace closer," Terror countered.

Dread settled in the pit of her stomach. "That is not what happened."

"Isn't it?" Terror tapped his finger on the table. "Didn't you see Menace buying flowers in the market that day and recognize his officer's insignia? Didn't you take that information back to your Splinter cell friends and concoct this plan to infiltrate the *Valiant*?"

Panic saturated her veins. Splinter cell? Was this guy batshit crazy? "That is not—I am *not* a terrorist!"

"No?" Terror flipped open the folder and started snatching out photographs. He smacked them down on the table. The old memories came flooding back as her gaze moved from one mug shot to the next. The constant hunger and cold. The fear. The depression. The anger. The desperation.

"Tell me the girl who ran guns for the Sixer gang out of The City isn't a terrorist." He shoved a photograph of a weapons cache across the table. She recognized the bag and packing material cradling the weapons. She couldn't be sure that exact shipment had been one she'd ferried on her back but it was possible.

"I didn't…I was just a stupid kid. I was hungry. I wanted a home. I needed money."

"Spare me." Terror picked up his tablet. "We all have sob stories. I'm not particularly interested in yours. What I am interested in is this." He spun around the tablet and showed her gruesome images of burned and mangled bodies.

Naya recoiled. "I don't know anything about that."

"Don't you?" Terror pushed the tablet in front of her so she couldn't look away from it. "You sent the information about last night's weapons shipment to your Splinter cell contacts. We have the data burst record that emanated from the *Valiant*. You just happened to be spotted entering an engineering access point around the same time the burst was sent. How do you explain that?"

"I can't."

"Your transmission worked. They attacked our ship last night. All of the weapons were stolen. Men were killed and maimed." He sat back and gestured to Pierce. "Men like him."

Feeling the situation spiral out of control, Naya said, "Look, I know I did some terrible things when I was a young, dumb kid. No one knows that more than me. But I am not a terrorist. I don't know anyone involved with the Splinter movement."

Terror guffawed rudely. "You just can't stop lying."

He slammed his hands onto the table so hard the tablet jumped. Startled, Naya inhaled a shaky breath. Was he going to hit her next?

Shaking his head, Terror retrieved two photos from the folder. He pushed them closer. "You're going to sit there and tell me you don't know these two people?"

Surprise rippled through her. Nattie? She touched the photo of her older brother. The years hadn't been kind to him. He looked so thin and drawn. The pockmarks on his face and his brown, brittle teeth shocked her. What kind of trouble had he gotten into now?

The other photo took her a moment to recognize. Her mother had aged considerably in the nearly eighteen years since she'd left. Like Nattie, her face was also scarred, but in a different way. Someone had slit her cheek from the corner of her mouth to her ear. It had been sewn back together crudely and left a thick, bumpy scar.

Her voice husky with emotion, Naya said, "This is my brother, Nattie. That's…that's my mother."

"Two known Splinter cell members," Terror added.

Her gaze snapped to his face. "That's not true."

"You know it is."

"I don't. I haven't seen them in years."

Terror glanced at Pierce and chortled with exasperation. "Again with the lies!"

Irritation laced her voice. "I'm not lying. I haven't seen

my mother in nearly twenty years. It's been six years for Nattie."

Terror's mouth settled into a grim line. "Now I understand how Menace was so easily fooled by you. I'd considered that maybe he was that gullible, but no. You're a supremely talented actress. I almost believe that you're telling the truth."

Frustrated, she shouted, "I am!"

"You expect me to sit here and accept that your mother has been living in The City for ten years and you never once ran into her? I'm supposed to believe that you were running guns for her husband, Sandy Cragen, the leader of the Sixers, but you had no contact with your mother? Give me a fucking break, Naya!"

Head spinning, Naya tried to get a grasp on reality. What Terror said couldn't possibly be true. Her mother had left with a sky trader named Jaxon and escaped to the colonies. If she'd been in the City, Naya would have found out about it. She sure as hell would have known if she'd been running guns for her mother's husband! Someone would have told her. Danny would have told her. He knew everything and everyone.

"You're lying," Naya spat back angrily. "My mother is not in The City."

Terror waved his hands. "You know what, Naya? I'm done." He leaned forward with an enraged expression twisting his features. "Tell me where the hell my gun shipment is and maybe I'll let you walk off this ship alive."

Naya tried not to freak the fuck out. This man didn't issue empty threats. "I don't know where your guns are,

Terror."

He jumped out of his seat and kicked the chair behind him. "If I have to come around this table, you are going to regret it."

Lip wobbling and tears threatening to spill, Naya tried to make him understand. "I don't know! If I knew where the guns were, I would tell you." She didn't add that she was about ten seconds away from pissing her pants with fright.

Terror's nostrils flared as he inhaled long, deep breaths. Regaining some control, he said, "Then you're going to find out where it is."

"And how the hell do you expect me to do that?"

Terror gestured to the pages of her rap sheet. "Your history tells me you'll find a way."

Naya leaned back in her chair as the awful truth swamped her. "You're going to drop me on the surface."

"See, Pierce?" He glanced at his colleague. "I told you she wasn't as dumb as she looks."

She gritted her teeth at his cruel remark. The man was clearly trying to bait her into exploding. She wasn't about to give him the satisfaction. "I don't have the kind of contacts you think I have. If I start jamming my nose where it doesn't belong, there's a good chance I'm going to have my throat slit."

Terror straightened up and shrugged. "It's a chance I'm willing to take."

His coldness stunned her. This man was totally devoid of feeling. His arrogance sickened her. Had he even considered the possibility that he was wrong and that she was actually innocent?

And where the hell was Menace? He'd sworn to her that he would protect her. He'd promised to fight for her. Yes, she'd lied to him by omission and she had to answer for that, but to abandon her to this terrifying and danger-ous man?

"What about Menace? Is he willing to risk my life on your totally wrong intel?"

Terror pinned her with his ice-cold glare. "My intel is never wrong."

"It's wrong today."

"Pierce? Show her."

The wounded man walked to the one-way mirror and tapped the frame twice. She was able to see through the mirror into the adjacent and totally empty room.

"Menace gave you up. He's not coming to your rescue. Once I told him what a lying, thieving, terrorist-loving whore you are, he washed his hands of you." Terror plant-ed both hands on the table and leaned forward with his most frightening stare. "You're all alone, Naya."

Unable to hold his gaze, Naya glanced away from him. Seeing the empty room on the other side of that mirror had shattered her last sliver of hope. When things had gotten tough, Menace had done what everyone else always did. He'd cut her loose.

Feeling worthless, Naya gulped down the sob trying to escape her throat. She blinked rapidly and cleared the stinging tears. She had to get a fucking grip. The only way she had even the minutest chance of surviving was to cooperate.

Voice cracking, she asked, "What do you want me to do?"

Terror's face relaxed as he pocketed his victory. "You're going to meet with your contact and find the location of the weapons, the Sixer gang hideout or the headquarters of the Splinter cell. All three would be nice."

"My contact?"

"Dankirk, the Red Feather fixer," he clarified. "I know he has his dirty little fingers on the pulse of the Calyx underworld. You'll be given an address where you'll ask him to meet you."

She narrowed her gaze. "What makes you think I'm going to draw my friend into a setup?"

"If you don't, I'll have him picked up by one of my strike teams. I can assure you the amenities will be nowhere near as comfortable as these."

Naya didn't doubt him for a second. "Danny's not stupid. He's going to know something is wrong. He takes his oath to the Red Feather very seriously. He's not going to compromise the chain for me."

"Then you had better turn on the charm and convince him," Terror warned. "Or else it won't be just your ass on the line."

Who else could he possibly rope into this?

"I know all about Hallie's involvement with the Red Feather. Forgery. Smuggling. Maybe I'll haul her skinny little ass in here next. Wouldn't that be humiliating for Vicious? He'd find out that the wife he worships has ties to known terrorists. I can't imagine how quickly the government would jump in and sever their mate bond. With that useless, barren womb of hers, she's easily disposable."

Awash in horror, Naya could only stare at Terror. Hallie considered this man her friend and he spoke about her in that awful way?

"Let's not forget about Menace. He'll be stripped of his rank by the morning. Over two decades of honorable service gone like that!" He snapped his fingers. "He allowed a terrorist to infiltrate the armory and steal classified information. He's responsible for the deaths of eleven men. It's the firing squad for him if I don't put in a good word.

Even if I do, the Kovark—"

"Stop," she interrupted weakly. "Just stop. I'll do it."

Terror's mind was made up. The deck was stacked against her and she had no access to a lawyer or any kind of justice here. Her impending death had become a cold, hard fact. She refused to let anyone else be hurt because of the stupid things she'd done as a teenager.

"Pierce, take her to the segregation unit." Terror considered her for a moment. "Let her have a meal and unrestricted fluid access. We don't want her fainting on us before she finishes her mission."

"Oh, you're so kind." Naya rolled her eyes as Pierce hauled her out of the chair and guided her to the door. She'd expected rough handling but he was surprisingly easy on her. Apparently not all of the Shadow Force operatives were dicks.

Within a few minutes, she was locked in a tiny cell and uncuffed. There was a metal rack with no mattress or blanket and a silver toilet and sink in the corner. The door was solid metal with a food tray slot and observation window. Taking advantage of her moment of privacy, Naya used the restroom and washed her hands.

Alone in the quiet cell, she refused to cry. This wasn't the first time she'd been abandoned. She'd survive. She always did. The knowledge that Menace had turned his back on her hurt worse than anything she'd ever experienced. Part of her wished that Terror had put his hands on her, that he'd beaten her to a bloody pulp to extract the information he wrongly believed she possessed. At least then she'd have real physical pain to distract her from the gnawing, burning ache of ruined love.

"It's your own damn fault," she whispered angrily. It was. There was no denying that. If she'd told Menace everything about her past, he wouldn't have been blindsided and so easily convinced by Terror. After the way the Shadow Force agent had come after her, she could only imagine what tricks he'd used to convince Menace that she was a lying, murderous terrorist.

That Menace could believe her capable of something so sinister tore at her heart. She'd been certain he was going to tell her he loved her this morning. She'd been waiting with bated breath for him to say the words so she could return them to him without the fear of being rejected.

She hoped that his friends would rally around him and protect him from the blowback. Her love for him didn't end with this betrayal. She wanted him safe and alive, even if that meant she would never see him again. It wasn't his fault that he'd chosen and Grabbed her. Her sky warrior had no idea what he was doing when he brought her and her murky past into his life.

Metal hinges creaked. A food tray slid through the slot. She didn't hesitate to snatch it free from the door. If this was going to be her only meal, she needed to eat all of it. A flattened prisoner cup in a plastic package came through the slot next. She ripped open the package and assembled the thin paper cup. It had a leak along the bottom so she could only drink over the sink. Not the most glamorous situation, but it quenched her thirst.

After polishing off every last morsel of food, she placed the tray in the slot and pushed it through to the other side. She moved to the rack and tried to get comfortable on the cold metal slab. It reminded her of her early days of sleeping in alleys and on sidewalks. In those first days, she hadn't learned the various tricks to make her nights more comfortable and warm like salvaging cardboard, newspapers and blankets.

Sleep didn't come easy, but she managed to quiet her mind finally. If she had any hope of surviving and finding a way to save herself, she needed to recharge her batteries before they dropped her back on Calyx. She wasn't sure how long she slept, but it felt like hours.

Two loud bangs on the door startled her. She bolted upright. The cover on the window opened and Pierce's face came into view. "Five-minute warning. If you need to pee, you better do it now."

The window cover slammed closed and she jumped off the bed. Not wanting to have an audience, she used the bathroom in a hurry. She sat down on the rack again and clamped her shaking hands between her knees. The full weight of what these men expected her to accomplish crushed her. She didn't even know if it could be done, but she had to try. She couldn't let Hallie or Menace be hurt.

There was another knock before the cell door opened. Pierce dangled a pair of cuffs from one hand and a black hood in the other. Her gut soured at the sight of the hood. The man gestured for her to stand. He pointed to her neck. "I need your collar."

Naya took a step back and brought her hands to her throat. She touched the soft blue leather and the dangling silver tag. "Why?"

His expression softened. "Your bond has been dissolved. You don't have the right to wear it anymore."

Dissolved? Divorced. Like a pallet of bricks dropped on her head, the realization that she and Menace were no more left her dizzy. Her heart beat wildly and her chest constricted painfully.

With trembling fingers, she reached back and unbuckled the collar. Her eyes closed briefly as the memory of Menace locking it around her neck tormented her. She could almost feel the heat of his adoring gaze on her skin. Swallowing hard, she pulled the collar away from her neck and handed it to Pierce. His jaw twitched as he took it from her.

"I'll make sure he gets it back," he promised as he pocketed the collar.

His words gave her hope. "Is he all right?"

Pierce studied her. "Not really. He's torn up about this. You have to understand that he didn't want it to go this way, but the evidence against you..."

She found some consolation in the idea that he'd struggled with the decision to give her up. "Are they really going to send him to prison?"

Pierce motioned for her to extend her wrists and started to cuff her. "If they don't get the weapons or good intel on this Splinter cell on Calyx, he's got a one-way ticket to Kovark. Terror and Vicious won't let him go down for treason." He tightened the cuffs around her wrists. "If you're able to get Terror what he wants, it's very likely Menace will only get a year or two in prison. He's strong. He'll survive it."

She understood what he was saying. If she really loved Menace, she'd do whatever it took to get that information for Terror. It was the only way to ensure his life would be saved. "I'll do my best."

"If you hope to save your life, you'd better."

Naya took a chance. "You know I'm innocent."

"What I think doesn't matter. Terror has made his decision. There's no going back." Pierce glanced at his watch. "We have seven minutes until Terror expects us. I can let you record a message if you want."

She smiled sadly. "My last will and testament, huh?"

He looked uncomfortable. "Something like that."

"I don't know what I'd say." The pain was too raw for her even to contemplate a final message to Menace.

"Maybe you'd like to warn a friend."

His message came through loud and clear. Hallie!

Pierce retrieved a small recording device from his pocket. "You've got two minutes. Make it quick."

Naya didn't waste any time. She sat down on the edge of the rack, hit the record button and started to talk into the small screen. She prayed her friend would remember the old codes or at least be able to piece the information together. "Hallie, I'm sorry I missed brunch today. I got some bad news about an uncle of mine. I'm on my way to visit him. I'm hoping Aunt Ruthie isn't sick too. If I make it back, I guess I'll have to quarantine myself so I don't infect anyone else on the ship." She bit her lower lip before whispering, "Good luck, Hallie."

"Done?"

She handed him the recorder and stood. "Yes."

Pierce slipped it into his pocket and opened the hood. A few seconds later, the dark fabric covered her head. "Say goodbye to the *Valiant*, Naya."

A silent tear dripped down her cheek. Trapped in the darkness, she surrendered totally to Pierce's control. Her fate was sealed.

Chapter Seventeen

"WHY WON'T THEY let me see her?" Menace paced the length of Vicious' office. He'd been freed from custody earlier that morning after his court-appointed attorney had poked a million holes in the case against him. "It's been twenty-six hours since they arrested us. My lawyer says there's no reason we can't see each other."

"I don't know, Menace." Looking haggard, Vicious rubbed his face with his hands. Not only was Vicious trying to deal with the fallout of a suspected terrorist living onboard the ship for over a month, but there had been major malfunctions in the *Valiant*'s many systems overnight. "I'm getting stonewalled by Pierce. No one will tell me where Terror is or where he's put Naya. I'm assuming he has her in one of the segregated cells in the Shadow Force sector. Only Orion has the capability to override the passcodes there but the malfunctions have frozen him out."

Menace's gut turned queasy. "I need to see her. I need to get her an attorney."

"You can't." Vicious wouldn't meet his gaze. "You can't do anything for her anymore."

"What?" Cold crept up his neck. "Why not?"

"They severed your bond yesterday afternoon. She's in legal limbo at the moment. She isn't one of us and she's no longer a citizen of Calyx. I don't even know what rights she has but I've got my legal team looking into it. This terrorism charge complicates things even further."

Menace felt as though he might puke. "Vicious, this isn't right. How the hell can Terror just railroad us like this? The evidence he presented to me in that interrogation room looked impressive but my lawyer is right. It's all circumstantial. They can't prove Naya has ties to anything criminal."

"They don't have to," Vicious said. "Terror's position is bolstered by the recent changes to our laws. The Shadow Force can hold suspected enemy combatants for six months without charging them."

"Six months?" The bottom dropped out of his stomach. He didn't even want to imagine the horror she would endure in that amount of time. "Vicious, I made a mistake yesterday. I have to talk to her and apologize. I have to make this right."

"Menace, I want to help you. I'm doing everything I can to—"

The door to Vicious' office burst open and Hallie stormed into the room. The general's secretary was two steps behind her. "Ma'am, you can't just barge in here! You have to follow the proper procedure."

Hallie pinned the young soldier with a glare. "You can stuff your proper procedures where the sun don't shine." She pointed to the door. "Now get the hell out!" The secretary didn't linger. He beat a hasty retreat and closed the door. The furious little sprite turned her gaze on her husband. "What have you done?"

"Good morning to you too, Kitten."

"Don't 'Kitten' me, Vicious!" Hallie's hands were drawn into tight fists. She was shaking with anger—and fear. "Am I next?"

Menace watched his friend's face contort with confusion. Vicious walked around the side of his desk. "Hallie, what are you talking about?"

"I know what happened to Naya." She wiped at the tears now dripping down her face. "I know what you did to her. I'm not stupid, Vicious. I can read the writing on the wall."

"You are not stupid." Vicious caressed her face. "There is no writing on the wall, Hallie."

"Don't lie to me!"

Menace hated to interrupt the couple's tiff but he needed answers. "Who told you Naya was arrested?"

Hallie narrowed her dark eyes at him. "She told me herself."

Menace reeled with shock. "They let you see her?"

Hallie shook her head. "She sent me a message. It arrived twenty minutes ago but the time stamp was from last night. I got the warning loud and clear."

Vicious stiffened. "What warning?"

"That she's been compromised and I'm not safe."

"Compromised?" Vicious cupped Hallie's face. "Do you know something about Naya's activities with the Splinters?"

"Is that why she's being persecuted?" Hallie gripped her husband's wrists. "Naya is no more a terrorist than I am. Anyone who thinks that our work with the Red Feather was in any way connected to the Splinter cell on Calyx is crazy."

"She ran guns," Vicious said forcefully. "She didn't deny it during her interrogation."

"And I forged documents," she countered. "A lot of us did shady or stupid things back on Calyx. It doesn't make us terrorists."

"No," Vicious agreed, "but Terror's evidence against her is persuasive."

Hallie pursed her lips. "You better than anyone should know that Terror isn't infallible. Do I need to rehash my trip to the colonies when Terror was my escort?"

Vicious paled. "No."

Menace wanted to ask Hallie if he could see the message but the door opened again. This time it was Admiral Orion crossing the threshold and he looked pissed.

"Orion?" Vicious let his hands fall from Hallie's face and stepped beside her.

"We have a huge problem, Vicious. Your man contravened a direct order."

"My man?"

"That one-eyed son of a bitch," Orion shouted. Recovering from his outburst, the admiral shot Hallie an apologetic look. "Excuse me, ma'am."

Vicious growled in frustration. "What did Terror do now?"

"Yesterday he requested two pilots and a stealth ship to conduct a covert mission. After the Splinter attack, I ordered all unnecessary missions grounded for forty-eight hours so we could reassess the security situation. That electrical spike that fried so many systems last night? That was your man sabotaging my ship so he could go off on one of his covert ops."

Menace swayed on his feet. "Naya, sir?"

Orion's mouth settled into a grim line. "I believe he took her to the surface. She wasn't on the stolen ship when he returned fifteen minutes ago. I've got him under arrest outside the Shadow Force sector but he's not talking."

"We'll see about that," Vicious ground out angrily. He turned to Hallie as if he meant to send her back to their quarters but stopped himself. "You're coming with me. I'm not letting you out of my sight."

She relaxed with relief. "Thank you."

Vicious crooked his finger at Menace. "Let's go get some answers."

Nodding, Menace fell into step behind Vicious and Hallie. Two of Orion's top officers joined them in the lobby. The elevator ride was cramped but short. They entered an area of the ship Menace had never before visited. He'd never even seen this section on the schematics.

Wearing black cargo pants and a gray shirt, Terror leaned back against the wall outside a door. He looked calm and peaceful. Menace had never wanted to hit his friend harder in his entire life. Did Terror have any concept of the hell he'd wrought? Did he even care? For the first time in their many years of friendship, Menace finally understood why so many people hated Terror. He was a bully. Period. Full stop.

Toe-to-toe with the man he'd once considered a best friend, Menace glared at him.

"Where the hell is my wife, Terror?"

"Don't you mean ex-wife?"

Menace drew back his fist but Vicious grabbed him, stopping him from striking Terror. Regaining control of his fury, Menace asked, "What have you done with her?"

"What I should have done the moment I realized who she was," Terror replied. "I punted her ass back to Calyx where she belongs."

"You contravened one of my direct orders," Orion interjected. "I realize you and Vicious are friends and you two tend to confuse the chain of command between yourselves, but that shit doesn't fly with me. I am the admiral in charge of this entire sky battalion. When I give an order, it's followed."

Terror didn't even blink. "I exist outside the chain of command. If you don't like the way I handle the affairs of the Shadow Force, you're more than welcome to contact my superiors."

"Is that so?" Jaw set, Orion glanced at one of his men. "When we're done here, ready a ship for Terror and his men. I want them off the *Valiant* within the hour. If he refuses to leave, vent him."

Terror's stone-cold expression didn't slip. "As you wish, Admiral."

The door to the Shadow Force sector hissed. Surprise registered on Pierce's bruised face as he peered out into the hallway. "We're less than two minutes from the agreed meeting time, Terror." He frowned at the group assembled. "It's going to be a tight fit."

Terror stepped toward Pierce. "They're not coming."

Menace grasped Terror's arm. "The hell we aren't."

"Seeing the proof of her treachery won't ease the pain, Menace. Let it go."

"And if you're wrong?"

"I'm not."

"Well, I'm not as arrogant as you. I know I was wrong to trust you. You showed me some incriminating things but there wasn't one piece of real evidence that tied Naya to any of this. How else do you think my lawyer got me out of holding?"

"I don't need a smoking gun, Menace. My gut tells me everything I need to know."

"My gut tells me I screwed up yesterday. Whether or not Naya did all those things you accused her of as a teenager, she wouldn't have done this. It's not in her character to hurt other people."

"And like always, Menace, you're a day late and a credit short," Terror replied. "You should have made your case yesterday. It's too late now. What's done is done. She's not coming back."

"We'll see about that." Vicious shoved his way by both of them, dragging Hallie right along behind him. "Menace, let's go."

Vicious cleared a path to the control room where Pierce and some of the soldiers who had tossed Menace's quarters were working. A flat-screen display covered one wall. A live feed from Calyx flashed onto the screen. A digital label in the lower corner marked it as a feed from a hotel in The City.

The familiar sight of Naya's dark ponytail zinged

through him. He took a step closer to the wall. She walked back and forth in the small hotel room. What the hell was she doing there?

As if reading his mind, Pierce offered the answer. "It's one of the locations we use to meet informants. It's wired to transmit live sound and audio. There's a four-and-ahalf minute delay to us, but we've got a guy in the room next door listening." He glanced at his watch. "She's probably already talking to her contact."

His mouth went dry. "Contact?"

Pierce shook his head. "No, not that kind of a contact. He's the fixer you ran into during your trip to retrieve Flare's bride."

"Dankirk?"

Pierce nodded. "From what we can tell, the man knows everyone and everything that goes on in the seedy underbelly of The City and Connor's Run. She still maintains that she has no ties to the Splinter cell or her mother and brother, but she didn't deny that Dankirk might be able to help her find them. He'd be an interesting asset to catch."

Menace wondered what kind of pressure Terror had applied to Naya to make her lure a friend into what was very possibly a trap.

On screen, the door opened and Dankirk appeared in the room. Menace held his breath as he watched the two old friends stare at each other. Dankirk cursed loudly, closed and locked the door and then rushed to Naya. The sight of her collapsing into the other man's arms ripped out his heart. It should have been his arms that held her tight, that gave her security and support, but he'd turned his back on her like a coward.

"What in the blue hell is going on, Naya?" Dankirk cupped her face. "I don't hear from you in weeks and now this? Did he hurt you? Is that why you ran?"

Naya shook her head and wiped at her wet face. She took a step away from him and turned her back on the camera. "It's worse than that, Danny. They know."

The man's face slackened. "About you running guns as a kid? Shit!" He rubbed his face. "I tried to get one of my guys on the inside to grab your records, but they were already gone."

"They have it," Naya confirmed, using her hands to emphasize. "They think I'm working with the Splinter cell that attacked one of their ships and stole a weapons shipment. They told me that the guns are here in The City. Is it true?"

Dankirk nodded and started to pace. "Of course it's true." He jammed his hands in his pockets as he walked. "You knew when you left that line of work that the Sixers were getting into bed with those Splinter dicks. The day that bomb went off, what did you tell me?"

Softly she answered, "That the risks and consequences were real now. That I couldn't compartmentalize what I was doing to justify the money I was making."

"And I told you to run, to get out of that line of work and start over," he said. "You built a good life for yourself but then what the hell did you do? You just had to swoop in and save Jennie. That backfired, didn't it? Now you're the one who needs saving and all you've got is me."

"We've gotten out of tighter scrapes."

Dankirk dropped his hands to his side in resignation. "I don't think we're getting out of this one."

"We'll see." Naya wiped at her face again. Knowing she was crying and he couldn't do anything to soothe her pain killed Menace. "Danny?"

"Yeah?"

"They told me something else."

"What's that?"

"That my mother is here in The City." She hesitated. "That was just one of their lies, right? That was just some tactic to trip me up and make me beg for a deal, yeah?"

Dankirk perked up. "Did you? Cut a deal, I mean? Because if you did, I get it, Naya. I won't mind taking it in the neck for you."

The realization that Dankirk was willing to go to prison to protect Naya made Menace feel even worse. It drove home the point he'd been mulling over all night. He didn't deserve her trust. In his rush to protect her from the threat of Terror unleashing Torment, he had capitulated too easily. He should have demanded to see her first, to speak with her, to let her know he loved her and would find a way to save them. Instead he had trusted in the justice system and left her to believe the very worst of him.

"No, I didn't, Danny. Stop trying to change the subject. Is it true? Is my mother here?"

"Yes," Dankirk reluctantly answered. "She's here."

Naya inhaled a noisy breath. "How long have you known? How long have you kept that from me, Danny? Months? A year?"

"Ten," he said finally. "Ten years, Naya."

She sobbed loudly. "Ten fucking years, Danny?"

"She didn't want you," he said, tearing up now. "I went to her. The second I learned she'd come back with that new man of hers, I made my way there. You remember that summer when I left you in charge of the other kids in our pack so I could make a trip?"

Still crying, she nodded. "Yeah."

"Well, that's where I went," he said. "I found her and her husband, the leader of the Sixers, and I told her that you were alone and living on the streets. I tried to make her see how dangerous it was for a thirteen-year-old girl to be living that way but she didn't care. She was cold. Heartless," he added. "I couldn't bear to tell you. I couldn't break your heart again."

Menace's heart raced as the awful truth was spilled. All around him, the room had grown eerily silent. Like him, they were all affected by the ugliness.

"Her man, Sandy?" Dankirk continued. "He stopped me on the way out and asked me if you were smart or fast or useful. I thought maybe if he could find a job for you he might make your mother take you in and support you. I had no idea he was going to turn you into a gun mule. This whole thing? It's my fault."

"It's not your fault, Danny." She sniffled and used the hem of her shirt to wipe the moisture from her cheeks. "Even back then, I could have said no. I should have been smart enough to realize that they were using a homeless kid to do their dirty work because I was expendable. I was a nobody, a nothing, but I kept telling myself that I could use the gang right back. I could get myself off the streets."

"And you did," Dankirk confirmed. "You just didn't know the whole story. I thought I was protecting you."

She laughed harshly. "Well, a load of good that did me. I've got the whole fury and might of the Harcos forces bearing down on me as we speak. They think I have an inside line on my gunrunning, terrorist-loving mama."

"I'm so sorry I lied to you."

She reached for his hand. "It's okay. I would have done the same thing to spare you any pain."

Dankirk shook his head. "What are you going to do?"

She shrugged. "What I always do."

"What? The right thing? The honorable thing?" He scoffed with irritation. "Naya, just run! Let me cut that damn chip out of your arm. I'll take you away. They will never find you again. You can start over with me. You can have the life you've always deserved."

Panic seized Menace. What if she said yes? Would he ever see her again?

"I can't, Danny."

Selfish as it was, Menace exhaled in relief. He hadn't lost her irrevocably.

"Why not?"

"There's no starting over for me. I tried. I got taken to a whole new culture and lived on a spaceship and you know what? My past still bit me in the ass. I can't outrun it." She lifted her chin. "I have to face it."

"Naya, for once in your damn life, will you listen to me? Be a coward. *Run.*"

She shook her head. "You don't know the man who is after me. He is not the kind of man who lets loose ends live.

The second I stepped foot on that ship and he caught a whiff of my misdeeds, I was marked for death."

"But you're innocent," Dankirk insisted. "You had nothing to do with this terrorist bullshit."

"Do you think he cares? No, there's no justice up there. It's the same crap we've dealt with here." She smoothed her hands over her head and straightened her shoulders. "I won't put anyone else at risk. If I'm going to die, I may as well go out doing something noble. Look, those weapons are going to get so many innocent people killed. They're going to bring war to The City. I can't let that happen."

"There's no way you're getting into the Sixer stronghold."

"I have to try. Hell," she said sourly, "if I do manage to walk away from this, it's straight to Kovark for me. You know what that means."

Menace knew all right. It meant starvation, beatings and rape.

Dankirk cleared his throat. "I could record a message for Jennie, if you want."

"No," Naya refused gently. "She's got her new life. I'm not about to drag the stinking carcass of our old one into it."

"She's happy. I saw her last week. It was a good thing you did, helping her escape with Josef."

"I'm glad."

Dankirk hesitated. "When I met your man, I thought he—"

She held up her hand. "I can't."

Menace's chest ached at the pain filling her voice.

"Some things are too good be true, huh?" Dankirk remarked.

"Yeah," she said, her voice quavering. "Although, with my track record of being fucked over by the people I love, I should have seen it coming."

It took every last bit of strength and control Menace possessed not to crumple to the ground. She had all but admitted she loved him in the same breath she called him out for betraying and abandoning her.

"I never wanted to be one of the men who let you down." Dankirk said the one thing Menace wished he could say to her.

"I know." She inhaled a cleansing breath and cleared her throat. She spun around and hopped onto the bed. Her determined expression grew larger on the screen until Menace realized she was nearing the video feed. The view wobbled as she punched the ceiling and tore the camera free. Her beautiful tear-stained face filled the screen. "If you want your guns, come and find me, Terror. But you better move fast. I'm probably not going to make it to nightfall."

The satellite feed turned to static. Beside him, Pierce frantically tried to connect with the team on the ground that was supposed to be watching her. He pushed his earbud firmly into place and cupped a hand over his other ear. "What? You're sure?"

"Pierce." Terror spoke his fellow operative's name in a growl.

Pierce shook his head. "She's gone. The team rushed the room the moment they realized she was going to run, but they weren't fast enough. She and her friend went out a window. They tracked down her ID chip in an alley. They swabbed the blood spatter on the wall for DNA but it's obvious that it's hers. She got a sixty-second head start on them and four and a half minutes on us."

Menace rounded on Terror. "What's your gut telling you now, Ter?"

"That I'm going to get back our weapons and annihilate a gunrunning gang by nightfall," he responded matter-of-factly. "Whether she's guilty or innocent, it makes no difference to me."

Menace went numb with the realization that he didn't know this man. "No difference? You dropped an innocent, unarmed woman in a dangerous place and gave her an impossible assignment."

"Impossible? Hardly," Terror scoffed. "You obviously don't know your own wife, Menace. Her record and her history tell me that she's tenacious. With enough motivation, she'll accomplish any task."

"Motivation?"

"You and Hallie?" He gestured to Vicious' wife. "You're Naya's weaknesses. All it took was the threat of putting you in prison and having Hallie arrested and taken away from Vicious to convince Naya to use her considerable skills to our advantage."

Hallie gasped and Menace gaped at Terror. "What the hell is *wrong* with you?"

"Wrong with me?" Terror's voice slashed like a razor. "What the hell is wrong with *you*? Don't you realize we're at war? Every day, I have to make decisions that would make the rest of you piss your pants. Unlike you, I don't have the luxury of rigid principles. I'm charged with protecting our people. Whatever the cost."

Menace was reminded of something Naya once said to him. "Collateral damage."

Terror's hard expression faltered. "I never wanted it to go down like this, Menace. Hurting you was never something I wanted, but it was unavoidable. Naya's ties to these people, whether she was aware of them or not, were too rich a resource not to exploit."

Menace saw red as Terror moved to a console and picked up a radio and earpiece. As he gave instructions for grid searches, Menace tried to suck air into his deflated lungs. The viselike grip on his chest convinced him he was having a heart attack. The knowledge that he'd been so expertly played by Terror cut deep. The fear that Naya, his beautiful, stubborn Naya, might not see tomorrow made him sick.

Pierce approached him. He withdrew something and extended it to Menace. "We'll get her back."

Menace's throat tightened at the sight of the Naya's collar in the other man's hand. He took it from Pierce, running his finger over the blue leather and silver tag. It occurred to Menace that they might be successful in rescuing her, but he would never get her back, not in the way he'd once had her. She would never forgive him.

"I know The City very well," Pierce continued. "I have some contacts there."

"You don't know the people she knows," Hallie interjected, her gentle voice so out of place in the war room. "But I do."

Vicious turned toward her and put both hands on her shoulders. "No."

Hallie shot him a daring look. "Excuse me?"

"I'm not risking you."

"There's no risk, Vicious. Just get me on the ground. I don't have to go near the danger. I only need to talk to a handful of people."

Vicious glanced at Menace. Sympathy flashed in his pale eyes. "Even if I wanted to let you go, Kitten, it's impossible. You heard Orion. He's grounded all flights."

Orion shook his head. "I'm not about to rescind that order. If Naya wasn't the mole on the ship, there's still a traitorous bastard among us. Someone sent that data blast that gave away the position and timing of our weapon shipment. I won't put my pilots in harm's way."

Hope faded within Menace. If he had to, he'd mount a one-man rescue operation, but without a ship to take him to the surface it would be impossible.

"I know this is difficult for you, Menace, but my hands are tied. If the *hazard* were any smaller, I'd be willing to look the other way."

Hope surged within him. Of all the pilots in this end of the star system, Hazard was the only one ballsy enough to steal a ship and take a covert rescue mission to the surface while the threat of a Splinter attack loomed. "I understand, sir."

The admiral nodded and glanced around the room, silently communicating his permission. His gaze lingered on Terror. "I'll give you a reprieve until this issue is resolved. When it's done, my order stands. I want you off my ship and out of my sight."

"Happy to oblige, Admiral."

Menace couldn't believe how cool Terror behaved. The realization that things would never be the same finally started to sink into his thick skull. It wasn't only Naya who he would lose but Terror as well. He finally understood the kind of pain Naya had known when her own blood used and abandoned her. It was the same heart-rending agony that Terror had caused with his callous treatment of Naya.

Forgiving Terror for what he'd done seemed impossible to Menace. He could only hope that Naya's kind heart wouldn't shut him out indefinitely. She'd already proven herself to be a better person than Menace could ever hope to be. Whether she wanted him back or not, Menace would do everything in his power to save her. He'd promised to protect and fight for her. He intended to keep that promise.

Chapter Eighteen

"**Y**OU WANT ME to do *what*?"

Naya ignored Danny's outburst and continued to rifle through the box of clothing in the safe house bedroom. "I want you to go to your communications guy and wait for a message from Hallie."

"Why the hell would I do that? She's one of them."

Naya sat back on her heels and glared at Dankirk. "She most definitely is not. I'm sure she got my message by now. I also know that Terror is probably shitting bricks trying to track me down. She's his best chance at finding me. If she thinks she can help me, she'll do it. So you go back to your com man and wait."

"For what?" Dankirk grabbed the first-aid kit and sat down on the edge of the small bed. "Give me your wrist. You're bleeding again."

"Well maybe you shouldn't have jabbed your knife four inches into my arm!" Her wrist throbbed incessantly. Her friend's surgical skills were sorely lacking but he'd gotten the job done.

"I told you I didn't know what I was doing." He unwrapped her arm and applied another wad of thick gauze on top of the already soaked dressing. Like her, he'd learned enough first aid to know that removing the bottom layer of a dressing and dislodging the clotted blood was a no-no. "We need to get you some antibiotics."

"Why? I'm probably going to be dead by sunrise."

"Don't say that," he admonished. "You're going to make it out of this."

"And do what?" She'd been asking herself the same thing. The one thing she wanted she couldn't have any-more.

"Look, I know you loved him, but he turned his back on you."

The need to defend Menace overwhelmed her. "You don't know him. You don't know Terror either." All the things she had been thinking during the long flight to Calyx poured of her mouth. "I don't think he willingly gave me up. I think Terror played us both. Menace is so damn decent he probably believed that lawyers and judges would sort this out. He believes Terror is his friend. He has no idea what that man is really like."

"Maybe," Danny said with an unhappy grumble. "It doesn't really matter now. You can't go back to that world. In a few months, you won't even remember him anymore."

She didn't think that was possible. What she'd shared with Menace eclipsed anything she'd ever felt for any other man. She didn't know if her heart would ever recover from this one.

"Let me come with you," Danny pleaded as he wrapped her arm. "I can help you."

She shook her head. "You can help me more by getting a message to Hallie. She needs to know where they take me so the Harcos team that comes to retrieve me can get their hands on the weapons, the Sixers and maybe even the Splinter cell. If Terror gets what he wants, he'll leave Hallie and Menace alone."

Dankirk put up both hands. "Wait. Back up. Who is going to take you where?"

She rolled her eyes. "The Sixers, Danny! Finding their headquarters is going to be impossible. *You* don't even know where it is. Anyone who does know sure as heck isn't going to tell us. The only way to get to their stronghold is to have them drag me right into it."

"So what? You're going let them take you?"

"I'm not going to give them a choice. I'm going to make the rounds of the underground and drop crumbs. They'll have to come get me so they can question me. They'll want to pump me for information before they finish me off."

Dankirk grimaced. "It's a big risk, Naya. They might just walk up to you and pop you right on the street."

She swallowed hard. "They might."

"I'll put my eyes and ears on you but I'll tell them to stay back. They won't lose you. You better hope Hallie comes through."

"She will." Naya didn't doubt her new friend for a moment. If Hallie could help, she would.

"If those sky warriors engage the Sixer crew, the distraction ought to buy you some time to escape. It won't be much time but it's a chance."

"If I get an opportunity, I'll take it," Naya promised. "I'd love to see my twentyfourth birthday next month, but it's out of my hands."

Her arm patched up and her plan laid out, Naya dug through the secondhand clothing until she found an outfit. She stripped down to her undies and bra and hopped into the loose-fitting cargo pants and a blue-and-white-flannel shirt. An old belt helped keep her pants in place. She stuffed her feet in a pair of slightly too-large men's boots and shrugged into a brown jacket with an even darker hood. Winter had come a few weeks early to Calyx. She needed to stay warm.

"Here." Dankirk thrust a sheathed knife and small pistol into her hands. "You'll need these."

"Thanks." She slipped the knife into her boot and tucked the gun into the back of her waistband.

"My offer still stands, Naya. You can come with me and we'll go to the colonies. You can leave all this behind."

"I can't." She turned him down gently. "If it was just about me, I'd be tempted to say yes. I can't let Hallie or Menace get hurt."

"Even though he hurt you?"

Naya sighed. "It's not that simple, Danny. You can't possibly understand the kind of pressure Terror exerts. It's not like the secret police here. This guy—he's unfeeling. He's a monster. He doesn't care who gets hurt so long as he accomplishes his mission. I know what he did to make me come here and attempt this. I can only imagine how he twisted Menace's arm."

He looked as though he wanted to argue with her but didn't. Instead he hugged her tightly. "Good luck, Naya. Be safe."

She lingered in her friend's embrace, enjoying the comfort of another person's heat and strength. His friendship and love bolstered her courage. Pulling back, she cleared her throat. "I'll see you soon."

Naya fled the safe house through a side door. She breathed in the cold, crisp winter air. She'd gotten so used to the climate-controlled interiors of the *Valiant* that the chilly wind burning her cheeks and nose was something of a novelty. She burrowed down a little deeper into the brown coat and pushed her hands into the pockets.

Head down, she traversed the dirty streets in search of the bars, pawnshops and secret gambling dens where the kind of lowlifes she needed were sure to be found. She made sure to talk loudly and stupidly at every stop. She wanted people to hear her asking for a place to buy a gun or that she was looking for work of the smuggling variety. She wanted a big, honking sign on her back that said "kidnap me!"

She stopped for lunch midafternoon. The food carts that lined the retail sector of the city drew her closer. Danny had given her some money to tide her over. It was more than enough to buy a hot meal and a drink. She found a discarded cable spool and joined the handful of day laborers gathered there to eat. She savored every bite of the sloppy, spicy sandwich, fully aware it might be her last meal.

Her gaze moved around the bustling sector. A series of paper advertisements plastered on the crumbling walls caught her eye. The shock of recognizing an old acquaintance arced through her. Elladee, a fellow homeless child and orphan, had been part of Dankirk's pack of street urchins.

Even back then, Ella had been strikingly beautiful. Naya couldn't believe where that gorgeous face had gotten her. Apparently she'd risen from humble beginnings to find a career as a designer's muse. Naya was happy to see someone had escaped that hellish existence.

She finished her meal and drank the last of her tea. Naya scanned the area while she dumped her trash. The sensation of being watched had grown stronger. She'd spotted one of Danny's tails earlier but had lost track of her in the crowd. This felt different. No doubt the Sixers or maybe even the Splinter cell they worked with had gotten wind of her.

Flipping up the hood on her coat, Naya hugged her arms across her chest and started walking again. Her heartbeat fluttered wildly. She made a split-second decision to take a less crowded side street, knowing full well she was probably going to be accosted. She said a silent prayer that they wouldn't try to knock her out with a club of some kind. Nothing like a head injury to slow her down when the seconds counted…

It seemed the universe heard her plea and decided to do her a solid. She heard the rushing footsteps but didn't try to outrun them. Before she could turn around, two arms grabbed her around the waist. She threw back both elbows and hit her mark. Her attacker grunted but got the upper hand by smashing a wet cloth to her face. The sicklysweet scent invaded her burning nostrils. Her body went slack but she fought the urge to black out.

Her assailant turned her in his arms. Her sleepy eyes

widened briefly at the sight of the familiar face before she slipped into an unconscious state. *Nattie.*

When she woke, her head pounded so hard it made her nauseous. She rolled onto her side, wincing as cold, unyielding stone pressed into her flesh, and pushed up onto her hands and knees. The urge to vomit was too strong to deny. She retched pitifully onto the dirty stone floor. So much for her last meal…

"Here, pet." Nattie's familiar voice filtered through her dry-heaving. "Drink this."

Still groggy and unsteady, Naya crawled away from the mess she'd made and tried to adjust her hazy vision. She was in a dank cell. Her brother crouched on the other side of the bars and wiggled a bottle of water at her. "Nattie?"

"I think I hit you with too much of the sleepy juice," he said with an apologetic smile. "You'll be fine though."

Limbs trembling, she made her way across the cell to the bars and flopped down on her butt. Her nose burned so badly. She rubbed her forehead. "Why did you do that to me?"

He pressed the water into her hands. "Why did you come back?"

She fought with the lid and finally managed to twist it open. "You know why."

He sighed heavily. "It won't change anything."

Naya swished a mouthful of water and spit it into the corner. She gulped a few swallows of the expensive purified water and eased the pain in her throat. Her vision started to clear and she got her first good look at her brother. He looked even worse than the photograph she'd seen. Something had happened to his right eye. The iris was milky-gray. Red streaks marred the sclera. The pockmarks on his face were even deeper and harsher. His teeth were brown nubs in spots.

"Hell, Nattie." She reached through the bars and gripped his hand. "When did you start using Impulse?"

He glanced away from her. "After Sindee died."

"Sindee is dead? How?"

"A new strain of the cough got her in Safe Harbor," he said. "It came off one of the sky warrior ships. They took too long giving the treatment to the hospitals in the colonies."

She stroked his hand. "I'm so sorry, Nattie."

He shrugged, the movement twitchy and jerky. "It was a long time ago."

"That doesn't mean it hurts any less," she countered.

"Is that how you feel about me taking your money?"

Her belly lurched as the pain of his betrayal became fresh again. "Sometimes," she admitted.

"It was wrong of me to do that. I know what you risked and how hard you worked to get that money together. I should have taken you with me."

She sighed. "It was a long time ago, Nattie. We can't change what happened."

He didn't say anything. Instead he pointed to the ceiling. "They told me you got taken by one of the sky warriors."

She nodded. "His name is Menace."

"Menace?" he repeated with a laugh. "Not exactly warm and fuzzy."

"No," she agreed with a smile.

"Do you love him?"

"It's complicated," she answered honestly. "And what I feel doesn't matter. We're not together anymore."

"But you're doing his bidding," Nattie said and scratched at a phantom bug on his neck.

"I'm not doing his bidding. It's another man who sent me here. A very, very dangerous man," she insisted. "You don't want to be here when he comes."

Regret and sadness flashed across his good eye. "I don't have anywhere else to go, pet."

Even though Nattie had hurt her so much, she couldn't shake the need to gather him close. He'd always been so weak and so easily manipulated. It was no wonder he'd ended up in this position. "You could come with me."

He seemed to be considering her offer. Eventually he shook his head. "Where you're going, I'm not keen to follow. Come on." He rose slowly, using the bars for support. "Mama wants to see you."

Not exactly thrilled by the thought of her impending family reunion, Naya took her sweet time climbing to her feet. She took another drink of water. Shivering with cold, she finally realized they'd taken her coat and pistol. A flex of her ankle told her the knife was gone too.

Defenseless, she stood back as Nattie opened the door to her cell. He touched the gun holstered on his hip. "Don't make me use this, Naya."

"I won't." With his twitchiness, she didn't make any sudden movements. Being shot by Nattie wasn't on her bucket list. Side by side with her brother, Naya walked through a maze of hallways. The pungent scent of fuel and chemicals filled her nose. "Is this an old manufacturing plant?"

Nattie glanced at her. "They used to make batteries here before they got that newfangled solar power plant set up across town. The size and location makes it perfect for our needs. Besides, with all the toxic fumes and the dump site out back, no one wants to come here to nose around."

Naya tried not to dwell on the effect all those toxic fumes were having on her right now. She could almost feel her brain cells melting.

They passed through a set of double doors and entered the main manufacturing space of the warehouse. Most of the equipment had been cleared. A living space had been set up in one section and small mess hall in another. Dozens of hard-looking men and women stopped what they were doing to watch her.

One entire side of the room was taken up by stacks of crates. They bore the stamp of the central government and were labeled as perishables. Her brain pieced together the information. There weren't any food shortages and the Harcos treaties weren't demanding too high quotas. No, some corrupt bastard in the government was selling food supplies to the Sixers.

"It's a good deal," Nattie said, his gaze moving over the floor-to-ceiling stacks of food. "We get a wholesale price. Mama sells it to the Splinter guys for three or four times as much as we paid. They need supplies so badly they'll pay anything. They'll even do food-for-gun deals. You should see the shit they hijacked last night and traded us this morning!"

"So you get your hands on weapons and cash while the Splinter cell gets to agitate the people of Calyx," Naya murmured.

"You always were the smart one."

Naya's gut clenched at the sound of her mother's husky voice. The memories of her childhood, most of them painful and tear-ridden, flooded back. She turned slowly to face the woman who had abandoned her. Decked out like a low-rent general, her mother commanded the attention of every eye in the place.

"Hello, Mama."

She didn't reply. Instead she walked a slow circle around Naya. "You turned out prettier than I'd imagined. With your daddy's genes, I was sure you'd look like someone beat you with the ugly stick by now."

Naya let the insult roll right off her back. Unable to help herself, she gestured to her own cheek. "The scar's a nice look for you. Makes you look powerful."

"Keep it up," her mother warned. "I haven't forgotten how easy it was to make you cry. I've still got my strap."

Naya's jaw tightened. "You don't scare me anymore."

"I should. Who do you think controls this city? It sure as hell ain't the government. It's me." She touched her chest. "Me and my crew and my guns."

"You and your crew and your guns are in big trouble. The Harcos forces know you're working with the Splinter cell here on Calyx. They don't care if they get their hands on you or the Splinters. They just want their weapons."

Her mother laughed. "Honey baby, they've been trying

to pin me down for years. They haven't succeeded yet."

"I found you in half a day," Naya snapped. "You have no idea what kind of pain these people are willing to inflict to get their answers. All it takes is one set of loose lips and your operation is toast."

"Let them come." Her mother looked gleeful. "It will accelerate our plans but we're ready. People are already on edge because of the food shortages and the riots. All it will take is one spark and this populace will rise up."

"And what? You'll be right there to supply them with weapons?"

"And food," her mother gestured to the crates. "The easiest way to win hearts and minds is to give them what they need."

"You are insane. This plan isn't going to work. It's just going to get a lot of people killed." Naya pointed to a man decked out in stolen Harcos weapons. "Look, those weapons are fine for close-quarters combat but the sky warriors control the high ground. They have ships and bombs and weapons we can't even imagine. If they think they've lost this city to enemy control, they will destroy this whole damn place."

"Let them." Her mother shrugged cruelly. "I'll be long gone. Can you imagine the kind of sales volume I'll have then? Every backward country bumpkin on this planet will want one of my weapons."

Naya's stomach lurched. The Splinter cell and her mother's Sixer crew had it all mapped out. The cost in human lives was nothing compared to the profits they could expect. "You're a monster."

"Oh, sugar baby, don't look so sad." Her mother drew the weapon from her thigh holster. "You won't be around to see any of that."

Before Naya could react, her mother fired three rounds. The impact registered in her brain before the searing pain ripping through her abdomen hit. Hands clutching her stomach, Naya stumbled backward. Rich, dark blood spilled into her hands. She stared at the crimson fluid, her brain on the fritz from the shock and trauma of actually being shot. Even when meting out death, her mother had chosen the cruelty of a slow, painful demise over the mercy of a plasma weapon.

"Naya!" Nattie rushed to her aid, cradling her body as she crumpled to the floor. He put a hand to her face. "Mama! Why? You said you were going to give her to one of the Splinter men."

"You think I'm going to hand them a girl who has intel on us and our enemies? Grow up, Nattie!" Their mother tossed a gun toward him. "Drag her into the middle of the floor and leave her there. The rest of you? Get ready. They're coming."

★   ★   ★

MENACE NERVOUSLY CHEWED his gum while Cipher got his mini-drones operational. Once they'd touched down outside The City, Hallie had come through like a champ. She'd made contact with a man who quickly put her in touch with Dankirk. Naya's friend had been waiting for Hallie's call. Menace had been sick with worry as the man relayed Naya's plans.

In that moment, he'd understood why Terror had been so tempted to use her. She was tenacious—and reckless. He'd never had such a strong urge to swat her backside. She had to learn that her life was precious and worth protecting. Once she was safely at his side, he intended to do everything in his power to convince her that she was very much loved and needed.

From the staging point, Menace had a good view of the dilapidated factory. Their ship's environmental sensors had gone haywire as Hazard brought them in for a stealth and fully cloaked landing. It seemed the place had been a factory at one point. Most of the toxic chemicals and byproducts were still onsite. The sooner they got Naya out of there the better.

His earbud clicked twice, alerting him that Pierce, their strike team leader, was coming on the line. He stopped chewing and listened.

"Cipher tells me we'll have drone feeds within the next sixty seconds. The charges are set at the entry points. Once recon is complete, we make entry on my mark."

Menace glanced to his left where Raze and Venom had taken up their positions. Hazard crouched down just to his right. The pilot hadn't been hard to convince to take the dangerous mission. Pierce, two members of the Shadow Force and the other three members of the SRU team were ready to breach the old factory from another angle. Terror had remained behind on the *Valiant* to supervise from his war room. It was no secret that no one wanted to go into battle with him right now.

Menace pushed his tactical glasses into place. The polarized lenses displayed a realtime feed from Cipher's drones. He glanced away from the picture, not at all interested in the swooping turns the devices were making.

But when a drone entered through a broken window and provided a full view of the main factory floor, he grew very interested. Menace spotted the open barracks-style housing section. The stacks of crates stamped *perishable* interested him the most. Naya's stories of food shortages and riots came to mind. Was this where all that food was going?

The silent drone began to slowly shift its view. There, finally, Naya came into view. She wore strange men's clothing. Her gait seemed off to him. Had she been drugged or hit on the head?

As if reading his mind, Cipher came across the radio. "Target in sight. Will put medical on standby for possible head injury or sedative exposure. Acquiring audio feed in ten, nine, eight…"

Menace's earbud crackled. A moment later, Naya's sweet voice filled his ear. "While the Splinter cell gets to agitate the people of Calyx."

A woman dressed in men's tactical gear came into view. He recognized her from the photos Terror had shown him. *Turn around.* He silently urged Naya to see the woman coming up behind her.

"You always were the smart one."

Naya stiffened. She faced her mother slowly. "Hello, Mama."

His gut clenched as the woman took her time studying Naya. He waited to see what she would say to her daughter.

"You turned out prettier than I'd imagined. With your daddy's genes, I was sure you'd look like someone beat you with the ugly stick by now."

He spotted the tic in Naya's jaw. *No, sweetheart, don't poke the bear.*

Naya pointed to her flawless cheek. "The scar's a nice look for you. Makes you look powerful."

"Shit," Menace whispered. She simply couldn't stop those smart-ass remarks from leaving her mouth.

"Counting twenty-seven armed on the main floor," Cipher informed. "I read a dozen heat signals in other portions of the factory. Will engage and separate enemy with drone missiles on command's mark."

"Affirmative," Pierce answered.

Down on the factory floor, Naya and her mother continued to face off. He'd missed some of their conversation. He was sure it had been a doozy.

Her mother grinned. "Let them come. It will accelerate our plans but we're ready. People are already on edge because of the food shortages and the riots. All it will take is one spark and this populace will rise up."

The whole evil plan came to light. Menace had to admit it was a tried-and-true method for fomenting revolution.

"And what?" Naya shouted. "You'll be right there to supply them with weapons?"

"And food. The easiest way to win hearts and minds is to give them what they need."

Naya glared at her mother. "You are insane. This plan isn't going to work. It's just going to get a lot of people killed. Look, those weapons are fine for close-quarters combat, but the sky warriors control the high ground. They have ships and bombs and weapons—"

"Prepare to breach." Pierce interrupted the feed. "Cipher, give us a sixty-second countdown."

"Yes, sir. Breaching in sixty seconds."

"Can you imagine the kind of sales volume I'll have then?" Naya's mother asked. "Every backward country bumpkin on this planet will want one of my weapons." Naya's shoulders slumped. "You're a monster."

"Breaching in forty-five."

"Oh, sugar baby, don't look so sad."

Menace's heart skipped two beats as the other woman raised her weapon and aimed right at Naya. Before he could even shout the word no, Naya took three to the stomach. The world went still around him. He couldn't breathe. He couldn't think. He choked on his gum as his instinctive swallow pulled it down his throat. Awash in horror, Menace watched Naya fall backward into her brother's thin arms.

Blood soaked her shirt and spilled onto her hands. He'd seen enough stomach wounds to know that she didn't have much time. They had to get to her. Now.

"Breach! Move! Move!" Pierce shouted the order. "Cipher, blow that back room."

On autopilot, Menace ran forward with his team. Small, controlled explosions rocked the facility. Tunnel vision took hold. His only thought was of reaching Naya in time. The reality that she could die alone clawed at him. If she died without knowing how much he loved her, Menace wouldn't be able to live with himself. It would be too cruel for her to leave this world without knowing the warmth of his love.

Two explosions Pierce's men had set took out the doors and granted them access to the building. They hit the factory hard and fast. The sight of Naya in a pool of blood in the center of the floor made his heart leap into his throat. Bloody streaks marked the path she had been dragged. Rapid gunfire and plasma bursts rocketed over her writhing, hemorrhaging body.

Raze and Venom were pinned down on one side of the room. Hazard had a shield with him but he was too far back. Every time he took a step, he drew heavy fire. Frantic, Menace looked around for something, anything, to use as a shield so he could pull her out of harm's way.

"Hang on, Menace. I'm coming for you."

The shock of hearing Terror's voice in his ear left him momentarily stunned. In another instant, the Shadow Force operative was at his side with a heavy shield. Terror grabbed his arm. "Let's move."

He didn't even ask how Terror had gotten there. He didn't care. This was his only chance to save Naya. He was grasping it with both hands.

Bullets and plasma bursts ricocheted off the heavy-duty and specially coated shield. They kept low and moved quickly. Pierce shouted commands over the radio, ordering Venom into a sniper position. Whether he would get there in time to help Menace and Terror extricate Naya was anyone's guess.

Menace dropped to his knees next to Naya. Her eyes widened at the sight of him. He shook his head. "Don't talk.

Conserve your energy."

"We don't have much time, Menace. Work quickly," Terror grunted as he kept the shield in place, shifting it ever so slightly to provide the most coverage for Naya.

Menace grabbed a trauma dressing from the med kit strapped to his thigh and pressed it hard to her belly. She cried out in pain. Blood dribbled from the corner of her mouth. "Just hold on, sweetheart."

She gripped his wrist. "I'm sorry. I should have told you but—"

"Don't," he cut her off before she could finish the apology. "None of that matters now." He caressed her face. "I love you, Naya. I love you. Just focus on that, sweetheart."

Her pained, panicked expression softened. "I love you too."

"Touching as this is, we need to move." Terror glanced over his shoulder and frowned at them. "Get her up, Menace."

Even though he worried lifting her would cause even more damage to her internal organs, there was no other choice. If they stayed here, she was going to die. She screamed in pain as he gathered her in his arms. Her hot, slick blood coated his hands and soaked his uniform. The bitter scent of it made his stomach churn.

With Terror at his back, Menace ran toward their team, who provided constant suppressive fire. Up above, Venom picked off the enemy one by one. Finally unpinned, Hazard rushed out to join Terror with another shield, providing enough coverage to fully protect Naya's wounded body. Bullets whizzed and snapped by them, but the two men ran them out of the factory.

A second ship, this one a so-called dart, often used to evacuate medical casualties, waited near the ship Menace and the team had used. Was that how Terror had gotten to the surface? Even though the dart could make the surface-to-*Valiant* trip in less than an hour, it was still too much time for Naya.

Hallie came running out of the bigger ship where she'd been waiting with Cipher. Her pale face said it all. Two medics ran out of the dart and hurried to assess Naya's injuries. Menace carefully placed her on the stretcher. Unconscious now, she was barely breathing.

"Take the dart, Menace," Terror urged. "Get her to the *Mercy*. She won't make it to the *Valiant* in this shape. The medical installation is still in lower orbit. It's fifteen minutes tops."

Menace nodded and rushed after the two medics who carted her to the safety of the dart. Inside, the pilot was already prepared to take off and was in the process of radioing the installation to let them know a critical patient was incoming. Both medics attached tether cords hooked to harnesses on their jumpsuits to clips dangling from the ceiling to minimize their jostling and the effect of the upcoming gravity loss as they worked. The second her stretcher was secured, the pilot lifted off and began the rough, fast ascent.

One of the medics pushed Menace into a chair to get him out of the way. As he buckled his safety belts, he stared at Naya's limp body. Blood poured onto the floor. Vents strategically placed under the stretcher clamps drained it away so the medics had a safe working space.

They hooked her up to various monitoring devices, stuck her with multiple IVs and pumped her full of medications. She was intubated and placed on a ventilator. Trauma dressings were soaked with synthesized clotting preparations to stem the massive blood loss. Plasma and units of blood were dispensed via the overhead med box. It seemed that as fast as they pushed it into her, it ran out onto the floor.

Needing to feel her, Menace reached out and grabbed her cold hand. Holding it tight, he dropped his head. For the first time since childhood, he prayed.

Chapter Nineteen

HOURS LATER, MENACE sat in the waiting room outside the surgical unit on the medical installation *Mercy*. Naya had been much too fragile to move to the *Valiant*. Luckily the trauma surgeons on board were fresh from the front lines and highly skilled. He was glad her life was in their capable hands.

The papery-thin blue scrubs he'd been given by one of the medics felt alien against his skin. On the chair next to him sat his pile of weapons and a bright-orange biohazard bag holding his soiled uniform. They kept the place uncommonly cold. He blamed his trembling limbs on that.

The sound of heavy boots squeaking on the highly polished floor caught his attention. He glanced to his left and spotted Vicious and Hallie walking toward him. He didn't have the strength to stand. Vicious grabbed the weapons and biohazard bag from the seat and moved them one spot down before sitting. With a heavy sigh, he stretched out his legs and leaned back in his chair.

Hallie took the empty space on his other side. Always so kind and gentle, she grasped his hand in both of hers. She didn't ask any questions or try to start a conversation. She seemed to understand that he couldn't talk right now. What he needed was support.

The minutes ticked by as they sat in companionable silence. An hour or so after arriving, Vicious rose from his seat and disappeared down an adjacent corridor. He returned with a bottle of rehydrating sports drink and two energy bars. Vicious thrust them into his hands. "Eat this, Menace. You need your strength."

He didn't argue. Unwrapping the energy bar, he noticed the red stains on his cuticles and in his calluses. Naya's blood had marked his skin. No amount of scrubbing in the hospital bathroom had been able to wash it away.

Hallie must have noticed him staring at them. "I'll go ask one of the medics for some peroxide wipes."

She left him alone with Vicious. Menace bit the bar and drank some of the slightly tart drink. He hated the berry-flavored version but didn't let it stop him from devouring the snack. Vicious had been right to insist he eat something. Naya was going to need him to be strong for her.

"I'm sorry, Menace." Vicious broke the silence finally. "This shouldn't have happened. I should have done more to protect you and your wife."

Menace stuffed the empty wrappers into the drink bottle and screwed on the cap. "This wasn't your fault, Vicious."

"Wasn't it? I should have found a way to rein in Terror."

"After seeing Terror in action, I don't think that's possible. He may be beyond restraint."

Vicious wiped both hands down his face. "I don't know when it got so complicated."

Menace didn't either. He took aim at the garbage receptacle in the corner and shot the bottle toward it. It hit the rim and bounced into the can with a satisfying *thunk*.

Hallie rounded the corner with two familiar faces in tow. Venom and Cipher followed her to the seating area. She handed Menace the disposable wipes, started to sit but then counted the open seats. Realizing there weren't enough, she glanced at Vicious, who opened his arms and patted his lap. Vicious slid his arm around her waist when she perched on there. His lips brushed her temple. The sight of the couple sharing a tender moment gutted Menace.

Venom sat in the spot Hallie had once occupied. He hesitated before asking, "How is she?"

Menace shook his head. "I don't know."

Venom squeezed his arm. "The surgeons on this installation are amazing. She'll be fine, Menace."

He wished fine had a more concrete definition. The shots she'd taken had caused a great deal of damage. Not wanting to think about the awful possibilities, he changed the subject. "Did you get the guns?"

Venom's face showed surprise. "Menace, we don't have to talk about the mission. Let's just focus on Naya's recovery."

"She almost died trying to complete Terror's mission. I want to know if she succeeded."

"She did," Venom assured him. "We got the weapons cache and a huge amount of intel on the Splinter cell on Calyx. They've already grabbed three of them by instituting a planet-wide dragnet. One Splinter ship tried to flee the surface when they got wind of our raid on the factory. We snatched them up and took them in for questioning. Dankirk called in his friends from the free press to photograph the food stockpile and disseminate the information to the people of Calyx."

"She did a great deal of good today," Cipher said. "Her bravery saved a lot of innocent lives."

Menace supposed that was some small consolation. "Her mother?"

Venom shook his head. "Pierce tagged her in the arm and chest but she managed to escape. We'll find her. With those injuries, she can't have gone far."

"And her brother?"

"Dead," Venom said. "He got hit with friendly fire. Hazard swears he saw the mother pop him but who knows."

Menace wouldn't put it past the old broad. "She probably considered him a loose end."

"With that drug problem? He would have been easy to interrogate. A promise of Impulse and he'd sing like a bird," Venom replied.

"His body?" Menace hated to ask the gruesome question but it had to be done.

"We brought him back with us. He's in storage in the mortuary. I wasn't sure if Naya would want to bury him properly."

"She will." Menace couldn't imagine Naya doing anything less. No matter how badly her brother had treated her, he was still her family.

"I thought you would want this back." Cipher held out Naya's red notebook. "I've already given a decoded copy to the Shadow Force unit."

Menace grasped the small book and ran his finger over the red leather. Protecting her privacy seemed a moot point now. "What was in it?"

"Not what Terror expected," Cipher answered honestly. "It was her record of favors owed and debts repaid. She kept inventories of her acquaintances. Just initials," he explained, "but tied to their occupations. I think it was her way of knowing who could help the people who came to her with various needs. The back section was filled with contact information for various shops and warehouses in Connor's Run and The City."

Regret gripped him. "I should have let you decipher it the night it came into my possession."

"Hey," Cipher said gently, "you couldn't have possibly known what was going to happen. You did the right thing respecting your wife's right to privacy."

"A lot of good it did her," Menace grumbled. His gaze swept the lobby and settled on a surgeon coming toward them. His heart stuttered and he leapt to his feet. Hands clammy, he fisted them at his sides—and waited.

The doctor nodded at the crowd. He stopped in front of Menace and smiled. "She came through the repairs beautifully."

All around him, there were sighs of relief. Vicious clapped him hard on the back.

The surgeon gestured in the direction he'd come. "If you'd like to come with me, Menace, I can let you see her. We'll move her out of recovery into a private room in a few hours."

Menace glanced at his friends. Vicious sent him an encouraging smile. "Go. We'll be here if you need us."

In lockstep with the doctor, Menace walked to the double doors leading to the surgical unit. Once they were inside and away from his friends, the surgeon began to give him more facts.

"It was touch-and-go in the beginning. We were able to gain control of the bleeding and repair all of her injuries. She responded well to treatment in the operating room. We're holding back on administering accelerated healing drugs. I worry that the shock to her fragile and very small system might be too much at this point. We hope to begin a slow, steady infusion in the next two or three days."

"Whatever you think is best," Menace croaked, his voice thick with worry. He glanced around the recovery ward. The rooms were large and filled with beeping, hissing machines. Medics sat at computer consoles outside each room and monitored their patients' vital signs.

The surgeon stopped outside a room. He gripped Menace's shoulder. "You should know that one of her ovaries was damaged beyond repair. We were forced to remove it and the attached fallopian tube. Her uterine artery suffered a nick, but we're extremely confident in its repair. She will be able to have children, possibly requiring the help of some medical intervention, but not for some time."

Numbness spread through his chest. His stomach lurched painfully. How was he going to tell Naya? Even though she hadn't wanted to start a family immediately, she'd made it clear she wanted children. The thought of her losing out on that dream because of this clusterfuck sickened him.

"I've recommended that she be fitted for a contracep-tive device before she's discharged. If she chooses to stay," the surgeon amended. "I understand that her status is still in question?"

Menace's jaw hardened. "Yes."

The surgeon didn't ask him to elaborate on the situa-tion. Instead he left Menace alone. Reluctant to see Naya's battered body, he entered the hospital room with some hesitancy. She looked so small and pale in the big bed. Tubes and wires snaked out of her limbs and mouth. A ventilator breathed for her while they kept her in a medical coma to heal.

He made his way to the chair next to her bed. Desper-ate to feel the life coursing through her, he reached for her hand and softly stroked her skin. His fingertips drifted to the underside of her wrist. He felt her reassuring pulse. For the first time since rescuing her, he believed she would live.

Touching his forehead to the bed, Menace let his tense muscles relax. He tried not to let any of the troubling what-ifs invade his mind. Right now he could only focus on sending her the most positive healing thoughts. He prayed that she could feel his love wrapping around and cradling her broken body.

The medics and doctors who came in and out of the room did their best not to disturb him. They adjusted her medications and refilled her IV fluids. When she'd proven stable enough to move to a private room, the switch was made quickly and efficiently. His confidence in the medical team on the *Mercy* grew exponentially.

Half an hour after settling her into a private room, Menace heard a knock on the door. Hallie poked her head inside. "May I come in, Menace?"

He nodded. "Please."

She stood at the end of Naya's bed and stared at her friend. He read the sadness on her face. "Gosh, this brings back memories."

Menace chuckled softly. "Except you were the one in the bed that time."

"Yeah." She came closer and rubbed his upper back. "Look, she's going to be sedated for a day or two. She's stable and doing well. Why don't you go back to the *Valiant*? You can take a shower, get a hot meal and pack a bag. Take a nap if you want. I'm happy to stay here with her until you return."

If anyone else had made the offer, he would have turned it down. Knowing that Naya shared such a strong bond with Hallie made it easier to accept. "Thank you, Hallie."

Menace kissed Naya's forehead and smoothed some of her hair out of the way. He lowered his mouth to her ear. "I love you."

Out in the hallway, Menace found Venom, Raze and Vicious waiting for him. Vicious gestured to the closed door. "Raze has agreed to stay here in case Hallie needs something or you need to be reached."

"And you and Venom?"

"We're coming with you to settle a score." Vicious' tense features said it all. "We've had the sparring room cleared. Terror is waiting for you. Pierce and Torment will stand with him. Terror agrees the old way is the only way."

Though brutal and violent, the Harcos way of settling feuds worked. Bloodlust exploded within Menace. By the time he was finished with him, Terror would need a bed onboard the *Mercy*.

WITH A LONG, slow inhale, Naya surfaced from the heavy weight of sleep. She gazed at the strange silver ceiling for a few seconds before finally remembering where she was. She'd been in and out all day, never able to stay awake for longer than a minute or two before being dragged back down into the warm embrace of sleep.

Her brain worked overtime to piece together all the clues. She'd been shot—by her mother. That memory was crystal clear. She remembered the full-on assault and the firefight. Menace came to her rescue—with Terror of all people! The wonderful sensation of Menace's fingertips gliding over her face and his deep, husky voice confessing his love for her spilled over Naya like sunshine.

He loves me. He came for me.

Warmed by that thought, she glanced around the room. She was in a hospital of some kind. A dull ache throbbed through her entire body, but there wasn't any real pain. The machines beeping and swooshing all around her probably had something to do with that.

Her gaze fell to her bedside where she discovered Menace in a cramped chair. He had his long legs stretched in front of him but held her hand. Head tilted back at a terrible angle, he snored. The sound brought a smile to her face, but the sight of his right arm and hand in a heavy cast made her frown. She noticed the bruises on his face and neck.

Movement near the doorway drew her gaze. Terror stepped out of the shadows. Her heart monitor beeped wildly as she laid eyes on her tormentor.

"Relax," he said gently. "I'm not here to finish you off."

"Like I believe that," she snapped back, her voice gravelly and throat sore. Now that he was fully illuminated, Naya saw the awful bruising on his face. His nose was broken and taped. One of his hands was in a brace. He leaned all his weight on his right foot because the left was in a cast. She spotted the crutches leaning against the wall.

She looked at Menace and then back at Terror. "Did he beat you up?"

"There was no other way to restore my honor and pay for what I did to you. I'm sorry by the way. For almost killing you," he added lightly.

She pursed her lips. "Apology not accepted, Terror."

He chuckled. "I didn't think you'd be an easy sell." More seriously, he said, "You'll be happy to know I'm leaving the *Valiant*. I think it's best for everyone involved if I find a new home base for my operations."

Good fucking riddance. She gestured to her broken body. "You'll understand if don't make it to your going-away party."

He smiled, the subtle curve to his mouth softening his harsh face the smallest bit.

"No offense taken."

Still irritated with him, she asked, "Did you get what

you needed?"

"I did. Your actions saved the lives of countless citizens of Calyx and members of the Harcos forces. It won't be forgotten." He glanced at Menace. "I didn't give him any choice when it came to you. He thought he was helping you by giving me permission to interrogate you. He believed that if he showed cooperation I would remember our friendship and not unleash hell on you."

"I figured as much." Naya narrowed her eyes at him. "After the way you twisted my arm, I could only imagine what you'd done to him."

"That's my job," he answered simply. "Menace loves you, Naya. In my line of work, I see how very rare it is for two people to share what you have. After all you've been through together, you'd be a fool to let him go now."

Her eyebrows shot up at Terror's relationship advice. Maybe it was the meds making her hallucinate, but she actually thought it was sound advice.

"Besides," Terror said with an evil grin, "think of the ammunition you'll have to use against him the next time the two of you have a domestic dispute. You'll win every fight from now until the end of time."

Naya groaned. "Really, Terror?"

He laughed. "What? Is it too soon for the ammunition joke?"

"You are such an asshole."

"I know." He grabbed a small red envelope from the rolling tray near the door. Hobbling, he brought it to her. "I thought you two would want this as soon as it came through the office."

She grasped the envelope. "What is it?"

"Open it when I'm gone and when he's awake. I'm sure he'll want to experience the good news with you. Oh and you should be receiving your settlement offer in the next few days."

"Settlement offer?"

"We did almost kill you after wrongfully accusing you of terrorism," he pointed out. "I wouldn't be surprised if it's a rather large sum." He considered her for a moment. "Maybe you could use the money to fund that little import-and-export business you had in mind."

Naya gawked at the Shadow Force operative. "How the hell—"

"It's my business to know everything that happens on the *Valiant*." Then, with a smirk, he added, "Plus, Hallie has the biggest mouth when it comes to bragging on her friends."

She made a mental note to thump Hallie the next time she saw her.

Limping, Terror made his way to the door and grabbed his crutches. He waved his hand in front of the frame. Pausing in front of the open door, he looked back at her. "You know, if you decide to leave Menace, we could use a woman like you on our team. Your skills are quite impressive."

Naya glanced at Menace, who snored even louder now. Love blossomed in her chest. "I'm flattered, but no thanks. I'm staying right here."

With a final nod, Terror left the hospital room. She ran her finger along the edge of the envelope. Out in the hall, something noisy and metal hit the floor. The ensuing clatter ripped Menace from his dead sleep. He jumped to his feet and turned his body so that he shielded her on the bed.

She smiled at the sight of him protecting her and caressed his arm. Menace jerked as her touch registered. Spinning around, he gazed down at her in surprise and wonder.

"Naya?"

"Hey." She didn't know what else to say.

"Hey, sweetheart." His grin quickly morphed to a tight line of concern. "Should I get a medic? Are you in pain?"

"I'm good." She rubbed his fingers. "I'm a little groggy, but I feel okay."

He eased onto the bed and caressed her cheek. "I'm so glad you're finally awake.

It's been six days since I brought you here."

Her eyes widened with shock. "Six?"

"Yes. They kept you in a medically induced coma for three days and then weaned you off the sedative and on to some accelerated healing drugs. From what I understand, it takes a lot out of your smaller bodies. Exhaustion is a side effect."

She glanced down at the hospital gown covering her stomach. "Is it bad? The scarring, I mean."

He didn't lie to her. "It's not pretty, but they tell me it will heal nicely. You've seen my scars. Yours will look the same in time."

"I guess that's not so bad." Better than the alternative, she thought grimly.

"Naya, some of your injuries required certain repairs that might upset you."

Gruesome images flashed through her mind. Weakly she ordered, "Just tell me."

Menace held her hand. "They had to take one of your ovaries. Your uterine artery was damaged."

The shock of it left her dizzy. After avoiding pregnancy for most of her adult life, the thought of never experiencing one cut deeply. "Can I—will I be able to have babies?"

"Yes," he answered quickly. "They assured me that in time there's no reason you can't have children. They'll monitor you more during pregnancy but you'll be perfectly fine."

Relieved, she took some slow breaths to still her racing heart. "Next time, you might want to lead off with the good news, Menace."

"There had better not be a next time, Naya." He brushed his fingertips along her forehead and down her jawline. "You scared the hell out of me. I thought—" He stopped himself and gulped. "I know I screwed up, Naya. I know you probably hate me and you'll never trust me again, but I still love you. I'll always love you. Even though I don't deserve you."

"Hush," she whispered. Emotions warred within her. She traced the hard lines of his face and gazed into his light-green eyes. "You're a big, stupid sky warrior and, yes, you broke my heart and my trust. I'm not saying it's going to be easy to start over but, Menace, you're the only man in the universe who can help me piece it all back together."

Menace exhaled roughly, the sound very near a sob.

Eyes glistening, he blinked rapidly and pressed his forehead to hers. "I'll do whatever it takes to make this right."

Eyes closed, she savored his heat and scent. "You could start by telling me you love me and giving me a kiss."

Pulling back, he peered down at her with such adoration. He claimed her lips in a tender kiss. "I love you."

"I love you too." She remembered the envelope and found it next to her hip. She lifted it up for Menace to see. "Terror brought this."

His gaze turned murderous. "That bastard was here?"

"I guess beating the crap out of one another wasn't enough to settle up?"

"Not even close," Menace growled. "Why? Have you forgiven him?"

"No, but I'm not going to waste energy being angry at him." She rubbed her thumb across his mouth. "You shouldn't either."

He didn't say anything. Tapping the envelope, he said, "You better open it."

Her gaze fell to his cast. "How long are you in that thing?"

"Three weeks if the bone-knitting injections work."

Amazed by the kind of medicine and technology the Harcos possessed, Naya opened the red envelope. Official-looking papers were tucked inside. She pulled them out and showed them to Menace. His expression instantly brightened. "They rescinded our forced divorce and reinstated our bond."

"That was fast."

Menace's happiness deflated. "You don't have to sign

the contract again. I don't expect... Not after..."

She rolled her eyes. "What happened to the rough, possessive sky warrior who chased me down in the forest and tossed me over his shoulder? Aren't you supposed to just *tell* me that I'm signing the contract again?"

"I'm sorely tempted to give it a try." Chuckling, Menace reached into his pocket and retrieved the blue collar he'd chosen for her. Somber and with such emotion lacing his voice, he said, "I don't expect you to start wearing it anytime soon but when you're ready, you let me know."

"Well, isn't this quite a change? You're actually asking me what I want this goround?" She laughed softly. "The last time you had a bonding contract in hand, you had me gagged and cuffed and already wearing your collar."

He flashed her that sexy grin she loved so much. "Sweetheart, you'll be out of here in no time. Believe me. That can be easily arranged."

The promise of good times to come made her smile. She grasped the front of his shirt and dragged him down for another kiss. Smiling, she ghosted her mouth across his. "Baby, I'm counting on it."

The End

About Lolita Lopez

The alter ego of *New York Times* and *USA Today* bestselling author Roxie Rivera, I like to write super sexy romances and scorching hot erotica. I live in Texas on five acres with my red-bearded Viking husband, our sweet, mischievous little girl and two crazy Great Danes.

You can find me online at www.lolitalopez.com.

Also by Lolita Lopez

GRABBED

Grabbed by Vicious

Caught by Menace

Saved by Venom

Stolen by Raze – Coming Dec 2015

Dragon Heat

Dead Sexy Dragon

Red Hot Dragon

Wicked Dark Dragon

Renegade Dragon – Coming Soon

Holiday Menage

Be Our Valentine

Margaritas and Mayhem

Fireworks For Three

Trick or Treat Trio – Coming Soon

Mistletoe Menage – Coming Soon

Ringing in the New Year – Coming Soon

Made in the USA
San Bernardino, CA
05 December 2017